ONE MINUTE AFTER MIDNIGHT

By Ken Knight

This is the work of fiction.
All persons and events portrayed
Are fictitious. Any similarities
Thereof are coincidental and
Unintentional.

Original Insert designs and Cover-Art by TIM TEWALT

Copyright © 2001 by Ken Knight
All rights reserved. No part of this book may be reproduced,
stored in a retrieval system, or transmitted by any means,
electronic, mechanical, photocopying, recording, or otherwise,
without written permission from the author.

ISBN: 0-75960-295-6

This book is printed on acid free paper.

1stBooks – rev. 1/17/01

Thanks Tim! --Kenny

HELL HAS NO FURY.......

*Marriage to a woman he doesn't love isn't what
Ray Torelli wanted in his troubled life, but with
What happened on a dark, rainy night on a lonely
Road, he is in no position to argue with his lovely
New Bride...He soon discovers that things aren't
What they seem to be, that an "accident" may not
Be so accidental afterall, and his young Wife's
Love for him may prove to be his worst nightmare overall.
Smart, sexy, and conniving Marissa has determined that
Nothing will separate she and her husband....not over
His dead body, or anyone else's............*

For CHRISTY CANYON
Forever The Finest!

MY CHAINS OF SORROW

To taste the fruit of forbidden love
Is what I crave to do
How I savor the sweet nectar
Of my one and only you…

But you say we are no longer one
That your heart is empty and dry
How can this be? What have I done?
To deserve this relentless cry…

From chains of sorrow I can't break free
I must win you back no matter the cost
As this pain swells deep within me,
I wonder the streets in search of love lost

My life is void and without meaning,
I need you to make me whole.
I pray that I will wake up screaming
And somehow in control…

But the truth hits me with such clarity
That this fruit was never mine
To persuade your love would be charity
Perhaps not now but maybe in time….

      -Roderick Osborne

Chapter 1

Aynor, South Carolina
June 4th:

The brew tasted so good accompanied by a cheroot cigar, only after two shots of tequila. Sitting at the bar with three other patrons flanking him, Ray Torelli was undoubtedly the strongest drinker here tonight. Blowing smoke toward the ceiling, the 23-year-old white man clad in jean jacket and jeans, sat on the barstool in relative silence.

With the exception of the friendly bartender, Ray Torelli spoke to no one else, not even the shapely waitresses passing by.

Ray had other things on his mind tonight, much more pressing matters than most here cared to learn about in conversation. After only six months, he had been fired from his latest job at the Rubber Plant.

His "attitude" was the cause-for-dismissal, because his words of wit had "offended" the sensitivities of a female co-worker.

The bartender had listened to the young man's story with interest; a familiar tale indeed. As the dark-haired, thick-bodied unemployed man sat at his usual end of the bar, he drank a little more than usual.

Ray Torelli could take it, though, despite his drive home. A lot pressed on his mind as he sat there in his favorite bar drinking, all the realities of jobless solitude and the fact that he might even get evicted if he fails to pay this month's rent.

It always felt better to drink whenever stress became pervasive, and yet Ray was confident enough to drive afterwards, every time. His lonely apartment better suited him when he was working, so he was in no hurry to return there tonight.

Another bubblegum-shooter, then another, how sweet it tastes, his brand of alcohol.

The bartender kept glancing at Ray as he worked the bar, and Ray guessed that he would probably cut-him-off soon.

Damn the simple-minded, he thought, and damn the drive back to his lonely apartment. After today's fiasco, he deserved to get drunk.

The barkeep filled his glass once more, eyed, nodded to Ray in expressive dismay. What the hell did he care? Ray thought, he probably has someone to go home to!

Loneliness was one thing that bugged him just a little in his personal life. Sure, solitude was cool, but not having female companionship for an extended period of time plays against a man's pride and self-esteem.

Then again, he thought, being alone was better than being paired with someone you were miserable with.

Yeah, take, for example, some of the women he has dated, like Marissa. She was an acquaintance from high school, and she had been one of the few young girls to pursue Ray Torelli, not the other way around.

She just ain't his type, he thought, and he spurned her despite her amorous attempts to seduce him their senior year. Last he heard, she went to SCU to study some wild shit like nursing or something. "Good riddance," he had said, finding cute-but intrusive Marissa Borders to be an annoying female pest. He chuckled as he recalled humiliating her at their Senior Prom.

Stepping off the barstool now, he stumbled only slightly, feeling the effects of alcohol more than before that last drink.

"See ya, Ray," chuckled the bartender as he scooped Ray's $10 bill from the bar top, watching his regular customer saunter toward the restroom now.

Ray stopped at the first urinal, unzipping his fly to urinate, closing his eyes in fatigue. He was able to drive home, he thought, with his only real concern being money right now. The goddamn rent was due this week and here he was, jobless again.

Zipping up, he turned around and walked back out of the restroom, heading straight for the bar's front door.

One Minute After Midnight

Rain. What a torrential fucking mess descending upon this southern town with a vengeance. Ray ran out from the bar in stumbling fashion toward his parked truck in the lot. By the time he was inside the cab, he was soaking wet and pissed off as well as intoxicated.

Slipping the key in the ignition, he thought about it. Fuck it, he thought, he deserved to get drunk tonight after getting fired!

Pulling out from the parking lot onto Rt. 501 north, he glanced at his dashboard clock, seeing the time to be 11:55 p.m. Home was only ten minutes away, so he would make it easy, no problem. Despite the windshield wipers going full speed, the pelting rainfall made for poor visibility. The glare on the slick roads made it even worse.

Driving at 50 mph in the torrential rainfall, Ray easily fell into highway-hypnosis, alcohol dimming his senses all-the-more. Traffic was scant tonight, as he drove into more rural territory, heading into Dillon County. The radio played country music but he was barely listening to the songs as he drove now.

Thoughts of the rent, other job prospects in the area and possible loss of his apartment, his truck, filled his mind in selfish horror. Getting evicted was no joke, the stark reality of such made him angry.

No, he kept thinking, there had to be more work for him out there and soon. There had to be a solution!

Rex Matthewson wearily maneuvered his motorized Moped bike along Myrtle Drive despite the inclement weather and near-zero visibility. If it were not for the street lights posted along this subdivision, he would have been unable to ride his new Moped back home tonight.

Rex was happy; no rain could dampen his mood on the night of his 20th birthday, especially after his parents gave him the ultimate: a brand new Honda Moped bike with a lock box on the back to carry his stuff!

The young retarded man was soaking wet and had a hard time riding his new scooter toward home in this thick rainfall, but he had been out to his favorite store and got caught in it. He knew his parents would be waiting and worried, so he rode non-stop, in the right of the 2-lane road with the bike's headlight on, barely able to see in front of him.

His eyes were hurting from the rain but he just groaned and took it, happy as a clam about the sweet prize he rode now.

The Moped was wide-open full throttle, and Rex knew he was only a few blocks from his home on 1300 myrtle. He didn't want his elderly parents to worry' no, not the two people who cared about him and took care of him when no one else even looks him in the eyes. He had been called many names growing-up retarded, especially in school.

Rex laughed as he remembered what his father told him to say to the tormentors in return: "I'm not retarded, I'm Irish!" His elderly Irish-descended parents taught him to take pride in that at least.

Maneuvering more to the center of the slick road, fearful of losing control, Rex locked his arms to keep the bike straight. His father had taught him how to ride this bike, but the rain was threatening to put Rex and his beloved new bike down.

With his helmet snug over his head and ears, the Moped's small engine rattle and the violent rainstorm raging around him, Rex failed to hear the vehicle approaching fast behind him suddenly, out of nowhere.

Ray Torelli didn't see any car or truck taillights up ahead, so he thought the road was clear, not taking in the fact of poor visibility in the night's storm. He felt like falling asleep now, eager to get home and crash into sweet, intoxicated slumber.

Rex swung to his right in compensation as his tires slipped on slick road suddenly, maintaining feeble control of his Moped as he slowed down.

Still, he failed to notice the pickup truck's headlights circling him quickly as the vehicle moved up behind him at a much higher rate of speed.

"Jeezuss!" Ray bellowed at the sight of the biker directly in front of his hood ornament, too close to react, even if his senses were not impaired tonight. Rex felt the ½ ton punch of the huge vehicle's front end as it devoured the rear of his Moped on impact, propelling him to bounce off the frontal hood and flop forward as the Moped fell under the front axle.

It was a sickening "crunch" sound to Ray, and he yanked the steering wheel to the right instinctively. It was enough to avoid crushing the Moped rider's chest beneath his big tires and half-ton weight. Instead, young Rex hit the pavement on his side and was caught by both front and rear driver's-side wheels rolling over his legs at the knees.

The violent, racking motion crushed bone and cartilage as the monstrous machine drove over his legs mercilessly. Rex howled out in the horror of the unstoppable seconds of hell that had captured him quicker than lightning.

"No...jeezus, no!" Ray barked in shock as he jammed on the brakes, halting his 4x4 Chevy in the middle of the road, shifting to park and shoving open the door. He flew out of his cab in realization of what had just happened. He had hit someone on a bike and run them over!

Everything was in slow motion as soon as he leapt from the truck, bounding around to the rear where his victim lay broken.

Even the pelting raindrops seemed to fall in slow motion as he stumbled toward the fallen man behind his truck. This can't be happening, Ray kept say8ing in his mind, this can't be happening!

Standing over the prone biker in stunned stupor, Ray watched as the young man pushed off his helmet, moaning out loud in the min-numbing pain. His legs were crushed, like twigs broken at the knees, and Ray could make out the biker's face in the truck's taillight glow, despite the rain. Omigod, he thought in added horror: I know this guy!

"Rex," Ray said out loud as he leaned over the quivering body of his unintended victim, shaking himself in the rain. He remembered Rex from high school. Rex was one of those retarded "Special Ed" kids who shared a gym class with him his senior year!

"Migod, Rex, I'm sorry…jeezus, I'm sorry!" Ray shouted down at the weeping victim, not realizing that Rex was going fast into shock.

"Omigod, what have…I done?" Ray spit up at the relentless rainfall and the dark sky that offered no assistance. The bleak realization hit him like a brick in the face: I am drinking; if the police come and question me over this, I'll go to jail for felony DWI!

Ray looked down the dark roadway, seeing no other traffic coming, and he looked around at the houses nearby, seeing no outward signs of residents looking out at this tragedy or anyone coming out to assist him now.

His next thought was a simple conviction: No one else saw this accident!

Ray glanced at his wrist watch, seeing the time: 12:01 a.m.; one minute after midnight.

Rex howled in pain, spitting up blood now, coughing and crying in sheer agony, his legs crushed at the knees. No telling what other internal injuries the kid had, Ray thought. This couldn't be happening! He kept repeating in his mind over and over.

It was happening, and he was to blame.

Staring down at the hobbled young man he had run over, Ray saw enough in the truck taillight's glow to horrify his soul. Rex was a victim of his! Life as he knew it was over once the police found out. As Ray stood over Rex, looking down at the retarded man's bloody face, his first priority came to focus.

He stepped a few paces back, his mind drumming up ways of escaping this unfortunate accident. No one saw it, and Rex was too fucked-up to see Ray clearly in the dark rainfall, too injured to even remember who Ray was if he did catch a glimpse.

Rex lay on his back on the wet pavement in excruciating pain. His legs were broken at the knees, smashed by the weight of Ray's truck. He couldn't see due to the rain and blood in his eyes, but he had heard someone yelling fearfully at him a minute ago, then he could do nothing but cry and scream.

Ray back-stepped to the truck's cab, reeling inn stunned reaction, his thoughts on self-preservation now. No other witnesses, no other cars driving by.

He was suddenly convinced that he could get out of this situation if he left now. Leaving Rex lying there in the road was not something he wanted to do, but it was the only choice over a jail cell for him.

"I'm gone...gone, outta here...jeezus," he cried to himself as he hopped into his truck's cab and shifted into drive.

Soaking wet and crying, Ray spun tires in acceleration, driving away from the gruesome accident he caused, the horror of the moment lacking his psyche even more.

"Dammit!" Ray shouted with emotion, wiping rainwater off his face with his left hand as he drove with the right, speeding to the end of Myrtle Drive, turning left onto Parsley Cove, where his apartment building was located. "This isn't happening...goddamn Rex, you retarded motherfucker...you fucked things up!" Rex bellowed as he brought his truck to an abrupt halt at the apartment building's entrance.

He would go to jail if he went to the police or even called 911, and he knew it.

Sitting there wet and traumatized, Ray Torelli sobbed in anxiety, his thoughts focused on self-preservation first. He kept one thing clear to himself: if he calls the cops or if he had stayed with Rex back there, he would have been arrested for Felony-DWI, drinking-and-driving and hitting a man on a Moped! He knew enough about the law to realize that his life would be even more useless as a convict in prison.

No, he thought, better to leave the scene and let Rex be taken care of by the next passing car. He couldn't believe this had happened to him! What if Rex dies? What if he somehow knew or remembered Ray? What if he dies? Ray kept questioning in his mind, shivering as he sat behind the wheel.

In his sudden rush to leave the accident scene unnoticed by other traffic, Ray failed to look in his rearview mirror before he sped away. If he had, he would have spotted a jogger trotting up behind his truck at that moment, stopping at the screaming victim Ray had run over.

Rex wasn't screaming as loud as he had been; shock gripping him almost entirely now, blood and rain soaking him as he lay on his back, helpless.

The jogger stood over him with hands-on-hips, and young Rex caught a glimpse of the hooded person just before he started losing consciousness.

The lone jogger lowered her parka's hood, letting her short hair get drenched as she gawked down at the victim of the hit-and-run.

"Ray Torelli...what have you done, you son-of-a-bitch...." The young woman spoke out loud, crouching next to the quivering victim. She knew the truck, and had seen Ray get out and look at the man he ran over as she was jogging up this road toward her home. He got back into his truck and drove off before she could stop him.

Looking down at the twisted mongoloid face with bloody mouth and nose, Marissa Borders vaguely recognized the victim, too, from back in high school.

A car's headlights lit up the darkness behind her, so Marissa stood up and turned to see an on-coming vehicle approaching slowly. She waved both her arms as she came into its beams, and the car slowed to a halt about seven feet in front of her and the hit-and-run victim.

"I'll call 911," the man said next, holding up his cell-phone.

"No need, I'm a nurse," Marissa said as she touched a hand to Rex's face, making his eyes flutter in semi-consciousness.

Chapter 2

12 noon
The next day:

The "South Of The Border" theme-park was situated on the border between the Carolinas, just west of Dillon County. Despite its Mexico-theme stores and restaurants, the place had a peculiar draw to it, and tourists almost always stopped off Rt. 95-south, and rested, shopped, or ate here.

One place to eat here in this theme park was "Pedro's Diner", a quaint little eatery with the best grilled chicken sandwich and sweetest ice tea in the Carolinas!"

It was also one of Ray Torelli's haunts, mostly because of the food and peace of the place. He sat at the counter in Pedro's Diner today, with a lot on his mind. Fear and gut wrenching apprehension was all he worried over as he sat on the big padded stool. He never felt more alone than right now.

Taking another bite of his grilled chicken sandwich and washing it down with tea, Ray thought about how he could explain what happened last night to the police if they ever found out what he had done.

No, they won't find out! He kept telling himself over and over in repetitive torment. No one else saw him last night; no one he could see anyway, and he made the decision to leave Rex there like that in order to save himself from the cops.

That kind of trouble wasn't what he could live with, despite what happened to poor Rex. Rex Matthewson: a name he had forgotten until last night, since he hadn't seen him since high school. He remembered him last night, though, like a foolish ghost from the past.

Rex had been in his junior and senior year gym class with a few other retarded "Special Ed" students in the school. Ray remembered the young Rex attempting to play basketball with the normal seniors, and wet his pants when he accidentally scored a basket, on the wrong end!

Ray made-fun of Rex back then.

Looking over at the diner's huge grill and the cook attending it, Ray shivered at the thought of Rex lying there on the pavement back on Myrtle Drive, crying out in agony in the driving rain.

He felt even worse about the prospect of going to jail last night if he had remained there and called 911. No, for self-preservation, he drove away, his decision a selfish but realistic one.

"What the fuck was he doing out on a Moped at midnight...in that rainstorm anyway?" Ray asked himself softly, then sipped his iced tea again.

"Damn you, Rex," he sneered as he raised his sandwich to his mouth and took another bite.

He had left his apartment early this morning and just drove around aimlessly, unable to sleep after last night. Part of him felt like maybe the cops would bust down his door any moment, another part of him felt that he would get away with it entirely. The latter was the only reason why he didn't turn-himself-in.

Just the idea of jail made him cringe. Even now, he would face not Felony DWI, but Felony Hit-and-Run! Either way, he looked at it, he would go to prison for what happened at 12:01 last night. Fleeing from it, though cowardice, was self-preserving and a decision where another man's worth was weighed against his own.

Ray had been drinking, yes, but in that weather...it might not have mattered. No, he thought, Rex was in the wrong place at the wrong time, and he paid for it.

Taking another bite of his delicious chicken sandwich, Ray silently told himself something more "realistic". He was a normal young man who was struggling to stay afloat in life, and Rex was a retarded young man who wasn't productive anyway, so he left him there.

That thought made Ray kind of hate himself, but it was the momentous decision he made at 12:01 last night, and he had to live with it forever.

Funny how little spur-of-the-moment decisions make for life-long regrets. One simple turn-left, and you might never be the same.

Finishing his sandwich, Ray asked for a refill on the iced tea, forcing a smile at the black waitress as she took his empty glass.

The front door of the diner swung open again, a lone patron entering off to Ray's left but he paid her no attention as he sat there, stewing in his thoughts.

The casually-dressed young Caucasian woman walked into the diner in a slow stride, eyes on the man seated at the counter instead of a booth.

What a greasy-spoon joint, she thought as she looked around for a second, then turned back to Ray Torelli on the stool.

He looked incredibly sad to her, like a man lost. He looked like a loser sitting there, and she almost didn't say anything but remembered why she had tracked him down today. It was of the utmost importance to her, and Ray Torelli was a big part of her plan.

Last night's accident on Myrtle Drive opened a door for her, an opportunity she relished while Ray was painfully regretting it.

As she stepped up behind him, she recalled how he got back into his truck and drove away after running over Rex Matthewson.

By the looks of him today, she guessed that it was eating-him-up. Now was the time to grab an opportunity. Like her mother once told her: If you see something you like, go for it!

"Ray," she spoke up politely, standing behind him with hands in the pockets of her designer jeans.

Ray turned to see who spoke his name and felt his heart sink in recognition of the young woman standing before him now. Another face from the past had shown up rather unexpectedly in his life, and Ray was not pleased.

"Marissa...Marissa Borders?" he sighed in feigned surprise, turning on his stool.

"Ray Torelli, so nice to see you again after all-this-time," she said with a pleasant smile, tapping him on his forearm. Her smile gave Ray a renewed felling of uneasiness, like this was some sort of weird prank. How does she pop-up after all this time, and why now?

"Yeah, Marissa, it's been a while...since high school," he answered her meekly, watching her take the stool next to him. She looked good physically, an athletic-looking woman with short brown hair combed much like she used to wear it years ago, back and over-in-front, wavy.

Those eyes of hers he remembered, too, just like back then; the eyes of a predatory cat. Marissa had been one female he avoided back in school, a girl who, in return, hounded him relentlessly with misspent affection.

"We've got to talk, Ray," she said as she sat next to him on his left. He looked at her blue sweater and the bulges indicating well-formed breasts. Wow, she had grown nice tits in the past five years.

Ray couldn't imagine what Marissa would have to say after five years, and after how he humiliated her during their senior prom.

He looked at her with a poker face, eager to hear what she came to talk about. It was too coincidental that she found him here...or was it? He didn't know what to say.

"Ray...we've known each other since grade-school," she began in a smooth voice.

"Yeah," he sighed, slightly embarrassed by how he had treated her back then. Surely, she would bring that subject up.

"I'll cut-to-the-chase, Ray...to hell with small-talk..." she continued in a sterner tone. Ray nodded, nervous about her intentions now.

Marissa stared him square in the eyes, felling her own nervous heart pounding in her chest.

One Minute After Midnight

"I was there last night," she said hesitantly, "and I saw what you did!"

Ray's heart sank again, and he couldn't even swallow, petrified by those words she spoke.

He looked down at the shoes she wore: expensive sneakers on small feet. He was helpless in disbelief, imagining how in all the four winds could Marissa Borders been there last night?!

"I was out jogging as I do every night, and I saw you and your truck there after you hit that retarded guy on the Moped...you left the scene," Marissa said smoothly.

"I don't believe this," Ray managed to speak with cotton mouth.

Marissa smiled slightly, her tone practiced and soft as she continued.

"You got in your truck and split before I could get your attention...I recognized your truck immediately," she said rather calmly.

"How?" he asked gruffly.

"I see you every now and then around town...I still live in Dillon, ya know, and you just didn't notice me, as usual," she said matter-of-factly.

"Jeezus Christ...so I take it that...tha cops know and they're...looking for me," Ray groaned in nervous speech, quivering in apprehension.

"As a matter-of-fact, they don't know...not yet, which brings me to the next point-of-interest," Marissa said coolly, eyeballing Ray.

He remembered her as always talking like this, condescending and blunt.

"I didn't tell the cops that I knew the driver was you, Ray, but I still can...especially since it's a homicide," she continued with a poker face. That smooth, moon face of hers had the look of a jackal, and she scared the hell out of him as he sat in front of her now.

"Rex died?" he sighed, then swallowed hard. She nodded slowly, her mouth quivering as if trying not to smile.

"He died in my arms...Shock mostly, plus retarded people often possess poor health anyway....The paramedics said his heart failed," Marissa explained calmly.

"Omigod," Ray sighed in misery, his worst fear a realty now. The diner seemed to turn 3-dimensional around him as he sat there, stunned by the news.

Why Marissa hadn't gone to the police about him was a mystery. He hadn't seen her in at least three years, and considering the way he treated her back in school, she had every right to inform on him.

"Hey, it's okay, Ray...I took care of it and no one else knows it was you who ran that retard over last night, so don't worry about the cops hunting you down...right now, anyway," she added rather casually.

The way she said "retard" made him frown in wonder of her intentions. He had no money, so it couldn't be blackmail, no. She had to have a reason for doing what she did and another reason for confronting him here, today!

"Fuck him, he's worthless anyway, Ray, and I covered you because I have a proposition for you to consider, big guy," Marissa continued, tapping him on the arm.

"Proposition....? Marissa, we haven't talked in a long time and I uhh...think we last parted enemies if I recall?" Ray retorted in surprise of her statement. He then took a big swig of his iced tea, swallowing fast, wishing it were alcohol.

"That's going to change, Ray," Marissa answered with a grin.

"Whoah, hey girl...if it's blackmail, you're talking about, I'm broke and unemployed right now; I might have a hundred dollars in the bank," he told her in a huff.

"I want something from you, Ray, but it's certainly not your money," she said flatly, eyeballing him as she spoke.

"What could that possibly be, Marissa, after all this time...after I'm now a wanted man on a manslaughter rap?!" Ray sneered in a lowered voice. He couldn't believe this shit.

"No one but me knows it was you, Ray, and no one else has to know, so you're free as a bird, if you help me out in return," Marissa said with a slight smile across her pretty, mad-up face.

"What the hell could I possibly do for you?" he asked her out loud, not wanting to look her in the eyes.

She smiled that cat-like grin, eyes seeming to sparkle when he said that. Marissa touched her right hand to his shoulder and moved closer to the extremely nervous man.

"I have you by the short-hairs, true, but I can offer you a sweet deal in return...hmmm...the police will never know who that hit-n-run driver is, as long as you and I can work together," Marissa said softly.

"This is blackmail, my god," Ray sighed as he shrugged her hand off his shoulder.

"We work together, Raymond, and you won't have to worry about a thing...not even your truck getting repossessed," she continued, then took a sip of his iced tea.

The young man hung his head in defeat, eyes on his empty plate, smelling the grilled steak-and-eggs cooking over yonder. How could she have seen him last night like that?

She knew too much, too much for him to oppose her, and her motive was still a mystery. Why, after all this time, was Marissa Borders back in his life?

Why was she jogging in that rainy mess? He didn't remember passing a jogger.

"Work together...what do you mean, Marissa?" he asked feebly.

"I want you, Ray...you," she whispered in his left ear. He looked up at her in shocked silence, his arms still shaking.

"Marry me, and it's all taken care of," Marissa said softly, eyes portraying sincerity.

Ray leaned back in awe of the words she just spoke. And the woman was serious!

Marissa nodded as he just sat there, staring at her in shock. He couldn't believe her offer, but then the underline sank in: This was no simple offer, it was a demand.

"Why...migod, why?" he managed to utter with a cottonmouth.

"I've always wanted you, Ray, you know that, and now is a perfect time for you and I to hook-up," she added happily.

Ray gawked at her with an open mouth, wanting this to be some form of sick joke.

"Marry me...and you've got nothing to worry about; I'm even getting an inheritance from my deceased grandmother's estate once I'm married," she said with a wink.

"My first instinct is to say fuck-off," Ray sneered with a scowl, eyeing her.

Marissa nodded, her face going blank again.

"Okay, that's fine...hope you don't mind prison food, Ray," she whispered with hesitation.

"You bitch," he growled loud enough for the waitress to hear.

Marissa winked at him, expecting that response.

"Why do you want me to marry you? Jeezus, you're good-looking enough to get any other guy around here, shit," ray spoke more calmly.

"I've always liked you, Ray, even when you treated me like shit, and you should be grateful to me for covering your sorry ass last night," she added with a chuckle.

Ray was awestruck by her audacity in this. Rex was dead, and here was the only witness to the hit-n-run asking for his hand-in-marriage-or-else!

"So, you go to the cops if I refuse to fuckin' marry you?" Ray asked her in a hot whisper.

Marissa nodded with that sly smile of hers. She enjoyed this, having him over-a-barrel.

"Huh, what about love, romance, all that shit?" he snorted with emotion, looking around in hope no one else could hear their sordid conversation.

"Hmmh, that'll come later, honey, but first we can marry: I'll get my inheritance, and you will be in better straits as my husband," Marissa answered in confident tone.

"Your husband, huh....Marissa, I don't like you, remember?" Ray chortled in a loud whisper.

"Doesn't really matter, considering the position you're in, Raymond," she said impishly. He hated her back in school and he was felling that hatred once again.

"I didn't mean to kill Rex, godammit, it was an accident in a bad storm...shit, it was an accident," he told her in an emotional reply.

"Then, why did you flee the scene?" she asked him softly.

"I was drinking, and it would've been a Felony-DWI, huh...." Ray snarled.

"Now it's Felony Hit-n-Run plus manslaughter," Marissa reminded him.

Ray nodded in agreement.

"I don't believe this, I'm ruined," he sighed, hanging his head in shame, arms on the counter weak and trembling.

"No, Ray...marry me and you are free and good, hell...I'll even pay off your truck for ya," Marissa said boldly, hand on his shoulder again.

"And if I say no...." he whispered with eyes to the floor.

"Then the Dillon County Sheriff's Department will know everything, and you'll go to jail, more-than-likely be convicted and get twenty years," she replied casually.

"You could be in trouble for withholding information," Ray injected.

"No, I can afford a good lawyer, and claim something like lapsed memory or something, trust me, Ray....I've planned this out since this morning; all bases are covered," she answered him stoically.

"Really," he groaned in disbelief.

"Try me and you'll be eating dinner in a jail cell tonight, honey, and I'll do it," she said in a whisper.

Ray looked at her again and wanted this whole thing to be a bad, bad dream.

"I'm a Registered Nurse now, and my inheritance will be a little over a million dollars plus some real estate, so we'll be set as a married couple, Ray," she added softly.

He didn't want to say anything to the conniving young woman now, listening in horror to his predicament.

"I want you with me, Ray. Sorry I have to do it this way but my mom once told me to go after the man I want mercilessly," Marissa said next, hand going down his arm slowly.

"Blackmail," he sneered under his breath.

"Yeah, but it's a good deal for you, too, Ray…wealth and a woman with a tight body," she told him frankly.

Ray shook his head in disbelief.

"What do you have without me, Ray?" she asked coyly, "nothing but troubles."

"Yeah," he sighed in defeat.

"Please believe that this is sincere on my part, Ray. I do care for you and I know once we get to know one another more, you'll care for me, too," she injected timidly.

"I don't think so….Besides, you'll have an ax over my head forever," Ray said as he thought about it more.

"No, I won't hold it against you once we're married, but if something were to happen to me, the authorities will receive a package of info on the unknown driver who killed Rex Matthewson," she said with a rather graceful voice now.

"And, I suppose divorce is a no-go?" he chuckled in spite of himself.

Marissa shook her head in the negative. "Marriage is forever, until death-do-us-part, remember?" she retorted out loud.

"You want a lifetime commitment from me or you get me thrown in jail for manslaughter," he snickered in sarcasm.

"In a nutshell, yeah, but I'm a better deal than a lot of women you'd likely meet, so think of it that way," Marissa responded, her hand on his now.

"I can't believe this is happening, and you of all people," he said with a forced grin, eyeing her casually-dressed physique. He couldn't stop thinking of Marissa back in school.

"Hmmm...you're a good man, Ray, and you can do a lot worse than what I am offering you," she said frankly, looking into his eyes again. Those sky-blue eyes she remembered from high school days' some things about a person never change.

"Worse...you're hemming me up and I either marry you or go to jail, jezus!" he quipped, indignant.

"Life is a series of choices; one choice takes you into left-field like prison and another gets you a good deal like what you'll get when we're married," Marissa said politely.

"Man, if only I hadn't been drinking last night...we wouldn't be talking," he sighed.

"Well, it happened, can't bring it back, but you can help yaself out by saying yes to me," she sighed softly with that cat-like smile of hers.

"Marry you?" he snapped in a chuckle, still finding it difficult to swallow. This chick has a lot of nerve...a lot of nerve.

"Yes, and you won't regret it, honey," she said sharply, sensing he was close to agreeing.

"My first instinct is to tell you no," he said softly, looking at his glass of tea.

"I know, but you're a smart man, even if you didn't go to college, and you know I'm telling the truth....Plus, I know you don't want to go to jail," Marissa answered in confidence.

"Hmmph, maybe, maybe not," he snorted in contempt.

"You're all alone, Ray. No girlfriend, no job, no family to speak of...and now you've done something you can correct only if you take me up on my lucrative offer," she explained calmly, drilling it into him more and more.

"You fuckin' bitch," he sighed, feeling as if he was hyperventilating.

"Yeah...mmh-hmmh, I'm a bitch who can make you or break you, it's your choice, homeboy," she retorted indignantly.

"You know me too well, how's that?" he asked defensively.

"I like you, Ray, and I have watched you, even when I was attending the University of South Carolina," she answered flatly.

"Fuck this, I don't know what to do," he spoke with emotions again, his eyes betraying weakness. Marissa loved every second of it, he plan working like a charm.

"For once, if only once, Ray, put trust in me, and you'll be clear of Rex's death," she told him again. She didn't mind repeating herself this time.

"You remember Rex from high school?" he asked meekly, trying not to show a tear from his watering eyes.

"Oh, yes, he was one of those special-ed idiots they made us share gym-class with, and he still lived with his elderly parents over on Pico Drive, not far from Myrtle Drive where he ran into you," she replied with a shrug of avarice.

Ray nodded in agreement.

"Hey, he was a toad, a stain....Certainly not worth going to prison over," Marissa said with a chuckle of sarcasm.

A stain. Marissa was cold-hearted about the dead Rex Mathewson. He wondered what the newspapers were saying about the incident. Was there a description of the truck?

He knew she had him by the balls, and he couldn't think of a way out.

"Ahh...I guess you got me, Marissa, there's nothing I can do," he said in a huff, turning on his stool to face her.

"Trust me, Ray, and marry me," she said with a grin.

"When?" he asked in surrender.

"August first, here in Dillon," she responded calmly as if she had planned the wedding as well. Damn her, he thought.

"Wow, Rex is gone 'cuz of me, and I'm forced to marry a woman I don't love," Ray said next to spite her.

"Love comes and goes, but like I said, life's full of choices," she added with her smile.

"Yeah, what are we to do in the meantime?" he asked, weak-in-the-knees now.

"You got a place to go for awhile, like another state or somewhere for a month or more?" Marissa asked next.

"Why?" he quipped in wonder, then took a sip of his iced tea.

"Till this blows over, you-know," she whispered.

"Uhh...I guess I can go to Fayetteville or maybe Atlanta, but I can't afford to stay long, plus my next month's rent is due," he said painfully.

"Make it Fayetteville....Call me when you get there and I'll take care of your apartment if you give me the key," she said insisting.

"All right, but I uhhh...." He stammered, unsure of the whole thing, even himself.

"Here's fifteen-hundred dollars cash and my Visa Card...motel's on me for a month. Just stay out of here until July, so I can make sure of my plans and so you can chill out and recover from what happened last night," she explained, pulling out a big wad of bills with a credit card out of her jeans' pocket, handing it to him.

"Marissa, I don't think I ever will recover," he sneered as he plucked his apartment key off his key-ring and handed it to her.

"You know where I live, too, I suppose," he said as she took it.

"Yep," she whispered with a grin.

"Don't even think about turning away, Raymond, because I'll turn you in if I don't bet a call from you by tonight...and don't worry about a thing. Just think about my offer more and don't tell anyone else about what happened," Marissa continued, standing up now.

"Hell no, and it's looking like I've made my choice," he said to her, feeling perversely relieved about her offer now.

"Good, you won't regret it, Ray, 'cuz I think we're gonna get-along great," she said in earnest, patting him on the back.

"Does today's paper say anything about the accident?" he asked, watching her jot down her phone number on a napkin. She then stuffed it into his jean jacket pockets.

Ken Knight

"Stay away from the newspaper, honey. It'll just stress you out more," she told him, running her hand up his back.

He gripped the cash and credit card in his left hand, glancing over a shoulder at her. Ray still couldn't grasp this situation completely. "Lunch is on me, honey, call me tonight," Marissa said as she put a $10 down on his plate and then to quickly exit the diner.

Chapter 3

It is better to marry
Than to burn.
    --St. Paul

Marissa relaxed now, content with her success thus far. She wanted to call her retired parents in Florida and tell them she was getting married soon but decided to wait...maybe next week.

The hot water of the bathtub felt damn good, exhilarating to every inch of her bare body now as she laid back here in her bathroom.

Tomorrow, she thought, she would get her nails done and go pick out her wedding gown, maybe go to the spring shop and have her invitations made up.

It had worked out great, she thought, as she lay in the bathtub, water up to her breasts. Despite the tragic accident involving the retarded Rex Matthewson, fate had smiled upon her, and she seized the opportunity to get the man she had always wanted, all the way to the altar. The scent of potpourri was in the air from her spraying the sweet scent all over the house earlier. She glanced at the clock on the wall, seeing it to be 7:05 p.m. Ray should be calling her any time now, and she knew he would. She knew him well enough.

Much like her mother, she possessed an uncanny "track" fro reading people like a book, and 98% of the time she was right.

Ray was a lonely man down on his luck, and recently struck by a lightning bolt of tragic circumstance, namely Rex, so she knew he would take her offer.

Being sent to prison was not something he could take, she guessed, and with a timely accident last night, sealing his fate to her, Marissa was taking full advantage.

Why not? She asked herself. Since he spurned her friendly advances years ago and humiliated her like he did, she deserved

Ken Knight

this opportunity. Marissa still adored him, though, her desire never wavering even after high school.

Ray was lonely and so wash she.

She ran a wet hand through her neck-length, short brown hair, and then reached over to the small stand next to the tub where a fresh glass of orange juice sat. Bringing the glass of OJ to her lips, she sipped in delight. This was an evening to celebrate.

Then her cellular phone ran, as expected. She picked it up off the toilet seat and pushed "send" to receive the call.

"Marissa," she said in bland greeting.

"Yeah, it's me...." Ray Torelli spoke softly from the other end.

"Hello, Ray, good to hear from you," she answered in kind, smiling to herself as she rested back in the tub with the phone to her face.

"I've thought about what you're offering, long and hard," Ray spoke in a smooth, calm voice.

"Really," she sighed.

"Yes, and I'll do it," he said.

"You'll marry me?" she asked insecurely.

"Yes, even though part of me doesn't want to and I hate you for putting me in a bind like this, but yeah...guess we're getting married," Ray said in reluctance.

"You won't regret it, honey, and don't worry...no one else knows or suspects," she added with a snicker of triumph.

"What do the papers say?" he asked next, curious.

"Just that Rex Matthewson was the victim of a hit-and-run driver and no suspects at this time....It also states I am the only witness, so don't sweat it, Ray, you're covered," Marissa explained politely.

"Huh, I don't really even know you that well, Marissa; I still don't believe this is happening," he sighed in rebuttal.

"Hey, life's like that sometimes, but you're getting a good deal yaself, Ray, do don't gripe," she told him flatly.

"Maybe," he whispered over the line, some static heard now.

"Don't worry, and stay away from Dillon until July first at least….Trust me, Ray, it's all gonna be taken care of," Marissa said with a sterner voice.

"Yeah," the man on the other end sighed in conclusion.

"'Bye," Marissa chimed, then canceled the call.

She placed her cell phone on the toilet top again and relaxed back in the tub's hot water. Her parents lived in Charleston, SC, both of them having struck it rich in her grandmother's real estate venture recently.

Marissa's grandmother, Bernice Gunderson, was a real estate investor in her sunset years, and lucked out. When she passed away last year of leukemia at age 68, Bernice had stipulated in her will that once her only granddaughter, Marissa, marries, she'll receive one million dollars of her estate.

Marissa like her grandmother and missed her, but that inheritance money was so very appealing now. All she had to do was get married, and now that was sealed!

Ray Torelli had agreed to marry her and she would hold him to it. At age 23, she was going to be a bride and it felt good. Yeah, a rich bride!

Closing her eyes, head against the porcelain tub's rear, Marissa thought about her husband-to-be. Ray Torelli was a handsome man, even back in school, and she like him since, even though he spurned her and even humiliated her more than once back then.

There was a quality she always like about Ray, a unique "ruggedness" that appealed to her. Despite his lack of a career, she wanted him. It was the kind of "want" of another human being that was a mixture of both love and obsession.

Now, she had a home of her own, thanks to her parents, co-ownership of her grandmother's house in Aynor and $1 million dollars after she marries the man she has always desired.

"Mmmhh…life is good, hmmh-heenh, what luck," she cooed to herself in happiness of the moment, the hot water feeling so good to her bare flesh.

Ken Knight

An only child, Marissa had grown up alone and knew what loneliness is. Now, she didn't have to be alone anymore, nor did she have to settle for a man she didn't really want.

"What luck," she said again, running a hand over here breasts in the water.

Fayetteville, N.C.
9:00 that night:

No way he could sleep, not tonight and not after the events of the past two days kept replaying in his head.

Ray Torelli lay on the motel bed in just his jeans, eyes staring up to the ceiling in aimless gaze. This had to be some surrealistic nightmare! A retarded man is dead and a woman he thought he had seen-the-last-of was blackmailing him into marrying her!

Her words still haunted his mind; what she told him in the diner earlier today. About her witnessing his crime: Rex dying in her arms, and if anything happens to her, the police will find out about him and last night's fiasco.

Damn her, he thought, and damn Rex Matthewson for being out on his Moped in that storm last night. Damn them both!

Fear ate at his gut like never before; the fear of the police investigation, a trial, imprisonment, and fear of the young woman he used to call names back in high school.

Marissa had him over-a-barrel, and he couldn't imagine escaping her without ending up in jail for Rex's death.

She had changed some since high school, he thought, her body having developed well, but those eyes of hers still portrayed something sinister, and he took her at her word.

IF he refused to marry her, she would go to the cops even if she gets in trouble for waiting so long! She had him by-the-balls, and it hurt. The image of Rex lying there on the road broken and bleeding kept reappearing as well, and added to his inability to sleep.

Poor Rex, he thought, despite his handicap, the guy didn't deserve that fate. No one does, but Ray didn't deserve prison either.

"Hmmph, I'm getting married...fuckin'ay," he chortled out loud in sarcasm. It might not be so bad, he kept telling himself.

Marissa turned out to be a fairly good-looking, physically-fit woman with a nice ass and tits on top! Maybe, he kept saying to himself over and over.

He was alone. Hell, he couldn't even find a date for the "Summer's Eve Dance" at the Firehouse in Dillon last month!

Now, Ray had a fiancée with ax hanging over his head forever. Maybe it'll work out fine, maybe Marissa is now a cool chick who is good in bed? He told himself as he lay there motionless. She did give him $1500.00 cash plus her credit card, so he knew she was loaded like she said she was.

He would get to sleep with her, but as long as it had been since his last fucking, Ray would rather pass on her right now. This was a bona fide "Talk Show" case, he thought next. Yes, sir: An intoxicated young man on the way home from a bar, hits and kills a retarded man, then flees the scene to protect himself; only to become a victim of blackmail by a lovelorn woman who has wanted him since high school!

"What the hell were you doing out there like that, Rex...Better yet, what were you doing, jogging in that storm, Marissa?" he asked out loud in tensed voice. He wondered about the coincidence which was too good to be "accidental" for Marissa.

Damn, she had him by the balls, and Ray could see now way out but to call her bluff and then be sent to jail for manslaughter.

It became clearer as he kept "justifying" leaving Rex there in the road to save his own skin from the cops and from likely being sued by Rex's parents.

It was a selfish move, but he regretted it nonetheless. Knowing that he had caused someone's death shook him to his soul.

"Jeezus, I'm sorry, Rex...I'm so damn sorry," he said in a whisper, then sat up on the bed, fighting off tears again.

"Man, I am so fucked up," he sneered in self-hatred as he got up and sauntered into the motel room's bathroom to shower again. He still felt dirty as hell.

Thinking of his parents, who divorced when he was ten, Ray couldn't imagine telling them any part of this sordid tale. His mother who lived in Myrtle Beach now, would be thrilled that her youngest son was getting married, regardless how! His father would just get drunk and laugh at him. His older brother would laugh, too.

He undressed and turned on the shower nozzle, not bothering to wait until it was hot to get in. Standing beneath the cascading spray getting soaked, Ray closed his eyes and remembered the look on Rex's bloody face last night.

That shocking horror on the mongoloid face of Rex Matthewson would probably haunt him forever, because it was so vivid and lucid in his memory.

The shower water felt like the rain last night, beating down his head and shoulders relentlessly. Just standing beneath the spray, Ray Torelli wished in silence that he was dead rather than Rex. Regret and guilt were choking him now, as they would for a long time to come.

Dillon SC
June 6th:

Dillon was somewhat of a "sleepy" community just north of North Carolina's border near Hammer SC, and the "South Of The Border" theme park. Many retirees and life-long residents lived here, despite the jobs located everywhere else but in Dillon. In rural southern counties like Dillon, there lived some rather unique people if one looked for them.

One Minute After Midnight

Authors, poets, retired generals, defrocked priests, geriatric politicians, and computer hackers all seem to enjoy the solemn quiet of a rural county such as this.

Samuel "Spaz" McCracken was one computer hacker who was not originally from South Carolina. Matter-of-fact, he was a New Yorker up until his 18th birthday when he was arrested for "computer piracy" and pretty much disowned by his strict Irish Catholic family.

"Spaz" came to Dillon, South Carolina to get away and on-his-own, as well as for the quiet Dillon offered.

He even scored a rented house near the "Motel Dixie Dream" on Rt. 501 for just $400 per month. It was neat as hell, getting his own place like this.

Even better than that was the sheer lack of visitors bothering him. Until today, anyway.

The knock on his front door surprised the young man who was typing on his word-processor in his "study" before the interruption.

"Better not be no goddamn Jehovah's witness!" McCracken snorted as he walked to his front door in just T-shirt and cut-off jeans shorts.

When he opened the door, he gawked in silence at the attractive young woman standing there with hand on hips.

"I take it you're "Spaz" McCracken?" Marissa Borders spoke softly to the surprised young man with the Coke bottle-thick, round-framed eyeglasses.

"Uhh…yes, ma'am, Spaz…McCracken," he answered in nervous hesitation, looking her up and down in wonder how a woman like this would know him?!

"We need to talk, may I come in?" she said next, smiling sweetly.

"Yeah, sure…uhhmm…come in," McCracken stammered in uncertainty, allowing the nicely-dressed brown-haired female to enter his humble dwelling.

"My name is Marissa," she said softly as she stepped into the dusty, unkempt living room of the small one-level home.

"And, uhh...how can I help you?" Spaz stuttered nervously, ogling the 5'8" shapely brunette in wonder. She wore a tight-fitting blouse that was blue in color and a black cotton mini-skirt with black fishnet stockings. Expensive-looking black pumps fit her feet, and a sweet perfume met his nostrils. This had to be a prank.

"I need your expertise, Spaz...no bullshit," she said sharply as he stepped in front of her meekly. She sensed that he slightly feared her.

"How do I know you're not a cop lookin' to bust me again?" he asked her softly, adjusting the thick-lensed glasses on his nose.

"Do I look like some dyke policewoman, Spaz?" Marissa snickered in sarcasm.

"No particularly," he said in his soft monotone voice, eyeballing her nervously.

"I know your acquaintance, Billy Sharps, and he recommends you very highly as a hacker," Marissa continued in a soft tone, standing there boldly.

"Billy runs the PC shop down in Aynor, yeah," Spaz said matter-of-factly.

Marissa nodded, reaching inside the tiny purse slung over her left shoulder.

"I need someone to be hoodwinked," she said as she slowly removed a wad of bills from the purse.

"Killed?" Spaz snapped in surprise, not understanding her meaning at first.

"No, not killed, you idiot...I need your computer talent to pull the wool over someone's eyes. Know what I mean?" Marissa chimed with a smirk at the nervous be-speckled young hacker. Spaz nodded in hesitation, unsure of her.

She saw him as the poster boy for Geeks-R-Us, rather harmless but excitable and stereotypically one of those rare guys who can break into any computer system imaginable, and that's what she needed him for.

She smiled impishly as she held out the wad of bills. Spaz saw them to be $100 bills.

"You have a job, Spaz?" she asked casually.

"Free-lance," he said hesitantly.

"That's what I thought. Now, what's your fee for a job involving a hospital computer system?" Marissa asked, fingering the thick wad of money.

"Hospital?" he quipped in surprise as she stepped around the living room to check his place out. She glanced back at the blond Geek smartly.

"Unh-hunh, that a problem?" she retorted.

"No, buy why a hospital?" Spaz asked in wonder, watching her walk up to him with a sinister stare. She shoved the whole wad of bills into his waistband, then stopped inches from his face, eyeballing the nerd closely through his thick eyeglasses.

"No questions asked, Spaz...and you n' me can become the best of friends, know what I mean? Marissa soft but firm. She then circled him again and slapped a hand against his backside.

"Uhh...all right, maybe so, Marissa. Just promise me you're no...." He whined insecurely, watching her frown at him in anticipation of his words.

"Cop?" he chirped meekly in insecurity, taking the thick wad of bills from his waistband.

"I'm all alone here with you today, Spaz McCracken; no badge, no gun, no wire...only a lot of money and complete sincerity," Marissa said grudgingly as she unbuttoned her blouse to show him her brassiere-covered breasts where a wire tap could be hidden, then re-buttoned it up.

"Okay, I believe ya," Spaz muttered as she went to open her purse to show him no wire or badge existed there either.

"So, it's a hospital computer, that's cool," he added with a nod. Marissa paced the bland living room, seeing that he decorated with only a framed painting of a half-naked woman by a pool, as well as a big picture of a wolf on another wall.

Ken Knight

This guy was a dork, she thought, and obviously inexperienced around women, so she knew he could be easily manipulated and bought!

McCracken quickly counted the wad of money, coming to an even $2,000 all in 100's. This woman was too good to be true!

"Wow...wow...what do you want done?" Spaz spoke up nervously, excited by the cash, combing his short blond hair.

"Oh, that's just the first payment, Spaz, if you can pull this off," Marissa said cryptically, looking at his lean, lanky frame.

"Shouldn't be a problem," he added excitedly.

"Good, because I need this to be smooth, confidential and without any backfires," she said in her mild southern accent.

"I can do this," he told her boldly, pocketing the cash in his shorts.

Marissa smiled girlishly at her new cohort, walking around the room slow and cat-like. "Is your stuff al here?" she asked next.

"Yep, in the spare bedroom...I'm set to do almost any hack job you can suggest, Marissa. I'm up-to-date on all of the mew modems and software, and I dare say a hospital's system is cake...compared to a pentagon mainframe," he explained in rambling ardor, eager to please his latest "client".

"Excellent, honey, you're hired," Marissa said as she accompanied him into the next room where an elaborate computer terminal set-up sat on a cheap desk with printers and extra amenities she didn't recognize. "Spaz" was a hacker, all right.

"I'm impressed," she said as Spaz began to explain his PC "tools" of the trade, to include the lap-top computer he once hacked into the Federal Government's USENET system two months ago.

"You wanna get into the hospital's system; the hospital in Aynor?" McCracken asked hesitantly.

"Yes, the patient's logs...Can you add-to or delete?" Marissa asked in return.

"Most likely just add-to, otherwise we risk getting kicked off screen minus another password. Those systems are tricky since they catalog every patient for fifty years," he answered frankly.

"All right, I'll be in touch, Spaz....What's ya phone number, by-the-way?" she asked as she walked out his work room to leave. He told her quickly and she committed it to memory as she headed for the front door. Spaz followed, still in awe of her.

Marissa turned to face him as she pushed open the door to exit.

"Be seeing ya, Spaz," she said with a grin, then leaned forward to kiss him on the lips quickly.

Ken Knight

Chapter 4

Fayetteville:

The summer sun made him squint when he walked out from the motel room at 1:30 this afternoon, going for his parked truck.

Ray Torelli had finally gotten some sleep at last, but only a few hours. He started his truck and roared out onto the highway into downtown Fayetteville, his thoughts still burdened by the horror two nights ago. However, he thought more of Marissa now instead of Rex and the crime he is escaping from.

Driving north to try to find a decent place to eat, Ray began to think of Marissa a little more favorably despite the looming fact that she was blackmailing him. He took her advice and stayed away from the newspapers of South Carolina as well as the TV.

He didn't want to read or hear about Rex.

Pulling into a fast-food chicken place, he parked and decided to go inside to eat lunch. Ray got out of his truck and walked up to the front entrance to the place. Wearing just jeans, sneakers, and a light green T-shirt, eh was still hot in the mild 75° weather.

The restaurant smelled of greasy chicken, teasing his hunger even more so. Ray pulled out his wallet and looked over the stuffed bills inside. Nearly all of them were $100 bills, what his "fiancée" had given him for the month to stay out of Dillon.

Things had to "blow over," she said, but how do you buy an $8 meal with a $100 bill at a small chicken joint like this?! He snickered to himself in spite.

Standing in line at the counter, Ray looked at the people around him in silence. One diminutive old man stood in front of him, shaking in pose. Another stood behind him with a pair of crutches.

He glanced off to his left and saw a young couple in line with their arms in embracing affection. The guy looked like a soldier from nearby Fort Bragg judging by his "high n' tight"

Ken Knight

haircut, and the girl looked about 19 years old with a sexy physique clothed in jeans and a cut-off shirt.

He had always envied young lovers like those two, their affection so easily obtained it seemed. So goddamn easy fro someone like that soldier to meet and mate with a drop –dead gorgeous girl like that!

Ray watched the two lovers kiss lovingly as they stood in line at the counter. Eh was often dateless on weekends, and when he did have a date, it was usually with some semi-attractive unwed mother or some pudgy female cow he'd end up felling at a buffet somewhere.

Now, thanks to a tragic accident, Ray was being blackmailed into marriage by a woman who was attractive-but-unattractive on the same hand. Marissa had a body now, but her sinister disposition was too spooky to ignore.

Meeting a gorgeous lady like the one on that soldier's arm. Now, that would be nice! He thought. No, women like that always turned him down flat.

Springs Memorial Hospital
Aynor, South Carolina
4:30 p.m. next day:

Marissa was on a 10-hour shift at the hospital today, due to get off at 6 p.m. if she was lucky.

As an RN in the ICU area, she had a prime post in the hospital, especially for a new nurse fresh-out-of-college and an internship. Walking past rooms 10-C and 110-C where terminal patients lay on borrowed time, the white-uniformed Marissa Borders wanted to get onto the computer terminal now.

If "Spaz" McCracken was successful, then good news would be in the form of a secretly-hacked grid on the hospital's ER screen.

At the nurse's station in the center of the circular ICU wing, the computer terminal was vacant of the fat ass bitch who

One Minute After Midnight

normally parks there half the shift, so Marissa hurriedly sat down in front of the wide-screen DC-IB Micro pane Computer System and typed in her code and then the known password.

"Borders...check Ten-C if any urine sample is available in the catheter, then see what Mister Jones in Nine-B wants...he keeps hitting the call button," spoke the skinny Nursing Supervisor as she walked past Marissa at the computer.

"Yes, ma'am," she answered promptly, typing further to get into the Emergency Room screen and their continuous list of deceased patients.

"Cantankerous old bastard," she sighed to herself in thought of old Mr. Jones in ICU, room 9-B. Typing in the password she saw her supervisor use the other day, Marissa obtained access to the hospital's ER records rather quickly.

She typed in a name along the open line and pushed "Return", then waited seconds more.

The gold letters on the screen made her smile in success, for it was on there. The name and info she had told "Spaz" to put on the hospital's DOA list was there now. The hacker in Dillon County was no joke after-all, and her money had been well-spent.

Rex Matthewson was dead.

She quickly logged-off and left the computer to carry out her boss' orders for 10-C and 9-B. McCracken had come through, and now she considered using her services for something else since this succeeded. Hacking was an art form, and the four-eyed geek named McCracken was the artist!

Walking into 10-C, Marissa looked down at the terminally-ill man in the bed, barely alive on a respirator. Checking his catheter and its basin attached to the bed, she found no urine enough to bother with.

"Hmmh, see you in hell, Roberts," she sneered to the man lying near-death in that bed. He even looked like a corpse lying in a coffin, she thought.

Why not just euthanize people like this? She often wondered,

Ken Knight

Then again, this guy in 10-C probably lived more worthwhile and productive than both Rex Matthewson and Ray Torelli combined, she thought with a chuckle.

Back at the motel, Ray locked his door and settled in front of the TV with a cold soda before he happened to think of something he didn't consider before.

He could call anonymously to the hospital and inquire about Rex Matthewson.

Picking up the cheap phone on the nightstand, he dialed information first for the number, then the hospital administration office.

"Springs Memorial Hospital Administration," spoke the irritating soprano voice on the other end.

"Yes, hi...This is Jack Evans with the DILLON OBSERVER newspaper....I'm inquiring about a DOA you received on the early morning of June fifth," Ray lied politely.

"There's only a small amount of info I can give to the press, sir...what is the name?" replied the receptionist.

"Rex Matthewson," he said nervously.

There was a long pause on the other end after Ray said the name, making his heart beat faster with anticipation.

The receptionist was using the computer there. "Yes, sir...it's showing a Rex Matthewson, age twenty...DOA at zero-zero-forty hours, June fifth," the receptionist spoke robotically.

"Thank you," Ray said in conclusion, then hung up the phone. He was lucky he got that information, since hospitals generally let the police handle the press questions.

He wasn't surprised, because Marissa was there that night also, and Rex allegedly died in her arms as she was rendering first aid. With it, confirmed by the hospital, eh felt even worse. The ax began to swing.

Laying back on the bed with his cold soda, Ray stared at the TV set in stressful silence. "The Andy Griffith Show" was on the 25" screen, and for some strange reason, he enjoyed watching those old re-runs.

For a few minutes he forgot his predicament and just watched Andy and Barney. After two episodes and three sodas, Ray fell asleep sprawled on the bed, exhausted.

He didn't waken until 10:00 that night, and when he did, he just headed for the bathroom to take a piss.

Ray sauntered back out into his bland motel room and froze in his tracks as soon as he laid eyes on the intruder sitting in the chair by the window.

"Marissa...." He sighed in surprised disbelief.

"Hello, Ray. Your door was unlocked, so I let myself in...we gotta talk some more, honey," the casually-dressed Marissa Borders answered calmly, legs crossed as she sat there with a hand up to her face.

Her hair was well-brushed and back, down her neck in subtle curls, her face well made-up and those cat-like predatory eyes staring up at him.

"What about...more bad news for me?" he sneered in contempt, rubbing his eyes.

"No, good news actually; I told you not to worry, didn't I?" she chimed, enjoying his continuous fear.

"Hmmph, yeah right," he snickered as he sat down on the end of his room's bed, eyes on her intently.

"You been eating good, Ray?" she asked softly.

"The best fast-food around here, yeah," he said with a smirk.

"Hmmm...treat yaself to a real restaurant sometime, and if you need more cash, just ask," she offered next.

"My apartment cleared out?" he asked.

"Yes, and your stuff's been moved to a storage bin in Aynor, but you will lose the security deposit to ya landlord, of course," she answered casually.

"Fuck it," he sighed in defeat.

"When I am officially a married woman, I get one million dollars of my late grandmother's estate, so we'll be good-to-go," she reminded him, giving Ray another incentive.

"Marissa, the way I treated you back in high school...." He spoke hesitantly, recalling the times he cruelly spurned her flirtations and come-ons back then.

"Forget about that now, Ray. I forgive you, and I have made the first arrangements for our wedding in August, even got the invitations printed up since it'll be a small ceremony," she continued in her smooth, southern voice.

"All right, but you still haven't convinced me that the accident last week won't come back to haunt me," he said flatly, folding his arms.

"It's only going to haunt you if you let it, Ray...the cops won't know shit if you just stick-with-me," she said softly.

"Forever?" he replied with a frown..

"Yes, of course...I mean, you'd end up marrying one of these days, only to some trailer park chick with no money and a penchant for making babies, instead of me," Marissa said with a chuckle.

Ray hanged his head in lack of better response to her cynicism.

"Really now, which one is better for you, Raymond, since you're not college-bound or in the military...you can't otherwise do better than me?" Marissa repeated in proud tone.

"Maybe, but I don't have a choice, do I?" he retorted.

Marissa smiled girlishly at her fiancée, feeling sorry for him.

"Hey, look...you made a decision that night. honey, and fuck Rex...Retard shouldn't have been out on his Moped in that storm. He's worthless and you know it, so you bolted to save yaself legal trouble," Marissa said in cold demeanor, her brown eyes of evil piercing his like burning strobes from hell.

"Yeah, fuck him," Ray sighed in hesitant agreement.

"I'm taking advantage of your situation, but I know you'll one day see it was the best way to go," she added softly with a wink.

"Part of me want s to still tell you go-fuck-yourself," he said with a frown at her.

"Hunh, forget that, Raymond...just kick back, relax, and let me handle everything. Hell, you just learn to forget about the other night because it's taken care of, as long as you play-ball with me," Marissa added as she stood up and strolled across the motel room toward the bathroom.

"For the rest of my life...." He sighed in defeated realizations.

"And mine," she sighed as she disappeared into the tiny bathroom there. Ray laid back on the bed, eyes to the ceiling in hopeless gaze. He tried and tried to concoct a resolution to this crisis but Marissa had him covered too much.

Damn her, eh thought in contempt of the young woman. She had him by the short-hairs and was not about to let go. She wanted him for marriage! What blackmail...what conniving shit! He told himself as he lay there in defeat.

The death of Rex weighed heavily in his mind still, haunting him as he knew it would probably forever. He killed a man by foolish accident and now he was paying for it.

Yeah, Ray thought in silence of the room, maybe this "punishment" was better than prison. Either way, he was a prisoner.

When he opened his eyes again, he glanced over to see Marissa Borders coming out of the bathroom, completely naked.

"Marissa...uhh..." he stammered in surprise, ogling her well-shaped, lithe physique as she stepped up to the bed.

Staring down at Ray with hands on her bare hips, Marissa smiled slinky at her fiancée.

"Mmmhh...make love to me, Raymond, and I promise you won't regret it," she cooed softly as she knelt onto the end of the bed, eyes beaming sincerity.

Ray surrendered quickly, sitting up as her left hand grabbed his shirt to remove it.

"Marissa, you're too much," he sighed as he took in her body in admiration as well as desire, from her full breasts and washboard stomach to her muscular thighs and trimmed snatch between them.

She was on top of him in the next second, hands working to strip off his clothes. Their mouths met in a fluid kiss, then Ray eagerly kicked off his jeans and boxers, wanting her now.

"See...that's not so bad," she whispered in his ear, fingernails clawing down his hairy chest.

It had been a long time since he had been with a woman, and despite what had happened, at this moment, he welcomed Marissa.

Marissa looked down at his stiffening erection as she leaned back, running her hand down his turgid pole.

Ray reached his hands up and pawed her boobs in glee, anxious to indulge now, but she was in control now, in control like she had been since that goddamned night of June 4th.

Marissa lowered herself over his torso, kissing his chest, belly, then slid down to his raging groin area, taking the rock-hard cock in her right hand.

Knowing what she was going to do, we rested his head back to enjoy something he had never known before today.

Marissa faced his raging penis with a grin, then kissed the head, making him shiver.

She smiled cat-like over his chest at his bewildered face, then took his manhood into her mouth. Watching in sheer delight, Ray couldn't believe how easily she devoured him.

"Ohh...yeah, baby...sooo-good!" he bellowed out loud in ecstasy, enjoying her fellatio as he lay there at her command. Marissa bobbed up-and-down, fellating his cock eagerly, expert at the delicious act.

Running her hands up and down his hairy chest as she slurped on his erection, Marissa kept her eyes on her lover's face, seeing that he was obviously enjoying the blow job.

After another 30 seconds or so, she raised her head up with that wicked grin of hers, then she rose to her knees, straddling his hips now.

Before he could move an inch in response, she was on him, taking his cock up inside of her sweet, wet canal. She felt so good as she began to move on him now, hands gripping at his chest. Her face contorted in delight of the penetration as she increased her pace, up and down o his manhood as he lay beneath her enthralled.

"Ooohh, Ray...ooonnhh, Ray...yeah-baby, finally...fucking!" Marissa chimed in ecstatic ardor, riding him faster all-of-a-sudden.

Ray reached up and pawed her bouncy boobs again as she moved like a human piston, absorbing his cock completely inside of her.

"Unnh...ooaahh, Marissa...uhhh, shouldn't I wear a condom?" Ray asked in a groan, running hands all over the bouncing woman's sweaty body.

"I'm on-the-pill, silly," she chuckled with a slap to his chest, then stopped on his tool for a moment. Ray raised up and embraced her as she sat on him. She ran her hands through his dark hair, kissing his lips in passionate vigor.

"Mmmhh...you feel good," Ray moaned when their lips parted again.

"So do you, stud, now shut up and let's fuck like husband n' wife should," Marissa chimed, pushing him back to the bed.

She continued her carnal ride on top of him, and Ray guessed this was the way she like to make love, in control and on top. Foreseeing the future with this energetic, curvy young woman, he knew there was no way she could make him love her, no matter how they made love in bed.

Marissa awoke at 1:30 a.m., lying in the motel bed next to Ray. She didn't move, only looking up to the dark ceiling, then over at the digital alarm clock on the night stand.

Feeling the naked man asleep beside her made her happy. She had him now, the one she wanted all these years, and he was a good lay on top of it all!

She snuggled next to him on his left, her free hand touching his chest as he slept hard. Marissa remembered something in that moment, something she only recently forgave Ray Torelli for.

Ken Knight

High School: 1994, their junior year and prom night was upon them. Ray had taken a rather slutty blonde named Theresa to the dance and told Marissa to "fuck off" when she had asked him first!

Marissa had decided to go to the junior prom regardless since her mother had bought her dress and all, even though she didn't have a date. There at the prom, Marissa remembered being teased by some of her peers because she came alone.

To top it all off, she was singled-out by guys that night as well, targeted for a cruel prank.

Marissa remembered strolling out from the "dance hall" of the school toward the double-doors to go sneak a smoke, out in the parking lot. Without warning, two tuxedo-clad boys from her class ran out of the men's bathroom as soon as she passed by and tossed a can-full of toilet water on Marissa Borders' beautiful blue dress.

One of the guys with the toilet water was non-other-than Ray Torelli. She remembered how he laughed at her as she stood there in her ruined prom dress. Others came out of the woodwork, it seemed, laughing at the gangly young girl with braces on her teeth, victim of Ray Torelli's cruel prank at prom night.

It wouldn't have happened, she thought, if she had a date that night, if she had not been the only girl on from prom night without a date! They all laughed at her in humored cruelty.

She'll never forget the wicked laugh of Ray Torelli that night, and the humiliation of what he and the other asshole did.

Marissa kissed his stubbled cheek, feeling him more slightly beneath the covers. Damn him, she thought, for what he did to her back then. She still loved him in a unique way, a way that allowed her to do what she has done to make Ray marry her. The feeling of "victory" over him made it all worthwhile.

She snuggled closer to him, sliding her left hand down his abdomen to his groin, feeling his flaccid organ that earlier had been inside of her. Marissa felt complete at that moment there in the dark room, and she didn't worry. Worry was not in her plan, since she planned well.

"Mmmhh, for one brief moment...life is good," she said to herself as she closed her eyes again to return to slumber.

Ray opened his eyes wearily at 3:45 a.m. and turned in the warm bed only to find Marissa pressed up against him. Still sleepy, he hugged her into him gently, and lightly kissed her face. She felt so damn good, that body of hers an energetic sex-machine. He hated to admit it, but she was the best he had experienced so far.

Maybe it wasn't so bad; maybe she wouldn't be so bad to live with. She had a fit sexy body and know-how to use it in bed obviously, plus she was rich, according to her.

"Maybe," he said softly to the darkness, resting his head against hers on the pillow. He ran a hand up her torso to her breasts and she squirmed a little but didn't wake up.

Ray closed his eyes and for a moment, he imagined what it'll soon be like to be married to this woman, a woman he once rejected and cruelly teased back in school. Falling back asleep beside his fiancée, Ray drifted off quickly into dreamless slumber.

Ken Knight

Chapter 5

August 2nd:

Ray Torelli awoke in a cold sweat, raising his head up from the pillow, focusing on the head of his wife laying next to him in the bed. The moonlight beaming inside the cabin seemed to give her face an eerie "glow" as she peacefully lay there sleeping.

He was on his honeymoon now, aboard the "Atlantic Sea Prince" Cruise Liner with his newlywed wife, Marissa Borders, whom he married only yesterday back home in South Carolina.

The cabin was a plush one and the dinner they had on board last night was delicious, not to mention their first sex as a married couple earlier! Marissa can really be a slut in the bedroom, he thought with a snicker.

Here, he was in a honeymoon bed only 2 months after fatal accident involving a retarded kid on a Moped. Only 2 months after Marissa blackmailed him into marrying her. He wondered, thought, despite her promise to never use Rex's death against him once they were married, would she be tempted to once again wield that ax over his head should he oppose her in any future endeavor?

Divorce was out of question, since she could still turn him into the police even if it would look bad on her for procrastinating.

She says that she loves him. Lord knows, no woman has ever said that to him before, but he didn't feel that way about her even now. Resentment existed between them and Ray recognized it first hand. She resented him for the past, and he resented her for what she made him do this summer. "I did this," he told himself as he lay there next to his wife in the ship's cabin #24 on the Promo deck. He struck poor Rex that stormy night, and he fled the scene, complicating matters even more so.

Marissa was the only witness and she seized the opportunity like a champ.

Ken Knight

This was all his fault, though, because he started the ball rolling back on June 4th.

Their wedding was still vivid in his mind, clear and horrific to his psyche. Marissa decided on a small ceremony in the Dillon Pentecostal Church back home, and she even picked out the tuxedo she wanted him to wear, made him cut his hair shorter than usual and made him shave his thin mustache to boot!

His mother was there but not his father; his brother stood as his "best man" despite the fact that Ben Torelli was drinking before the ceremony, as well as after.

Marissa's family and friends were the most abundant in that small chapel, kind of strange people in his book. They were all wealthy like Marissa's going to be, now that she's married.

The reception at the house he's now going to share was strenuous for Ray because he had to meet all the people in Marissa's coterie whom he failed to meet before.

To top it all off, Marissa's father, Samuel Borders III, toasted their union by saying: "A lifetime of love, commitment, and as many kids as the hairs on your head!"

Kids with Marissa? My god, what a thought.

He raised in the bed and slowly brought his legs over to the carpet below. Ray stood up form the bed and glanced back at Marissa in the moonlight from the window.

A cruise on the Gulf of Mexico, stopping at Mexico's Acapulco resort was her idea. That was evident in this forced marriage: Marissa would call the shots. Personally, Ray didn't care right now because he didn't want to be here particularly.

The whole idea was still cutting into him; the idea of being blackmailed into marriage! He made his bed and Marissa Borders Torelli was sleeping in it.

Walking across the spacious cabin to the dresser where he had unpacked earlier, Ray found a pack of her cigarettes lying there. He glanced back at his wife in the bed, and then fished one of the cancer sticks out of the foil pack. He didn't smoke much until Marissa made her offer back in June at Pedro's Diner.

Now, like his wife, he enjoyed a cigarette more often than not, not caring if it became a habit.

He lit it with her Zippo and took a long drag, inhaling. Marissa moved in the bed, and Ray heard her moan for him, guessing that she would wake also.

"Mmmhh...Ray baby, where are you?" she groaned as she awoke suddenly, her head raising up slowly as her eyes tried to focus in the dark room.

"Right here, my little ball and chain," Ray answered her softly, blowing smoke toward the ceiling as he leaned against the wall by the bathroom. She smelled cigarette smoke, and made out his silhouette in the dark room, so she sat up and rubbed here eyes and yawned. It was now 4:30 a.m. "Honey, wanna catch the first breakfast at six?" she asked softly, eyeing the naked man across the room.

"Sure," he sighed in reply, not moving.

"Mmmhh...come back to bed, Ray, we've got 'till five thirty, and we can fuck until sunrise," Marissa chimed sweetly to her man, arms extended in gesture.

"Why not...hmmm...maybe I'll die getting laid?" Ray chuckled as he returned to her.

The two lovers embraced lovingly beneath the warm comforter, kissing in renewed passion. Ray moved between her legs, slipping his stiffening organ back inside her warm, but wet slot like before.

"Forever starts tonight," Marissa said in a moan of delight, repeating what she told him while fucking last night.

Ray just kissed her lips, chin and neck while plunging deep inside of her once more, enjoying the sensation of her flesh on his, her legs wrapped around his backside.

"Oooaahh, Ray...oohh, Ray!" Marissa wailed out suddenly in ecstatic delight of his penetration. He thrust harder as she voiced her approval, ramming into her canal with vigorous intent. Past lust, past contempt he continued fucking his wife in fluid ardor.

Ken Knight

"Feel so damn good...Marissa," he exclaimed in joy of the act.

"Ooonnhh...told ya you won't regret it, Ray...ooohh, Ray, you beast!" Marissa bellowed in torrid response, hearing the bed creek beneath their onslaught.

8:00 a.m.
The Promenade Deck:

The hot sun was baking the passengers looking for a tan as they laid out on deck chairs and towels all along the thoroughfare here. Ray's first impression was that this ship was too crowded.

Standing at one of the outside deck bars nursing a sea breeze with a lime, he glared out at the other passengers in wonder. Wearing only his cut-off jeans shorts and a green T-shirt with flip flops on his feet, he was in total R&R mode, despite his situation with Marissa.

She had to be somewhere around, he thought. "I'm not lucky enough to have her fall overboard and drown," he told himself in silence.

Within seconds more, Ray spotted his young wife walking in her bouncy stride toward him from the other side of the pool area. Clad in her yellow, string bikini, Marissa Torelli looked good, her body filling out the skimpy swimsuit gloriously, turning every male head within eye shot.

She wore mirrored sunglasses, too, her hair brushed back wet and down her neck. Marissa smiled at her husband intently as she stepped up to him on her bare feet. "Morning, big guy...." She cooed as she leaned in for a kiss. They kissed lovinglying in greeting, her hand going up his hairy chest.

"Good morning," Ray sighed as he looked her over. She did look delicious in that bikini.

"So, what do ya wanna do today, honey?" she asked softly, looking past him to the bartender behind the bar there.

"Maybe try that skeet shoot on the port side, and gamble a little," he answered her casually.

"Cool, just be careful with those slot machines, babe...they'll get away from ya," she told her husband as she turned to the bar, wanting a margarita.

Ray looked around at some of the other couples nearby in the sun. He wagered all of them were happy to be together. Sure, Marissa might look a lot better physically than half the women he'd seen on this boat so far, but he still didn't love her! He doubted that would change no matter how long they were married, no matter how many times they made love.

Marissa returned to his side with her margarita glass in hand, sipping it lightly as they began walking alone the sun splashed deck together.

"Ray, don't worry anymore, honey...try to put the accident behind you and we can make a life together," she said softly to her lover as they strolled past the pool and dozens of sun bathers.

"Don't think I can, Marissa....I mean, it's still overwhelming; one night out of my life I do something that could land me in prison for twenty years...but, instead, I'm forced to marry you, and here I am," he spoke in a hushed tone.

"It's not so bad, Ray, when you weigh the consequences otherwise," she reminded him coldly.

"Never thought I would be married. Shit, I had the worst luck even getting dates back home before," he chuckled in sarcastic reference.

"Majority of women nowadays are either married, engaged, or very, very picky," Marissa said casually as she looked out at the endless ocean around the big ship.

"Oh, they're unwed mothers looking for a meal ticket...or, they're lesbian schoolteachers," Marissa laughed mockingly.

"I could've gone to college like you did. It might've changed everything for me," Ray added.

"Maybe, and a lot of guys meet their future wives in college; maybe you would've fallen in love with me after all if we attended SCU together?" she suggested coyly, touching a hand to his back.

Ray took a swig of his sea breeze, and didn't want to answer that remark. Bull shit, he thought, no way he would have hooked up with her in college or anywhere else. No, she hooks him instead, on a fateful night which he now viewed as the lowest point of his life.

Stopping at the bow of the cruise ship, arms on the railing as they stared out at the ocean waters behind the boat, Marissa and Ray stood side by side in silence now.

Ray glanced down at the gold wedding band on his left ring finger.

"With this ring, I thee wed," Marissa had said as she slipped it on his finger at the ceremony only the day before yesterday.

He did the same for her, only Ray had no engagement ring for Marissa Borders. No way, since this was her idea, her blackmail! Still, he thought about how his life was going downhill before the accident on Myrtle Drive, before Marissa blackmailed him into marrying her.

No, he kept telling himself, this was not "better" for the most part. Sure, he wasn't alone anymore, and he was getting laid, plus his wife was wealthy now, but Ray still didn't want to be here.

"Have you been thinking about getting a new job when we get back home?" she asked him softly, breaking the silence.

"Yeah, I'll find something, don't worry," he answered her flatly.

Marissa raised her margarita to her lips, sipping it again as she thought.

"I'm not worried, honey, because we've got a home that's gonna be paid off and my job pays good, so we won't be hurting," she added with a grin.

"When do you get that one million?" he asked her hesitantly.

"As soon as the lawyer sends me the check…and I think I'll invest half of it," she said with a smile, looking up at the six foot man.

One Minute After Midnight

"Tell you what, though, I'll pay off ya truck for ya," she chimed impishly.

"I appreciate it, really," he answered her amicably. They then kissed once more, and fell silent in more contemplative thought.

Marissa drank her margarita faster all of a sudden, deciding to get at least a little intoxicated today.

"I love you, Ray, believe it," she said to him softly as the wind picked up.

"Sorry I can't say the same, Marissa," he answered her.

"Yet," she sighed with a wink, then downed more from her glass.

At 10:00 that night, Ray and his shapely young wife were back inside their cabin. Marissa was in bed asleep after running around all day, drinking with Ray, as well as fucking for an hour earlier this evening.

Ray, however, wasn't sleepy, so he sat on the cabin's sofa in silent observation of his sleeping wife. She looked really sweet, lying there prone, head on the pillow sideways, a pleased look on her dormant face.

Cruises like this can be boring, he thought, if you're alone. And he felt alone, even with his new wife. Damn her for making him choose like this, despite all of her "perks".

It was ironic, he kept thinking s he watched his wife sleeping in the dimly lit cabin. Ironic in that only three months ago he was broke, lonely, sexually frustrated, and self destructive. No, he was married, getting laid on his honeymoon, and was no longer financially screwed.

All for marrying a woman he didn't love; a woman who had his future under her control.

At least, Marissa was a 36D 26 32 female of young age and energy, not some cow, but she still had him on a leash with Rex's death, and he was indebted to her for the rest of his life.

There was no recourse, no reprieve from this sentence and part of him almost thought of what she had done to be "poetic justice". Ray killed a young retarded man while driving intoxicated, and he left the scene, leaving Rex Matthewson to die there on the road.

Was there a statute of limitations for manslaughter? He doubted it. Either way, what Marissa had told him awhile back popped back into his mind like a reminder: "Anything happens to me and the cops will know everything," she had told him back at Pedro's Diner in South Carolina.

So, if she dies in a car accident as no fault of his own, then Ray can expect the police to somehow learn about who ran over Rex Matthewson on June 4th?

Maybe that was a bluff on her part, maybe not. She wasn't talking about it anymore, and he didn't know how to ask.

He stood up from the soda and walked over to the bed again, staring down at the naked woman under the covers. He still hated her for blackmailing him the way she did, but he also like her physically and sexually, not to mention the money she had.

Maybe he could get used to this, if she doesn't turn on him later on. Crawling back into bed with her, he began to relax now, wanting to go to sleep because he knew Marissa would wake him at 6 a.m. for breakfast.

Snuggling close to the warm female body, slowly sliding his right arm around her torso, hand touching a breast.

She moaned slightly at this touch, but didn't waken. Her musk scent entranced him like before, making his penis go erect immediately. Just laying there, Ray laid his head behind hers, enjoying her smell, her warmth, her skin.

He didn't love her, but then, again, he couldn't say that about any other woman he knew so far, either.

At breakfast the next morning, Ray sat across from his wife at their table, eating his over easy eggs and bacon in minutes of silence. He also began to notice Marissa's penchant for eating fast, even when she wasn't rushed.

"I never asked…but, what about Rex's parents?" he broke the silence in a whisper.

Marissa put her fork down, glaring at him with those predatory eyes. Ray looked at her brushed up hair as she answered. "They were both elderly people; the old man is senile in a rest home now, and the mother died of a heart attack last month," she answered softly.

He could tell that she didn't want to talk about this topic. "Oh, just curious," he sighed with a nod.

"Don't worry, honey...everything's covered, and no one else knows squat, and they won't as long as we're together," she told him before mouthing more of her bacon and potatoes.

Marissa smiled slinky at the dark haired, round faced man who was now her husband, focusing on his broad, solid shoulders. She did love him, even if he never loved her.

"Ray, baby, you trust me, don't you?" she cooed girlishly.

"Yeah, so far," he answered.

"Rex is gone; a worthless sack of shit buried six feet underground in Remory Gardens back home," she said softly.

Ray remembered Remory Gardens as a small cemetery not far from the "South Of The Border" park on Rt. 501.

Rex wasn't "worthless" he told himself, just unfortunate, even more than he.

Marissa smirked at her husband in a gleeful stare. She perversely enjoyed watching Ray worry like this in his tortured silence.

She thought about his life before her ultimatum; an unemployed, lonely man with no real chance of a better life, a loser who was going to be evicted.

She had him, and was convinced Ray will soon completely agree with her.

She raised her left foot out of her shoe under the table and then snaked it between his legs and chair, toes touching his crotch in gentle gesture.

"Ray, baby, care to have some fun in the cabin before going out on deck today?" she cooed softly.

"Yeah, okay...." He answered his wife in slight reluctance, and she sensed it.

"Honey, you and I are gonna have a great sex life together, like it or not," she told him softly with a wink.

"Oh, I like it, honey, you're great in bed...really," Ray replied meekly, not wanting to piss her off this morning.

"Hmmhh...so are you, lover...and any time you want to make love, just tell me and I won't say no," Marissa said softly, grinning at the handsome man across from her.

"Okay, that's cool," he sighed, then ate more of his breakfast hurriedly.

"Just don't cheat on me, baby, and you'll have all the sex you want right here with me," Marissa added coldly, nudging her foot firmly against his crotch.

"Hunh, with who would I do that with...when I certainly wasn't getting' any before I met you again?" Ray retorted with a laugh.

"For future reference, Ray...forget about other women and taggin' other pussy," Marissa snickered softly.

"Well, I don't plan on it, honey, 'cuz you're better looking and better shaped than a lot of women I know," he told her in hopes of calming her tone.

"And now, I'm your wife," she chimed with a girlish smirk, then took a sip of her coffee. Ray felt like a victim at that moment, the cold realization coming back into his psyche once again. He felt so weak and leashed with Marissa now, like her slave in a way, her property, where he had no say.

Sure, the sex was great but to live with her as her lawful husband, that would take some getting used to. More than likely, he won't.

Looking across at this new wife, into her glossy black eyes, Ray saw Marissa as a predator and he was her prey, for a lifetime, perhaps.

9:30 a.m.:

Ray sat down on the chair by the cabin's port hole window, looking out at the sun drenched ocean outside the ship. Would tomorrow be as sunny when they would dock in Acapulco?

Marissa opened the bathroom door from the inside, and stepped back into the cabin. Ray looked at her now, and couldn't help but smile.

"Ray...can you do me a favor?" Marissa asked in a slinky voice, stepping to the bed completely naked except for her blue baseball cap on her head.

She knelt onto the bed and laid out on her back, legs open in invitation.

"What's that, Marissa?" he asked in return, eyeing her bare physique.

"Kiss the kitty," she said with a sleazy smirk crossing her face. She ran her right hand down to her furry cunt and fingered her tender lips in gesture.

He knew what she was requesting, of course.

After an hour of foreplay-turning-into-rough-sex, Ray was the first to hit the shower, leaving his wife in the bed exhausted but satisfied. Showering under the hot spray, he couldn't help but think of how he could get out of this "marriage" without being ruined for life. These were silent ideas which remained in his mind since June.

What proof would Marissa have besides being an eyewitness to Rex's death? She told him she had proof but refused to elaborate. Asking only angered her and a long verbal battle ensues.

No, he told himself, as he held his face under the hot spray: She had proof of some kind and could have him arrested for Rex's death any time she pleases.

That! That power she held over him made his blood boil the more he thought about it.

Here he was, on his honeymoon against his will, copulating with a woman who blackmailed him into marrying her. This was like a soap opera, only worse.

Will Marissa eventually grow tired of him like a lot of wives tire of their husbands? That would take years, even decade or two.

He did concede that she loved him in her way, because he felt that kind of affection for the first time, and it felt good, but he did not feel the same for her.

"Probably never will," he said out loud as he rinsed himself off.

Ray killed the water and stood there in the basin dripping wet, feeling the cooler room air striking his wet skin suddenly.

Rex made him feel so damn guilty, always lingering in his mind; that twisted down-syndrome face of his with blood streaming down from the gash in his face.

"Sorry, Rex, man...I almost wish I can trade you places," he said softly to himself as he reached to open the shower curtain.

"Why the fuck would you wanna do that for?" the voice of Marissa Borders-Torelli called out from inside the bathroom with him. Ray froze, realizing that she must have stepped in without him hearing her.

"Honey...I uhh...." He stammered in nervous reply.

"Wanna trade places with Rex, hunh...man, you're really a sorry excuse sometimes, Ray," she retorted as he pulled open the shower curtain to find her standing naked in the doorway.

"Marissa," he sighed in meek response, grabbing a towel.

"Did you forget that you are the winner in that debacle back in June...that you're now married and well-off, as well as a free man?" she continued in indignant pose.

"No, I just feel...." He stuttered again, gesturing with a hand to get a moot point across.

"Guilty?" she snapped with a coy smirk. "Guilty is bullshit, Raymond Torelli; and you should forget about the retard you smashed back home, forget him and focus on the future!"

"A future with you," he sighed in regret.

"Precisely, because unlike the other women over the years who passed-you-over for jocks or well-hung doctors, I saved you," she added.

"And we've got the rest of our lives for you to show your appreciation, lover," Marissa said in softer tone, walking up to the man in the shower stall.

"You're a real trip, Marissa," he said as he looked into those hypnotic, dark eyes of hers again.

"Peas-in-a-pod, you and me," she cooed, leaning forward to kiss her naked husband.

"Think so?" he asked as his penis grew erect this close to her.

"Know-so, and one day you'll know it, too, honey...me n' you are meant to be together, and that night back in June proved it," she answered as he dropped his towel to embrace her, pulling her into the shower basin, too.

"I don't love you though," he whispered as she snaked her hands around to his buttocks.

"Tell me that in five years," she cooed with a giggle, then kissed him lovingly.

"Still can't believe all this," he sighed again, hugging her into him.

"you're mine, Ray Torelli."

Ken Knight

Chapter 6

Men desire two things in life:
Danger and play. This is why
Men desire a woman; the most
Dangerous play thing!

--Nietzsche

Back home in Dillon, South Carolina was not Ray's first choice of places to go after the honeymoon. Upon arriving in his hometown on August 11th with his new wife, he wished he lived anywhere else but here. Here in rural Dillon County, his life was forever changed from the existence he once grew to accept before the incident on June 4th.

Driving Marissa's Dodge Stealth sports car with her next to him, he arrived in the driveway of her home at 7:30 p.m. sharp. He found it all-too-curious that Marissa's street was adjacent to myrtle Drive where the accident occurred two months ago.

This was his home now, in this two-story, $200,000 home made of brick, owned by his wife.

Getting out of the car, Ray popped the trunk by remote and proceeded to get the luggage when Marissa walked up to the front door of her home, leaving him to do the grunt work, of course.

The smell of the warm, Carolina air always made him feel welcome, but this evening he wished he was back on that cruise ship sailing for Acapulco. The Mexican resort city was a blast, and he wanted to remain there so damn bad.

No, he had to come home again and bake in the fires of guilt and fear over the accident involving Rex. Here in his hometown, the cops could so easily find out and arrest him for manslaughter.

In a place like Acapulco, who cares?

Ken Knight

Carrying the luggage into the posh household, Ray felt the pain of exhaustion the most now. They honeymoon had actually worn-him-out to a degree and he couldn't wait to hit the bed on the top floor and crash!

Marissa walked into the kitchen, turning on the ceiling lights first. She then checked the refrigerator and freezer there, both working smoothly still.

She was a "mechanophobe" in a way, scared of equipment breaking down, including the fridge. Walking into the living room, she found the air to be musty, so she found an aerosol can of potpourri-spray and sprayed the air of the living room and kitchen thoroughly.

"Ray?" she called out to the house interior, not hearing him now.

"Honey...?" she called up the spiral stairwell in wonder.

She walked up the carpeted, spiral stairwell to the second floor of her luxury home and stopped at the master bedroom. There, she found her husband lying face-down on their bed, sound asleep.

"Hmmhh...poor baby, worn-out," she said to herself as she leaned against the door frame, watching the man sleep in perfect silence.

"You and me, baby...to hell with anyone else," she sighed to herself as she turned to go back downstairs.

Romano's Bar & Grill
Hamer, SC
August 12th:

Ben Torelli took the stool on the far end of the bar, as usual. A regular here at Romano's, primarily because of its Wap owner, and he was Italian; Ben ordered his usual, a Michelob draft for starters.

One Minute After Midnight

Wearing just an old T-shirt, jeans and his work boots, Ben sat there, staring at his fresh beer in contemplation. He still couldn't believe his kid brother Ray was married now!

How that idiot managed to bag a babe like Marissa, so fast, he will never know. Ray mentioned that they had gone to high school together or some shit, but Ben just thought it was strange.

A "whirlwind" romance didn't sound like his skid brother at all, even if Marissa pursued Ray like he suspected. What does she see in Ray? Ben wondered in silence, thinking Ray would be "beneath" a successful chick like her.

"Hey, Tony...." Ben said to the bartender across from him, knowing the guy.

"Hey, what?" Tony responded as he glanced at the sullen-faced man with thick eyebrows, who he knew to be Ben Torelli.

"How the fuck does my younger brother get married to a good-looking broad so damn fast?" Ben chuckled jokingly.

"Dunno, but I know a little about Marissa, and she's a bitch-on-wheels; my sister knows her...one of those chicks you don't want to piss off, know what I mean?" the bartender reported matter-of-factly.

"Hmmph, well, she's my sister-in-law now," Ben snickered, then downed more of his beer.

"Good luck...and hope ya brother, Ray, survives," Tony answered humorously.

"Ah, fuck him, besides...I heard she's got money, too, so he's really on a leash," Ben chortled, then quaffed more beer.

"Man, never hook up with a chick who has lots of money 'cuz they will literally own your ass before long," Tony added with a smirk of contempt.

AA bartender's advice was always welcome to most patrons, even if he was full of shit.

Ben ran a hand through his neck-length brown hair and looked over at a passing waitress, eyeing her ample breasts in the red shirt she wore.

She caught his gaze and Ben smiled boyishly at her, remembering her name to be Kimberly. Kimberly returned the smile grudgingly, remembering Ben as one of those often-ingratiating "regulars" who hit on the waitresses every damn day they came in here.

One of the other waitresses called the type "Bar guys", those lonely souls who park at the bar of any restaurant or nightclub to drink and gawk at the waitresses without much to say or offer. Kimberly never got a tip from any of those type the two years she has been here at Romano's.

Ben watched her walk into the dining room of the joint, taking some old lady a plate full of chicken wings and fries. That waitress' ass reminded him of his new sister-in-law's; a slight "jiggle" as she walked.

"Ray, you're one lucky bastard," he said to himself in a chuckle, then downed more of his beer.

Ray had just finished painting the master bedroom when he heard his wife's car roar up the driveway at 3:15 p.m. She was off today, but was at the bank for the past two hours, straightening out the million dollar inheritance she was getting via her deceased grandmother's will.

As he came down the stairs in his pain-flecked old jeans and rag-of-a-shirt, Marissa was coming through the front door. The look on her face was one of absolute glee, and Ray winced slightly as she ran toward him with a giddy voice sounding off.

"I'm a millionaire, baby!" she exclaimed as she leapt into his arms in rejoice.

"Awwh, great, honey, so it went through?!" he retorted, feigning happiness.

"Yessir, the money is mine, and we are gonna be sitting fat," Marissa sang as they hugged. Then, she kissed him lovingly.

Marissa then bounced off into the living room to make a phone call on the cell phone there.

"Honey, fix me a glass of wine...." She said softly as he stepped up behind her.

"Sure," he said as he turned toward the kitchen, guessing that she wanted to get drunk and celebrate. Ray remembered a drunk Marissa one night on their honeymoon: she fucked him for an hour, then passed out for ten.

Fixing her a glass of wine, he watched his wife gibber girlishly on the phone with one of her friends obviously. He wondered why the few "friends" she has live so far away, like in Myrtle Beach or Fayetteville?

Marissa wasn't the kind to have a lot of friends, nor was she one of those women who had to have girlfriends around her all-the-time. That was another thing he was learning about his wife: she was a loner.

At least his lonely state-of-affairs was not his fault. Marissa seemed like she kept alone until she married him. The way she demanded marriage back in June reeked of frustrated ardor, and Ray will never forget that day.

Marissa hung up the phone and stood up as Ray handed her the wine glass.

"Let's go out tonight and celebrate, honey," she said to him lovingly, then sipped the red vintage.

"Okay, just let me wrap-up the bedroom and shower first," Ray said as he headed for the stairwell now.

"You do that....hell, maybe I'll join you," she called after him, then downed the rest of her wine. She was happy, like any new millionaire should be.

Just standing there, she thought about one inevitable bill she'd have to pay off and one more set of tracks to cover. She unbuttoned her blouse and stepped over to the spiral staircase twisting up into the home's upper floors.

"Now, I've got my money...my husband, and soon...my grand finale," she told herself softly in glee of the moment. "Hmmm...for a brief moment, life is good," she sighed as she slowly ascended the carpeted steps, undressing herself as she went.

The Steerage Inn was probably the most expensive restaurant in Myrtle Beach. It's probably why Marissa drove an hour here tonight with her husband in-tow.

Ken Knight

She was now a milli9onaire and wanted to dine like one this evening, so Ray couldn't complain. When else would he have been able to afford a place like this where the cheapest meal was $32.00?

The interior of the restaurant was furnished much like the dining hall of the cruise ship was, extravagant and cozy. Piano music played in the background, softening the mood as the two well-dressed lovers began to eat.

Ray never knew what broiled duck tasted like, until now.

Marissa was gorgeous in her blue evening dress and she made-herself-up real pretty before they left. She was a pleasure to look at, he told himself, in spite of her.

Ray was in a good mood tonight, and so was Marissa for obvious reasons, but something told him it would not last.

"Ray...I meant to ask you earlier: do you have any ideas for a job?" Marissa spoke up between bites, opening a subject he was afraid to discuss.

"Uhh, not really...but I'll get right on it starting tomorrow," he answered her meekly, hoping to end the topic.

"Good, because even though I've got money now...both of us gotta work still," she said matter-of-factly, spooning lobster meat into her mouth again.

"I know," he sighed as he stared down at his plate of expensive food.

"How do you feel about working as a clown?" she asked in sudden ardor, grinning across the table at him.

"A what?" snapped Ray in shock of her statement. She giggled in response to him.

"A clown...entertaining at parties, office gags, and such...I know the person who owns Pop N' Rock Entertainment over in Coneway, and they pay their people ten bucks-an-hour or better," Marissa explained in jovial tone.

"No fuckin' way...I can do construction work," he retorted with a frown.

"Construction's lousy around here lately, and you don't need experience to be a clown-for-hire, just a smile and humorous wit," she added with a grin of avarice.

Ray shook his head in refusal. It just wasn't him to be a "clown".

"Honey, it pays good and since I'll be paying off the house, paying off your truck, you'll be keeping most of your check," she continued, putting her fork down to take a swig from her wine glass.

"Marissa...me, a fuckin' clown?" Ray sneered in contempt, eyeballing her.

Marissa's cheery face soured fast, her disposition becoming more defensive as they discussed his job status.

"Motherfucker...you'll get a job soon or else, so take the clown job and like it...unless you have a college degree shoved up your ass I don't know about," Marissa sneered in a roll of anger, her dark eyes betraying her sudden contempt for him.

She had called him "motherfucker" only once before, during an argument they had two days before the wedding. He didn't like it one damn bit.

"Marissa, goddamnit," he managed to say as he squirmed in his seat, not wanting to make a scene in public.

"No, Ray, you're not gonna be an unemployed louse living off of me...I won't have it, so you better have a job by next week," she continued in her normal voice, making some of the other patrons in the restaurant look over at them.

"OR?" he chimed in curiosity.

"OR, you'll be sorry...." She sighed with a shrug.

"What, you'll tell the cops on me...now?" he retorted in wonder, smirking.

"Perhaps, or maybe your truck will get repossessed and your already poor credit-rating will become nonexistent," Marissa answered in a calm demeanor, sipping more of her wine.

"You can't...I mean...shit," he sipped in disbelief.

"I can and will, but it's so much easier if you go with the program," she added convincingly.

"Why do you gotta be such a bitch?" he asked in a whisper, looking around.

"Because I protect what is mine, and I want you to be happy, Raymond, and clowns are always happy," she said softly with a wink.

She's crazy, he thought to himself, certifiably crazy, and here he was, married to her! The ax was still hanging over his head, despite her promise to the contrary.

"I can't work as a clown, Marissa," he said hesitantly. She lowered her fork again and her moonlike face hardened into a mild frown, eyes burning into his.

"You can't work as a lawyer, or a doctor, or even as a policeman, either, Ray," she retorted coldly, continuing her dead gaze even as he looked down at his plate.

"I'll call the company tomorrow and get you an interview…enough said," she sighed in struggle to stop her aggressive tendency.

"Marissa…." He whispered in protest.

"Shut up and eat your duck," she retorted abruptly, not looking at him anymore.

Ray glanced over at the couple seated nearest them, wishing he had a gorgeous blonde like the woman seated next to the man accompanying her. Anyone but Marissa right now!

Driving home on Rt. 501, Ray was silent most of the time while Marissa drove. She talked in a milder tone than before, and he just listened, staring out at the black roadway.

"Hey, honey, just imagine where you'd be if we hadn't hooked up; broke, horny and alone, maybe homeless by now," she said once.

Ray didn't answer her. How do you answer someone who controls you like a puppet? He had gone from broke and lonely to this.

"At least I'm not some bitch-cow-baby-maker who cons you into raising another guy's kid in a trailer park…." She added for effect, glancing at him in the dark car.

"Hmmh, do you wanna have a baby?" Ray asked her flatly. It was the first time he actually had the nerve.

"Hell no, not yours, not any man's," she sighed easily. He was kind of surprised by that answer.

Chapter 7

> When in disgrace with fortune and
> Men's eyes, I all alone beweep
> My outcast state, troubling deaf
> Heaven with my bootless cries....
>
> > --William Shakespeare
> > Sonnet 29

Today was bright and gloriously sunny with a mild 73°F. A good day to chill and listen to the NASCAR race if Ray didn't have to help entertain his in-laws.

Mr. And Mrs. Wayne Borders of Florence, SC were two 50-year-old lovebirds who were even richer than their only daughter, Marissa. Mrs. Borders even remarked how Marissa and Ray need to buy a bigger house now that hey were millionaires, so they can raise a family.

No, Mrs. Borders, Ray thought to himself: Marissa has no plans of moving any time soon, and she hates children.

Of course, no daughter is going to tell their mom that there will be no grandchildren. Marissa put on a rather docile face while in the company of her parents, acting like "little Molly homemaker" instead of the ball buster Ray knew she could be.

Luckily, the lunch they all had together at noon went quickly, because Mrs. Borders talks too damn much.

Chatter-chatter-chatter, all about the honeymoon, the money, the houses they all owned and/or rented out. Ray couldn't stand it, so he ducked out when he could, going out back in the sun-soaked yard only to be followed by Wayne Borders himself.

"Ray...you n' me haven't really had a good opportunity to chat," the balding white man in slacks and silk shirt spoke up as he approached.

One Minute After Midnight

"No, sir," Ray said as he stopped in the green grass of the spacious backyard. He looked at the older man in asquint because of the sunlight.

"You and Marissa got together so fast, it's still a shock my baby girl's married now, but I mean it in a good way," Mr. Borders added.

No, you don't, Ray thought.

"It was a whirlwind all right," chuckled Ray in response. He hated lying like this, simply because he was bad at it.

"Hmmh, she loves you though, and I think she made a good choice," Wayne Borders added in complement.

Ray almost laughed at that statement. Boy, she had her parents buffaloed, too!

"Mister Borders...Marissa's a unique woman," Ray stammered in uncertainty.

"Tell me about it, she's unique plus-some....Hell, she's unlike anyone in either side of our family, and please...call me Wayne," the rich Realtor answered with a pat on Ray's back. Ray nodded in agreement as they stood there.

"Marissa knows things most people her age don't care to know, and she's smart as well as demanding at times," Wayne continued as he stepped around his son-in-law.

Ray didn't know what to say to that.

"Marissa said you got a new job?" Wayne asked in change of subject.

"Unh-hunh, as a clown-entertainer...pays good," Ray answered in embarrassment.

"Really, that's interesting," Mr. Borders remarked.

No, it isn't, you idiot.

Giving into Marissa's "clown job" wasn't as bad as having to tell someone else what the job really is. Pride was swallowed hard and dry at that moment. "Unemployed" sounded better than telling your father-in-law you got a new job as a clown!

Marissa had to be enjoying the fact that he caved-in to her demand about that fucking job. He starts Monday and he dreaded it.

"Wayne, you and Mrs. Borders have been supportive and we appreciate it," Ray bull-shitted again, walking the yard's perimeter with the man.

"We love our daughter and want the best for her...and, we think you-two will go the distance," he added matter-of-factly.

Ray nodded in agreement, keeping his façade.

The old man then touched Ray on the forearm, his expression suddenly one of hesitant malice. "I'll also warn you about my daughter, Ray; she's like a jackal when she's crossed...vindictive and downright mean, kinda like my wife, only worse," Mr. Borders described in a lower tone of voice, as if someone else could hear him all the way out here.

"Really?" Ray sighed in wonder. "You mean it could get a lot worser?" he wanted to ask.

"Yes, well, I probably shouldn't tell you his but...." Wayne stammered in hesitation.

"It'll be just between us, I promise," Ray whispered to placate him, wanting to hear more.

"Marissa's had a few boy friends in the past, not many though, and she was kinda possessive with them...she even physically abused one before they broke up," Mr. Borders told him slowly.

"Hmmm, we won't have that problem, sir," Ray replied, surprised to hear such.

"Funny thing is...she had this strange guy pursui8ng her just before she met you again; I never met the guy but Marissa said he was handicapped and was just a pest, that's all," Borders continued in reflection.

Ray didn't think nothing of that since Marissa was attractive after all. Why wouldn't other men pursue her affections?

Ray stopped walking the instant the idea came to his head. Thank you, Mr. Borders, you just gave me a card to play! He thought in silence.

"Well, son, I better get in before my wife thinks I'm sneaking a smoke," Wayne concluded as he started back toward the backdoor of the huge home. Mrs. Borders was obviously anal about smoking.

As he stood in the grass, feeling sweat on his forehead from the sun overhead, he thought more about what Mr. Borders had said about Marissa's other "suitors".

What if Marissa falls for another man? What if she has an affair with another man and chooses to leave me? It was a possibility and a beacon of positive light in his mind the more he pondered such.

He could be free of her if she could fall in love with someone else, someone better than he, better in her eyes! Surely, he wasn't her ideal mate, he told himself.

Another man, a divorce, and if she agrees, maybe even a juicy settlement from her hefty bank account? Things started looking brighter now.

Somehow, he had to find some guy to help him set her up for such a thing. It seemed possible, since she was good-looking. Then again, Marissa was too damn smart for her own good.

Sunday night:

Marissa relaxed on the plush sofa in the extravagant living room she redecorated this weekend. Alone in only her bathrobe with a glass of Scotch on-the-rocks, she stretched over the couch in quiet reflection.

Ray was upstairs asleep in the bedroom because he had to work tomorrow. She smiled at the success of getting him that clown job so fast. Hell, the owner interviewed Ray over the phone! It pays to know people.

Her husband the clown, just the thought of him in make-up, silly hat and size-20 shoes with a horn to honk, it made her laugh.

Serves him right, she thought. Ray didn't have a job when they got married, so why not take such a "demeaning" position?

Ken Knight

She laughed gently in spite of him, knowing it was a decent wage after all for someone like Ray.

"Heenh, if you were black I could get you into college real easy or get you hired at the Sheriff's Department, haanh," she quipped to herself. She sipped the Scotch, enjoying the "bite" of the strong alcohol in her mouth and throat. It would put her to sleep soon, and tonight she was content on sleeping on the sofa instead of with her snoozing husband.

Marissa promised herself that if Ray fucked up on this job she got him, she was going to give him hell for weeks over it. He took verbal abuse surprisingly stoical, so she guesses that she can say whatever she wants and he'll take it.

"Fuck him, if he ever hits me I'll have him locked up...that'll scare the piss outta him," she chuckled to herself softly, taking another swig of her liquor.

It felt good to be in control of money and men. Despite what has happened though, she loved Ray, but part of her wants a measure of revenge.

Yeah, that prom incident and the countless times he told her to "fuck off" or called her names like "bitch" and "dyke" back in high school. She was trying for his affections then, rather innocently, and he had to be so goddamn cruel. Why did he have to spurn her the way he did? She still wanted to know.

Monday
10 a.m.:

"Pop N' Rock Entertainment" was a rather lengthy drive form Dillon, but Ray didn't mind since it gave him time to consider skipping the horseshit job altogether.

Arriving at 10 sharp, the casually-dressed man walked into the office of the "Entertainment" company in the middle of a shopping center and asked to see the boss.

"So, Ray Torelli, you ready to become a clown and make people laugh?" the rather boisterous manager in a "Pee-Wee

Herman" suit asked Ray in feminine tone, escorting him to the back rooms of the place.

"Sure," he answered grudgingly, following the fag into the "prep room" where the clowns-for-hire got ready to perform, gag, whatever.

Rosemary is our best make-up person...and our most in-demand clown, so she'll show you how to apply your face and...then you attend clown school here for the next five days," the effete little man said girlishly as he led Ray into the well-decorated dressing-room with no windows.

"Wow," ray said in spite, frowning at the stranger with malice.

"She'll be in shortly, so just chill out and relax, then she'll show you your best face, okay?" the little man with effeminate voice and gestures concluded, pointing to the chair in front of the big mirror on the wall.

"Thanks," he said in reply to his new boss, faking enthusiasm. Part of him wanted to beat the shit of somebody right now. The fag was gone in two seconds, leaving Ray sitting there in agony over accepting such a demeaning job.

A minute later, when she walked in, Ray no longer had bad misgivings about being a clown for-a-living.

"Hey there, I'm Rosemary Jones, and you must be Ray," spoke the petite, overwhelmingly-gorgeous blonde walking through the door with a gleeful smile.

"Uhh, yes ma'am...Ray Torelli, nice to meet you," Ray stammered in awe of the young female's stunning appearance, standing to shake her hand.

"Hey...nice to meet you, Ray, and please call me Rosemary...or my clown name: Jiggles," the comely, buxom blonde answered him with a lion's grin.

Her mere presence was enthralling: a 5'3" Caucasian female of about 25, with plump, full breasts beneath the blue blouse she wore, a tight abdomen and well-rounded thighs with a full, firm ass in the designer jeans she wore.

Ken Knight

This was a goddess, he thought, and her oval face beamed beauty of eyes, lips, nose and high-cheekbones.

Her smile made him melt as she stepped up close to him, touching a tiny hand to his arm.

"You ready to become a clown entertainer?" she asked gingerly as she gestured for him to sit back down.

"Sure," he said nervously, staring at her in the big mirror while she pulled out a case of cosmetic face paint of various colors.

Her shoulder-length blonde hair looked natural and silky soft, her perfume even sweeter. Ray was delighted now, making peace with his unconventional job now that Rosemary Jones was his co-worker!

Jiggles, the clown...imagine that.

Ray sat patiently as the gorgeous Rosemary tried out three different kinds of make-up on his face. Skin tone and facial structure mattered, she told him. Finally, she found the colors that best suits his round, handsomely-even face: bond-white with blue around the eyes and dark orange lip gloss.

He sat there, enjoying every minute of the blonde bombshell's hands on his face. She ran her dry hand through his hair a couple times and it made him quiver in arousal.

"The face paint may itch some out in the hot sun, but you'll get used to it," she told him after completing the make-up job ion his entire face. Not bad for a former construction worker-turned-clown.

There, wow...it suits you," Rosemary said as she studied her work on his face.

"Yeah, it does," Ray sighed indifferently. He glanced at her bulging tits covered by the blouse she wore, wondering what ripe melons like that look like, minus the blouse?

"So, you want to be a clown entertainer, hunh?" she asked impishly as she sat down next to him as Ray looked at his painted face closer in the mirror.

"Yeah, something different than the usual jobs around here," Ray said boyishly with a grin.

"Oh, it's fun...and you get to travel some, too...you'll be doing a lot of kid parties, office gags, bar mitzvahs, and the like," Rosemary said in her mild southern accent, smiling at the handsome new employee.

"Really...so what's your specialty, if ya don't mind me asking?" he added in curious reply, staring into her sky-blue eyes.

"Me, I do office parties...bachelor parties, office gags, and strip-o-grams," she answered honestly.

"Oh, all adult stuff," Ray chuckled in realization.

"Yep, patents wouldn't like me doing my topless Jiggles-routine in front of a birthday party of ten-year-olds," she laughed in spite, gently touching his shoulder.

"So, you're a stripping clown," he said softly, nodding.

"Half the time, yeah, it's fun and an incentive to stay in shape," she said with a wink.

"I see," Ray said, looking back at his painted face in the mirror.

"I take it you were shown around by Pauly?" she asked, referring to the manager who escorted him back here.

"Yeah," Ray said in irritation.

Rosemary snickered in spite of him, knowing why Ray frowned at the mention of the boss.

"Pauly's queer as a three-dollar-bill but he's a good manager of the business and easy to get along with," Rosemary said in a whisper, smirking at Ray girlishly.

"So, you married...kids...work two jobs?" she asked him next, resting back in her seat.

"Married, no kids, thankfully, and this is my one job for now, how about you?" he replied politely.

"Hmm...single, no kids, this is the job I love, and I'm having too much fun to stop," Rosemary said softly with another wink.

"Will you and me work together any, by chance?" he asked hesitantly.

"Sure, if the order calls for two clowns at one place, why not?" she replied gingerly. Those sky-blue eyes of hers matted his resolve in seconds. Damn, she was gorgeous, and so well-endowed that she made Marissa pale in comparison. He couldn't believe she was single!

The small talk between Ray and Rosemary was easy, fluid, and interesting. She was so nice in demeanor, so "Bubbly" that Ray caught himself talking to her like they were old friends or something, disarmed by her witty enthusiasm. They talked of their past jobs and mutual interests for the next half-hour.

Rosemary worked at an exotic nightclub in Myrtle Beach before taking this job. She had been a stripper as well as a bikini-model, which suited her ample physique well.

Ray lied about his marriage, of course; can't tell a stranger about being blackmailed into marrying the sole witness to the hit-n-run you perpetrated, can you?

Rosemary then began to apply her own clown make-up much faster than she put Ray's on for him. They talked more as she did so.

Ray could tell that she had a lot of fun with this job of hers, as if the job was her purpose in life.

"Ray...what does your wife do?" she asked him as she smeared white over her nose thoroughly.

"She's a nurse over at S[rings Memorial Hospital, and she just got a big inheritance," Ray told her with hesitation.

"Shit, what are you doing, working here then?" Rosemary quipped in laughing response.

"Awwh, I gotta do something, even if my wife is rich," Ray chuckled matter-of-factly.

"That's cool, 'cuz a lot of guys I know would kick back and sponge off the old lady," she said with a nodding smile, applying her eye colors now.

She was an expert with the face paint, all right, a real artiste.

She was done in ten minutes: white paint over most of her cheeks and forehead as well as down her neck, then, a purple star painted over her left eye and her right eye surrounded by pink.

Then, her lips a blood-red with a smile painted past her mouth corners perfectly.

"Wow," Ray said as he looked at her. With her wavy blonde mane cascading down her neck and the make-up adorning her pretty face, she was unique.

"Clowns are people, too, right?" she chimed impishly as she walked to the door of the make-up room.

"Follow me and we'll find you some proper attire," she said with a hand gesture.

Ray walked out behind her, clown-face and all.

The "personnel room" of Pop N' Rock Entertainment was a spacious 38' x 45' chamber without windows, of course. Racks of clothing, clown outfits, exotic-looking jumpsuits, weird-looking shoes, hats, props and various tools-of-the-trade lined the walls, except where a long mirror was positioned.

"Here...is where you pick out your most useful clownage and props," she said as she walked him through the room, letting the door close.

"Clownage" was Rosemary's term for nearly all clown-related material pertaining to dress, even the red ball-noses and butt-horns. She was a silly girl, but sexy on top.

Ray surveyed the big room of clown wardrobe props, girlie stuff Rosemary wears, and some things he had no idea about. This was where he has landed in life, he thought.

At least his co-worker is a knockout blonde with big tits and he does have a wife to sleep with, he told himself.

Rosemary walked to one rack of clown clothes, pointing out how the floppy blue-and-gold jumpsuit might look great on him with his "style" of facial art.

Ray followed her like a puppy, transfixed about how her buttocks "moved" in those tight jeans covering them. God had created one thoroughly-sexy female when Rosemary was born!

"This is also where I rehearse for my strip routines...when I feel like I need to, she added as she walked to the wall mirror, touching the glass with her tiny hands.

Ken Knight

"Oh, yeah...hunh?" Ray sneered in wonder, checking out if the blue-and-gold clown suit fits him, and it did.

Rosemary watched the new employee in interest. She like him already, and asked herself why all the good-looking men are all married or gay?! Damn the luck, she whispered to no one.

She decided to "impress" him though, since no one else in the company was around today except for Pauly, and Pauly was a fag who didn't care what she did as long as she showed up for work.

"Wanna see one of my routines?" she asked Ray, slinky-faced.

"Hunh?" he retorted in wonder, watching her stop at the center of the space in front of the big wall mirror, hands on her hips.

"Be right back" she said as she then walked to a door on that side of the big room, going in.

Ray chuckled and looked back at the hung clothes on the racks, wanting to find a more conservative-looking clown outfit. There was no such thing!

Minutes later, Rosemary Jones reappeared inside the "personnel room", wearing a floppy white jumpsuit with multi-colored puffs on the front, huge shoes of blaze orange, and a fake red nose over her nose as well as a horn in her left hand. She made him jump slightly when she squeezed that obnoxiously loud horn.

"Hi there, guys...I'm Jiggles the clown, and I'm gonna make you smile one way or another!" Rosemary snickered in rehearsed announcement, stepping over to a small boom-box radio off the side. She popped in a tape of hers and pressed play. Ray stood about 10 feet away, eager to see what her "routine" was like.

The music was recognizable: "C&C Music Factory", a hip R&B tune that got Jiggles the clown dancing in a gyrating rhythm. The girl could dance!

She moved in a bouncy rhythmic dance, watching both Ray and herself in the mirror. This one was well practiced, and Ray stood there in silent admiration. After 30 seconds or more, she

One Minute After Midnight

unsnapped her jumpsuit's front and peeled the garment down while dancing to the music, all-smiles at Ray. He gawked at her in awe, seeing those beautifully plump breasts spill out from the clown suit, wonderfully bare. She jumped up and bounced in hip-hop dance fashion, her big boobs jiggling wildly as she moved.

Side-to-side and up-and-down, Rosemary danced in harmony with the boom-box beat, and before Ray could blink, she was out of the jumpsuit completely, and completely naked except for her face paint. Jumpsuit and clown shoes tossed aside, she danced in bouncing nudity before his eyes, unashamed of flaunting her assets.

Ray clapped in approval as the song ended, and the naked dancing clown slowly ceased her gyrations.

"You like?" she asked childishly, stepping slowly toward him now, breathing heavy.

"Hell yeah, wow, Jiggly...you're amazing," Ray stammered in response, eyeing her bare boobs and blondish crotch in arousal.

"Thanks, Ray, you're too cool...hmmh, that was my bachelor party intro-dance," she said with a grin, eyeballing the man intently.

"Too bad I didn't have a bachelor party," he chuckled nervously, sensing that she did indeed like him. Hell, he was still a stranger to her, and here she was, stripping for him to see!

"Hmmm...well, Ray, I think we're gonna work together just fine...." She sighed as she spun around abruptly and sauntered over to where her clown clothes lay.

"Hope so," he said, walking up behind her. Those ass cheeks of hers jiggled as she walked, adding credence to the name "Jiggles".

Her body was centerfold perfect: full, firm, and naturally-grown breasts with washboard belly, tight thighs and a full, well-developed ass. Ray loved that ass of hers the most, he thought; how prominent each cheek sat out and jiggled with movement of the legs, and her deep crack.

Ken Knight

That inviting blond muff between her thighs was perfectly trimmed and tantalizing to just look at; his penis throbbed in protest beneath his jeans.

What he would give just to fuck Jiggles once! He told himself that he would likely get to do that since she trusted him enough to strip alone with him today, and he would jump at the chance. For now, Ray played it cool.

"Now, Ray Torelli, consider yaself in clown school for the next week," she chortled as she pulled on her jumpsuit again, smiling sweetly at the new employee.

"Great," he said eagerly, watching those perfect boobs vanish beneath the jumpsuit again.

"It's lunch time already," she said, looking at the clock on the wall, reading 12:05 p.m.

"Wanna go out to eat with me?" Ray asked her meekly.

"No thanks, but you can…Just be back by one…and don't wipe your face off, please….Get used to wearing make-up in public," Rosemary answered him politely, gently slapping him on the shoulder.

"Deal, thanks for the dance, Jiggles," Ray said as he stepped past her with a gracious smile, tapping her on the back gently in return.

"Oh, you're welcome, buddy…maybe later I'll rehearse my strip-o-gram moves and you can watch while you try on more of these outfits, clown," she laughed after him as he walked to the door leading out of there.

"Thanks, Rosemary," he said in conclusion.

She honked the obnoxious horn in response to him.

Walking out to his truck in the parking lot, Ray couldn't believe what has transpired in four short months. From unemployed loneliness to a forced marriage, to a job as a fucking clown with a stripper as a co-worker.

He had lost his last job because he spoke "roughly" to a female co-worker and offended her neurotic sensitivities. Now, he had a job where his female co-worker dances naked in front of him to practice her clown routine! Go figure.

One Minute After Midnight

Climbing into his truck and keying the ignition, Ray thought about what it would be like to make love to Rosemary, the image of her bare physique buried into his mind permanently.

Cheating on Marissa was no problem, as long as the bitch doesn't find out. He decided that it'll be worth it if Rosemary wants to.

In typical male philosophy, he surmised that Rosemary wanted him, too, otherwise why would she have shown him her "routine" so soon?

"Hmmph, you-tha-man, Raymond," he said to himself, looking at his clown face in the rearview mirror.

Still, despite the deliciously-tempting "Jiggles", Ray loathed the idea of being a $10-per-hour clown at parties and such. Driving out onto the highway, he grabbed a towel from behind the seat and began to carefully rub off the makeup on his face.

Dressed casually with a clown face doesn't bode well in any restaurant, despite what Rosemary says.

For the money he can make plus the voluptuous co-worker named "Jiggles", he'll give it a try, even though the flamboyant demeanor of a giddy clown isn't in his nature to perform, beggars can't be choosers.

The idea of Marissa falling for another man still intrigued him and he thought about such a proposition as he drove west on Rt. 501, deciding on fast food today.

What a deal if Marissa decides to leave him! He thought. Damn the ax she held over his head.

A fucking clown. This is what I get for not going to college like my friends did, Ray told himself in cold regret.

Rosemary Jones got to the ringing phone before Pauly, answering it politely in the company's name.

"Oh, hi, Mrs. Torelli...yes ma'am, Ray's been here since ten and now he's out to lunch...I think he's gonna do fine in this business, 'cuz he's really a sweet guy," Rosemary told Marissa Torelli over the phone when Marissa asked about her husband.

"Yes ma'am, he will be back after one o'clock if you wanna call him back...." Rosemary continued as she leaned back in the

Ken Knight

desk chair, careful not to smear her makeup with the phone receiver.

"Me? I'm Rosemary Jones...I'm the one who is training Ray this week," she answered to Marissa's question as to who she was. "Would you like to speak to Paul?" she asked the rather land female voice on the other end.

"No, well okay, Mrs. Torelli, take care and have a nice day," Rosemary concluded when Marissa declined to speak with the manager.

They both said goodbye and Rosemary hung up the phone on her end. Strange, she thought, a wife calling her husband's new job to see if he was, in fact, there? A dominating bitch, she guessed.

Chapter 8

Ray pulled up into the driveway of his new home this evening at 7:00 sharp, after his first day of orientation in his raw profession. Part of him was pleased after hanging around the incredible Rosemary Jones at work, which made him horny.

Marissa had beat him home, which was unusual for a nurse to get off this early, or her shift, anyway. He walked up to the front door, finding it unlocked, so he went on in.

Marissa was on the sofa, wearing just her bra and panties, drinking one of her protein drinks.

"Hey," he said to her, dropping his keys to the kitchen counter as he walked through.

"Hey, honey...who is Rosemary?" Marissa asked in response.

"Rosemary? ....Oh, she works at Pop n' Rock," Ray answered nervously, wondering why she asked.

"I spoke with her on the phone today when I called there for you," Marissa said softly, sitting up straight as Ray approached the sofa.

"You checking-up on me?" He asked flatly.

"Sure, why not?" Marissa retorted.

"Jeezus, my wife spied on me the first day of my new job...I don't believe it," Ray sneered as he walked toward the spiral stairwell.

"My prerogative, Ray, so get used to it," Marissa snapped in defensive reply, eyes back on the TV. Ray went on up the stairs, wanting a shower now.

"Hmmph, gotta protect my investment," she said to herself in a laugh.

"Son-of-a-bitch...now you're a clown at ten bucks per hour..'cuz you can't do better...but you're my dead beat, so enjoy it," she said to herself softly with a smirk. She downed more of her protein drink, planning to go jogging at nightfall this evening.

Ken Knight

She put her bare feet up on the coffee-table her parents gave her years ago, and watched the glowing TV screen across the room. It was "Seinfeld", one of her favorite shows.

Ray cursed her under his breath as he got undressed to shower. She was going to make a habit of spying on him, even at his fucked-up job?! Damn her, he thought in simmering anger, damn her to hell for being such a castrating bitch.

He stepped in front of the bathroom's vanity mirror and stared at himself naked. He was a good-looking man with a decent physique, and certainly no pencil-dick; yet, here he was, forced into marriage and no other prospects could've beat Marissa Borders to it?!

IT was maddening, despite this nice home, money in his wife's name and his truck paid-off. He didn't love Marissa, though he didn't love any other woman so far, either.

Looking into his own eyes through the mirror's reflection, Ray ran a hand through his short, thick brown hair. Some men would consider him lucky, like his brother does, but the shackles Marissa put on him back in June makes it hard to just bend over and accept her ramrod-up-the-ass.

Damn her, he though, and damn himself for drinking, then driving that night, killing Rex. The warm shower felt strangely cold this time.

August 15th:

"Spaz" McCracken took a break from his keyboard, after three hours of hacking into a PC Game Company's "project" screens, semi-successfully. He walked to his small kitchen for a cold beer, and just popped the cap when the knock came to his front door.

Knocks-at-the-door for a man in his "business" could mean either the cops or some shady proposal from a shadowy character wanting a hack-job done.

One Minute After Midnight

When he stepped over to the window and peered out to see who it was, his blood pressure increased. Marissa, one of those shadowy characters who want his skills and pay cash up-front.

She always came right at dusk, this being the forth time so far. What, doesn't this girl know about wiring-money or E-mail messages? No, she shows up in-person alone, with a wad of money and verbal instructions.

As Spaz walked to the front door, eh reasoned why she does it this way: alone, so no one else is a liability, cash untraceable to either party, and verbal instructions because writing it on paper can convict you in court for sure. She shows up in person to make sure her job gets done, but it also told Spaz that she was a sole player in her scheme, alone in her plot against god-know-who. All Spaz knew was that the name Rex Mathewson had a lot to do with it.

When he opened the door, Marissa Torelli smiled sweetly at the young man, greeting him happily with a quick hug. She strolled past him in the doorway, into his humble abode while he looked outside for anyone else watching the closed door.

"Spaz...my homeboy, what you been up to lately?" she spoke up as she stopped at the center of the living room, hands on hips.

"Nothing as risky as you," he said with a chuckle, looking at her through his thick-lensed eyeglasses. She laughed at his remark, thinking he looks like an insect with those thick glasses over his eyes.

"Smart ass," she chided, looking him over.

A stained T-shirt, holey jeans, and bare feet were his wardrobe for today, not to mention the cheap aftershave she could smell in the room. He was a bad housekeeper, like most single guys, she thought.

Spaz smiled at the nicely-dressed woman, noticing her purple silk blouse over black cotton mini-skirt and black-stockinged legs with stiletto heels on her tiny feet. She was a damn attractive woman, which is why he let her walk all over him as usual.

87

"I've got another job for you, honey...should be easy for the skill you possess...." She said slowly, watching him go back to the kitchen area now.

"Really, what's the scope?" Spaz replied, opening the fridge again to retrieve his open beer bottle.

"A funeral parlor's system and ...my husband's credit rating," she said casually.

"Piece of cake, that all?" he answered as he walked back into the living room, with his beer and one for her. She took it reluctantly, wondering why this talented young Rube couldn't keep more than just beer in his cooler.

"I also want you to hack into the Social Security System's network, if possible, and delete someone for me...actually, two people if you can," Marissa calmly spoke, eyeballing him.

"You crazy, Marissa...that's not nearly impossible, it's bound to get me caught again?!" Spaz snapped in surprise of her offer. He walked around the room in disturbed ardor, upset by what she was telling him to do for her.

"Don't Spaz-out, Spaz McCracken, damnit. If you're good, then you won't be tracked," she retorted in a chuckle, watching him.

"No way, lady. The Secret Service will have my nuts if they catch me again, it's too risky...besides, the Federal data banks are too secure, might take forever to break-in once," he continued in a higher tone of voice.

"I want two Social Security members dropped, is that possible?" she asked coldly.

"Not impossible, difficult...because there is a back-up system in case of malfunctions, crash, or illegal tampering...you'd have to come up with death certificates, maybe a tax expert...." Spaz told her, hoping to discourage her plan.

"I want two men to show up on record as deceased or even better...never born," she said softly, stepping up to him.

"Deceased, maybe....I'd have to work through a funeral home's data base first, then hit the County Computer grid...hmmh, too risky still, because the Fed's system might spot the cyber-fake, especially at the Social Security Offices in S.C., shit," Spaz muttered in disdain.

"If you can do it for me, Spaz...I'll owe you big-time, and not just cash...but here's three-grand to start," Marissa chimed, pulling a thick wad of $100 bills from her tiny leather purse, placing the rubber banded wad on his coffee table near her.

He glanced down at the money, god-knows he needed it, but what she proposed could land him in a Federal Pen for 10-15 years!

Marissa smiled, then took a swig of her beer, eyes glued to him, watching his expressive body language. He was reluctant, but swaying.

"Who do you want to be deleted?" he asked her softly. Marissa rattled off two sets of nine-digit numbers, knowing Spaz easily memorizes.

"I can't, Marissa...it's too risky and doubtful. There's little chance I can do it completely the way you want...I mean, it might work, but it's fifty-fifty," the young hacker explained lamely, knowing that talking technical to her was useless, too.

"Life is fifty-fifty, Spaz," she chimed with her slinky smirk, staring him down.

"Hmmph, what do you want done in the funeral parlor computer system?" he asked briskly.

"Put in a name and number, date of death, June-fourth," she said casually.

"Rex Mathewson, right?" he answered back, then gulped down more brew.

"Correct...and my husband's credit rating," she replied with a snicker of malice.

"Better or worse?" he asked.

"Hah, make it go away, vanish into thin air," Marissa said with a wink. That made Spaz smile in spite of himself. She was really sticking it to her husband for some odd reason, especially since they were newlyweds! Spaz declined to ask her, though, because he sensed a "dark side" to this young woman, nor dormant, but he didn't want her angry at him.

"Now, about those numbers?" she asked.

"You sure you're not a federal agent?" Spaz retorted as he put his beer down on the sofa's wooden armrest, looking at her in contempt.

"Positive...Now, can you make someone's Social Security number disappear?" she responded harshly, gripping her beer bottle tightly in frustration.

"Maybe...I'll make no guarantees, but...." Spaz stammered back, wringing his hands nervously. Marissa paced around the living room with him, thinking hard on the matter, deciding on her private course-of-action.

"....but what?" Marissa chimed, sensing his apprehension.

"Uhh...Oh, I don't know...uhhmm...." Spaz rattled in discontent, eyes to the rug.

"Spit-it-out, damn you," she chortled with a smirk of humor, then took another sip of her beer.

"I think it's worth more than three, if it can be done," Spaz spoke flatly, not really wanting to demand anything.

"Ah....Certainly, my friend, certainly it's worth more, and I'm glad you do have the balls to say so," Marissa said with a smile.

He looked up at her and nodded.

"You succeed at the entire package, and you'll get another three-grand cash," she offered, watching him nod in agreement.

"No guarantees," he reminded her.

"Never are, so just go with it," Melissa sighed in angst, eyeing him intently.

Spaz stepped into the room where his "work table" of computers were to check on one thing before committing to such a risky task. Half of him wanted to refuse, but for $6,000 cash, he was leaning toward saying yes.

When he came back into the living room, she was nowhere to be seen.

"Marissa?" he called, seeing the wad of cash still on the coffee-table. Did she leave already? He wondered, stepping over to the dusty sofa.

Marissa Torelli reappeared from the kitchen, minus her clothing now. Spaz froze in place, awestruck by the sight of the naked female standing in his living room now, hands-on-hips.

"Still think I'm a cop, honey?" Marissa chimed girlishly as she posed provocative, seeing sweat on his face now. She raised her right hand up to her face, one finger in her mouth, sexy as hell.

"Omigod, wow, Marissa!" Spaz managed to say as he took a few steps toward her, shaking slightly.

"Heenh, work with me, stud, and we can fuck like rabbits...or, we can part-way now," she offered with a cat-like grin, eyes beaming sensuality.

"Oh, I'll work for ya, Marissa, no problem," he said in an anxious tone.

She smiled sweetly and then moved up to the nervous young computer nerd.

"When was the last time you been with a woman, Spaz?" she cooed, running a hand up his sweaty shirt.

"Uhh....Well, to tell ya tha truth...." He stammered, eyeballing her.

"You're a virgin? Wow...didn't think any existed these days...but it's cool," Marissa said softly, then leaned in for a kiss to his quivering lips.

He touched her arms first, relishing the feel of her soft skin, and her gentle kiss so enthralling. Looking down at her shapely, well-filled-out body, he felt himself go erect immediately, the thrill of it almost intoxicating.

"Mmmhh...I'm gonna fuck your brains loose, McCracken. Now, get out of those clothes," she sneered lustfully to her quarry, pushing him back with two fingers to his chest, toward his cluttered bedroom.

He smiled in giddy anticipation as he obeyed her order, the T-shirt, then the holey jeans, off in seconds. Landing on his

Ken Knight

single-sized bed with a raging hard-on, Spaz gawked up at the gloriously-naked Marissa entering his bedroom like a panther, kicking the door shut behind her. This was a first, his first! Right now, he'd do anything for her, and he marveled at what she was going to do to him, now.

Marissa looked down at the skinny guy lying there as she stood at the end of his bed, triumphant over him. "Hmmm...you want me, Spaz?" she asked, toying with him.

"Oh, hell yes," he said awkwardly.

Marissa smiled sleepily, kneeling onto the bed toward him, eyeing his engorged manhood. "It's about time you put this tool to good use, young man," she said impishly, touching it.

"Spaz" quivered in anxious anticipation as she gripped his rock-hard erection in one hand, grinning at him with a sleazy expression. Marissa then lowered her head to his organ, taking him in a way he had only seen in porno films. Her mouth had a life of it own. Wow!

The fellatio was so smooth and enticing, the sensation as she bobbed up and down like a human-head piston, sucking his flesh eagerly, nearly swallowing his pecker whole. She was good at this, he though, as he lay at her mercy, watching in delight.

"Oh, yeah, Marissa...oh, yeah, that's it." He moaned out loud in delightful rancor, running a hand through her short hair. She raised her head, licking her lips, eyes on him like a predator to her prey. She slid up over him, lying on his thin chest as her mouth kissed his neck eagerly, then his chin. Spaz snaked his arms around her soft body, hands hesitantly slipping down to her ass.

Before he knew it, his raging penis was inside of her, and it felt so damn good! Marissa cooed in reception of him and rolled over with Spaz for easy missionary-sex. Just like in those dozen porn films he had stashed in his TV drawer, this was pure, inhibited fucking and he loved it!

"Aaahh...heahh...ooaaahh yeah!!" he roared as he moved between her legs like a madman, thrusting into her vigorously in pumping rhythm, hands pawing her boobs as he leaned into her now. This guy was a virgin! She thought.

"That's it, baby...ooohh, fuck me, Spaz," Marissa chimed girlishly, egging him on, feeling better now that he was drilling her harder, faster.. At this rate, he'll be done in 60 seconds, she thought, hand exploring his torso as the young man indulged his first taste of womanhood rather sloppily.

She looked up at his sweaty face, wondering why he didn't take off those pop-bottle-thick glasses now. Spaz was in-the-zone, pumping into her sweet flesh in lewd abandon, his contorting face almost making Marissa laugh as she quaked beneath his onslaught. It felt good, though, even for a beginner like Spaz.

He was most comfortable in the missionary, so she didn't go for another position, letting the young man continue his speedy copulation. Spaz felt that peculiar sensation well-up fast, and he arched his back, plunging his organ as far as possible inside of her and erupted in sweet release, moaning out loud in triumph, raising upon his knees as he unleashed inside of the woman's canal.

"Whoah...big guy, you came already?" Marissa chided impishly as he slowed to a stop, breathing hard. He nodded with a grin, pushing his glasses back up on his nose.

"Hheenh, good boy," she sighed with a smile of avarice, staring up at him intently.

Spaz pulled out of her and felt weal all of a sudden, so he hopped off the bed and ran to the bathroom across the tiny hallway from the cluttered bedroom. Marissa heard him barfing violently in the bathroom, and she laid there, laughing in spite of him.

"Shit, he was a nervous wreck," she chimed as she laid her head back on a pillow, curling up on the sweaty bed in relaxation. She laughed in hysterics at the no-longer-virginal Spaz McCracken.

Ken Knight

August 20th:

A mockery of manhood, that's what he thought of this. Ray Torelli, all suited up in clown garb, happy-face and big red nose topped off by size-20 clown shoes and a funny red hat, played out the act for a kid's 5th birthday party here at 143 Pirates Cove in Florence.

The 5-year-old boy whose party this was for, was a bratty little snot, so spoiled that he had to be catered-to the whole time by his doting mother, the aunt, and, of course, the rent-a-clown, Ray Torelli. After an hour or so of gags, jokes-for-5-year-olds, and a surprise for little "Noah John", Ray was ready to quit.

The money was good, that's what he kept telling himself, and it wasn't physically hard work, either.

Little Noah John broke out crying when Ray, the clown, patted him on the back to say good-bye. Then, the kid spit food on his clown jumpsuit.

"Say good-bye to Bo-Bo, the clown, kids!" spoke the mother of the birthday brat as Ray waved, enroute to the back door of the house, where he entered earlier.

Bo-Bo: What a goofball goddamn name for anyone with a hair-shred of dignity, even at $10 an hour. That flaming fag named Pauly back at the office suggested "Bo-Bo" and Ray just couldn't bring himself to conjure a name on his own. Damn the luck!

Back in his truck, Ray lost the hat and gloves as well as the shoes, then lowered his white clown suit down to his lap, and drove onto the highway as fast as possible, heading back toward Aynor.

That was his 7th kids' party in one week, not o mention the weird office "gags" he was paid to work where he brought a secretary trick-flowers and embarrassed a boss with a honking visit at lunch time. At least, he wore makeup, so it wasn't too embarrassing for Ray, anyway.

"Say good-bye to Bo-Bo, the clown, kids…awhh fuck!" Ray snarled in contempt as he drove into faster traffic.

One Minute After Midnight

Stopping at a red light, Ray happened to glance over to the car in the lane beside him, seeing a young couple gawking back at him and grinning in ridicule.

Damn, his clown face!

"Hey, Bozo...I thought your show was canceled twenty years ago!" the male driver yelled out to him, making his comely girlfriend laugh hysterically.

Ray just looked at them in quiet anger, hands on the steering-wheel.

"Awh, looks like Bozo's gonna cry!" cheered the girlfriend, pointing at Ray in laughter. The light turned green and the couple roared on ahead in their sports car, probably still laughing at the clown in the Chevy 4 X 4.

"That's Bo-Bo, you assholes...and your girlfriend licks my balls," Ray chuckled to himself, driving on past the light, watching the hecklers speed up out of sight. He laughed in spite of himself, realizing that he does look ridiculous like this.

Driving toward Rt. 501, listening to country music, Ray couldn't wait for the day to end.

8:00
Same night

The Diamond Back was a country-western restaurant/club located in Dillon County not far from home, so Ray Stopped in for one drink after getting off from his job at 7 p.m.

He sat at the second bar there, on the end where he chose to smoke and have a beer. The place wasn't that crowded, and he liked it that way, so he could just sit there and listen to the music for awhile, and think.

Nursing his beer and puffing on one of his wife's cigarettes, he didn't notice the man sit down on the barstool next to him. Ray lost his thoughts for a moment and glanced at the black man in jeans, boots, and jean jacket next to him.

That was unusual, a brother dressed like that, in a country bar like this, by himself?

"Hey, man," the thirtiesh black man spoke to Ray, then motioned to the bartender for a draft beer. Ray nodded in return.

"Name's Giles...how ya doin'?" the man spoke when Ray glanced at him again. Ray extended a hand to shake and returned the greeting.

"Ray Torelli," he said casually, gripping the black man's thick hand in meeting.

"Man, this place is lame tonight, no women dancing, nothing," Giles said in a hearty chuckle.

"Yeah, but they're nothing but trouble, anyway," Ray chortled in reply.

"Awh, not really, brotha' ...women are the spice of life, man, like beer and music, only you gotta know how to charm them right, and tell them what they wanna hear, ya know?" Giles explained amicably.

I'm not your goddamn "brother", Ray thought to himself, glancing at the preachy "brother" named Giles.

"Maybe so," Ray replied with a shrug.

"I just gotta find me the right one, that's all...one that's fine-as-wine and sweeter than my grandma's sweet potato pie," Giles added with a laugh, then downed some of his beer.

Who was this guy? Ray asked himself in wonder, finding Giles to be very unlike the archtype.

The redneck-brother just gave Ray an idea with what he just said, and Ray had to laugh as he considered it.

He began to engage in small-talk with Giles, rapping in friendly dialogue as they sat there and drank beer. Ray even bought the man his second and third as they talked for an hour or more. Local boredom, country music, politics, sports, women, all topics of discussion between Ray and his new acquaintance.

They talked and talked, so much that Ray lost track of time and knew Marissa would be pissed about him coming home late, especially passed 10 p.m. To hell with her, he thought, because he had a plan to foil hers, anyway, and the smooth-talking Giles here was gonna play into it...maybe.

If Marissa could scheme a plan to twist his life into something he hates, then, by god, he can mind-fuck her in return.

Talking more about women, Ray learned Giles' "philosophy" about the subject, and the more Giles told him, the more Ray was convinced he could trick Marissa.

September 3rd:

Ray walked in the front door at 6:00 p.m. and found Marissa cooking in the kitchen. He walked up to her and they kissed lovingly, then she asked him about his day at work. Of course, he never told her about the benefits of long lunch-hours and getting to watch "Jiggles, the clown," practice her strip-dance routine in the wardrobe room of the office. No way she could find that out, and he hoped she never sees Rosemary.

Nothing like the presence of a gorgeous woman to stir the jealousy of your wife or girlfriend!

He did, however, entertain the notion of how jealousy could work against Marissa. Damn the thoughts of complacency, he thought as he sat down in the dining room to prepare to eat.

She was a good cook ,good in bed, and good to look at physically. Some...no, a lot of men would love to have her. And here he was.

Pot roast and steamed vegetables, with iced tea and a tiny glass of red wine. Marissa like dinner time and didn't mind cooking, even though she could afford a maid.

Sitting down at the 6-foot-lon dining table across from her husband, Marissa began to eat without saying anything at first.

"Honey, you haven't said anything about what you might do with all that money yet," Ray said after a mouthful of roast.

"Hmmm...rather simple, actually...a hundred grand into T-bills, another hundred-grand into stocks, and the rest on some investments I've decided on...maybe a new house, but then again, this one is big enough for us," she said with a casual shrug of indifference, forking a piece of meat into her mouth, chewing slowly.

In-other-words, Ray, it's none of your damn business, is what she was saying politely. He just nodded and continued eating, pausing for a moment to tell her this was a good meal.

Yeah, living here in her huge home that was too big for two people, near the exact location of the accident that changed his life forever.

And, a job that makes him feel like some kind of fag in a silly outfit, even though Rosemary Jones I pleasant to work around, this was the life! He thought in depressed consideration.

What worse punishment awaited him if he spent years as Marissa's latch-key hubby? Ray wasn't thinking about the good things like money, good food, great sex, and a home as he ate there, plotting hi supposing move against her.

She had to break off their marriage, and only then could he be free of her and the ax she held.

"How was work today?" she asked softly, eyes burning into his from where she sat.

"Usual…kids' party, then another right after that," he said casually.

Marissa smiled sweetly in response to his answer, and Ray stared at her soft, moon face in wonder. Damn it, she was enjoying this shit, him telling her about his clown job…it was a smile of malice aforethought! He thought.

He looked at what his wife was wearing now: a blue silk blouse and designer slacks with stiletto heels. That's right, she was off today, and he wondered why she dresses so good to go shopping? Yeah, another idea hit him square in the brain.

Marissa looked good when he still had on the clothes he wore from before they got married. Sure, she paid off his truck and bought him a Bulova watch, and a portable CD player with headphones, but nothing worth the money she has, nothing to say that she considered him worthy of expensive gifts.

One Minute After Midnight

Marissa was an A-class female with his C-class ass seated at her table. Why? It didn't make sense, except h=for her "love" for him. That, too, felt more like kinky possession.

"You know, I gotta go shopping for some new clothes," he told her softly, not looking at her.

Marissa nodded casually, dark eyes glaring at him as she ate.

"After we eat, you want to go out?" she asked casually.

"Sure, that's cool," he said as he reached for his drink.

Marissa smiled, then gingerly spooned some sliced vegetables into her mouth, eyes blued to Ray as if she were studying him.

"Don't suppose I might see a few thousand in my savings account?" he asked hesitantly.

"Sure, if you save your paychecks..." she chimed with a snicker of humor. It wasn't an answer Ray found funny...not at all.

"Honey, what was the fifteen-thousand I paid on your truck title?" she snapped before he could retort.

"I thought...just...." He stuttered in growing anger.

"That I'd share it all with you?" she laughed in response, putting her fork down and joining her hands in front of her face, elbows on the table.

"We might share our bed and our home, but a million dollars...when you barely geeked-out-a-living before we met?" she chuckled matter-of-factly.

Ray didn't know how to respond, his anger frowning to near boiling point.

"Honey, don't worry...I'll take care of it and you're getting benefits, so forget about sharing my cash," Marissa concluded on the subject!

Ray couldn't eat anymore, so he just downed the rest of his tea ad didn't look at her.

Benefits, she said. Benefits like an indentured servant! There he was, with a rich wife who didn't want to throw a couple grand hi sway because he was poor before she forced him into marriage. The bitch.

Ken Knight

He wanted to call her a bitch so bad he could taste it right now, but he refrained. She might buy him some clothes this evening...maybe.

Despite her sex appeal, part of him didn't want to fuck her anymore, either. Maybe that was a good thing, a "distancing" from the woman he didn't want to stay with. He couldn't be her "ideal man", no way. Maybe another would be...maybe.

Chapter 9

Lake Shore Mall
Dillon County
That night:

Ray walked hand-in-hand with Marissa as they entered the small shopping mall together. Marissa was dressed-to-kill as usual, and her husband casual, in jeans and a clean shirt. He looked to change his attire now that their lifestyle had more potential.

Clothes make-the-man, it's been said, though Marissa obviously didn't care about what he wore, obviously.

The place wasn't too crowded this evening, but a lot of couples were there, walking, browsing, shopping. Ray remembered not too long ago, when he couldn't even get a goddamn date to go malling or even out for a pizza in this town. Now, he was married to a rich nurse who dressed like a runway model just to go shopping.

As they walked together, he listened to her chirping voice commenting on the stores here in the enclosed mall. He also couldn't help but notice other men gawk at Marissa as they passed by. She was an attractive woman, unlike five years ago in school. She was also too damn smart for her age, too conniving and squared away.

Most women her age were still lost in college, pregnant by the wrong man, "experimenting" in drugs, booze, and lesbianism; but not Marissa Borders!

Ray thought it funny as he kept seeing other men eyeball his wife's figure. All these guys lusting after her, and here Ray was, her husband. His idea regarding another man continued to spin inside his mind. It was a god idea, getting better every time he pondered it.

He felt good tonight for some reason, good in prospective success, sure of himself for once. Holding Marissa's hand still, he headed into a men's clothing store next to a restaurant.

After selecting three pair of designer jeans and two silk shirts for purchase, Ray walked up to the cashier counter to pay for them, flashing his one credit card form his wallet.

The cashier ran his card number through, and waited while Ray stood there, watching Marissa as she strolled around the store aimlessly.

The cashier gave him a puzzled look, then ran the card through again.

"Sorry, sir, this card isn't valid," she said with a puppy-dog expression, holding the credit card in the palm of her hand.

"What...I've got about five hundred dollars more on my limit," Ray stammered in surprise.

"I'm sorry, sir, the machine is coming up invalid...I checked twice, and I'm supposed to confiscate this, but you can have it back," the cashier replied, handing him the card.

"I don't believe this shit," Ray sneered as he looked at his one credit card.

Marissa overheard the discussion and walked up to Ray with a pained expression. Way-to-go, McCracken, she thought to herself.

"Card no good?" she asked casually.

"Seems that way. It's sayin' invalid, but I've had this card for two years," Ray replied as he pocketed the card in disgust.

"It's okay, honey, I'll pay for ya clothes," Marissa said as she looked at the cashier, pulling her own credit card from her purse.

This was embarrassing as hell for Ray as he stood there like a little boy whose mommy had to pay for everything. Marissa paid for his clothes and even carried the bag on the way out the store.

"Man, that was embarrassing...Wait 'till I call the credit card company tomorrow, shit!" Ray sneered as they walked on down the mall.

"Don't worry, honey, it's probably just a computer glitch or something," Marissa lied softly.

"Hmmph, maybe," Ray fumed without looking at her.

"Let's get something to eat," she suggested, wanting to get his mind off of his no-longer-existent credit rating and credit line.

McCracken had done it, she thought.

1310 Courthouse Rd.
Dillon, SC
9:30 that night:

Jiggles, the clown, stepped into the living room of the house full of men and began her humorous "Clown dance" aimed at the groom-to-be seated in the center of the room while, all his buddies sat or stood off to the sides happily watching the act.

This was a bachelors' party, one of countless she had been hired to work.

And strip for.

Her giddy music blared from her boom box as she danced in hopping gyration around the groom seated in the center of the room. She slowly peeled off her floppy clown suit, teasing the on-lookers as she always did.

The men roared in delight as she released her big bare breasts, finally jiggling them madly as their approval bellowed louder.

Rosemary Jones danced in jubilant ardor for the grinning "bachelor" in the hot seat, shedding her clown suit slow and methodically, enjoying the whoops and cat-calls of her admiring room-full of men.

"Jiggles, I love you!" roared one of the more intoxicated revelers, making the clown-faced stripper laugh in glee, dancing to the rhythm of her hip-hop music playing now, completely naked;

Ken Knight

She purposely shook her boobs for her audience, letting them land on the groom's head a few times. This was why Rosemary called herself "Jiggles" the clown, and it's why locals from Dillon to Myrtle Beach called to reserve her time, with Pop n' Rock Entertainment.

Dancing in gyrating motion, she got too close to one guy and felt his hand touch her bare ass. Oh, well, he thought, they're fun.

The groom reached out his arms to hug the gloriously-naked female clown and Jiggles landed in his lap, kissing him square on the lips in conclusion of her extra dance for him. Sweat was smearing her make-up.

Lake Shore Mall:

Ray wasn't hungry, so he just had a beer while he and Marissa sat at the bar of "Ruby Tuesdays" restaurant here at the mall. She had a chicken sandwich and a glass of soda, again making him wonder how someone with her physique ate whatever she wanted.

Ray glanced around the restaurant and glimpsed someone he couldn't believe was there the same time as he, sitting over there at a table alone with a beer. He wouldn't have to go back to that dive "The Diamond Back" to find him after all!

Ray hopped off his barstool and walked over to the lone black man seated with his back to him now.

"Giles!" Ray quipped to get his attention. Giles turned around and grinned ear-to-ear as Ray extended an hand in greeting.

"Hey, Ray man, how ya doin', bro?!" Giles responded amicably, shaking his hand and gesturing for Ray to join him.

"Hey, man, I'm cool....Funny runnin' into you here...you with somebody?" Ray answered in turn, nodding in respect of the moment.

"Naawh, man, I'm just killin time, how about you?" Giles replied casually.

"I'm here with my wife...come on over and sit with us at the bar," Ray said insistingly.

"All right, I can do that," Giles said as he stood up, wanting to rap with Ray more and meet this wife he spoke-of back at "The Diamond Back."

"C'mon," Ray beckoned, leading the casually-clad Giles over to Marissa who was wondering who her husband was talking to over there.

"Marissa...this is Giles...Giles, this is my wife, Marissa," Ray spoke up in introduction. Marissa smiled sweetly at the black man in jeans, cowboy boots, and jean jacket, shaking his hand hesitantly.

"Nice to meet you, Marissa, I've heard a lot about you," Giles said first, smiling at the comely lady on the barstool.

He wondered why Ray told her he knew him from "way back" when they had only met a week ago? Oh, well....

"Sit down, man," Ray said sharply, gesturing to the stool next to Marissa.

Giles took the seat with his bottle of beer in hand.

"You-two just got married, hunh?" Giles asked casually, eyeing Marissa intently as Ray took the stool on the other side of her.

"Yeah, August first," she answered with a forced-happy face. Marissa was annoyed by this disturbance of Ray's "friend" while she was relaxing at the bar.

"Ray, my friend...you've done well for yaself," Giles chimed as he turned to look Marissa over more.

"Thanks," Ray said with a nod, then Marissa shot him a mean glance. That told him she was not happy with this interference.

"You married, Giles?" she asked him softly.

"No, ain't found the right one, I suppose," he answered, looking into her black eyes. Her eyes gave Giles an eerie feeling, kind of like he was looking into those of a reptilian, a woman's gaze, but that of an animal, like a jackal.

"You will bud, everyone does eventually," she said with a glance at her husband on her right side.

"Aahh, some people settle for someone, but not me," Giles said with a smirk.

"Ray and I are soul-mates," she added abruptly, looking at Ray devilishly, then took a sip of her soda.

"That's cool...." Giles said softly, suddenly feeling out-of-place. Ray fought off the urge to laugh.

"Be right back, y'all," Ray spoke up suddenly, leaving his stool to trot off to the bathroom, hoping Marissa might get to talking with the smooth-talking Giles Visor when he wasn't near.

Marissa watched him disappear into the restroom across the way, then grudgingly engaged his friend in small-talk. She never told Ray of her silent dislike of black people, because it wasn't important at the time, and the fact that racial opinions now-a-days are so "forbidden", one with dislike of some minority may find themselves like those accused of "witchcraft" 300 years ago...some free country this is!

Ray came back out of the restroom minutes later to find his wife talking with Giles rather steadily. He stood there, watching them converse for another minute, their backs to him. His idea blossomed even further as he slowly walked up to the two chatting acquaintances, and knew what to do next regarding Marissa and "another man". He heard what was being said now.

"Me? I'm trying to get hired on the local police, either in Aynor or Dillon..." Giles said to Marissa.

"Oh, you wanna be a cop, that's cool," she answered him with a grinning nod.

"You've got the size for that kind of work," she added, then sipped on her drink again.

"I do....Matter-of-fact, we've both got healthy bodies," Giles said softly as he smiled into her face boyishly. Then, Ray sat down next to Marissa on the other side.

She just smiled in response, resisting the urge to tell this "smoothey" to go stick his in a knothole somewhere. No, if he was Ray's buddy, then she would maintain appearances. Marissa felt something weird now though, as if something just wasn't right in Denmark!

After telling Giles good-bye and exiting the restaurant a half-hour later, Marissa and Ray walked in silence to the truck.

Getting in, Marissa asked him how he came to know Giles, and Ray told her he used to work with him a year ago. "Way back," yeah-right. She didn't press him further on the subject as they drove home.

"I love you, Ray," Marissa said after ten minutes of driving in silence, both of them staring out at the dark road of Rt. 501. Ray only nodded in acknowledgment of her statement. If he loved her he would say so, but didn't. He honestly didn't know that feeling, so he couldn't' care.

"I look forward to the day you say that back to me," she added softly, eyes on him in the dark cab of his tr4uck, watching him drive. "Maybe," he sighed indifferently.

"Liar...." She sneered in a whisper.

Ray glanced at her in contempt, breaking his somber mood. She was like that, though; one moment serene and pleasant, the next a bitch!

"How come you never mentioned this Giles Visor dude before?" she asked, deciding to re-hash the topic.

"Ah, just didn't ...no big deal," he answered with a shrug.

"And you just let him talk-smack to me like he did?" she asked politely.

"Hunh, what...he say something outta line?" Ray retorted, feigning concern.

"No, actually he's a nice guy, your friend. You oughta invite him over sometime," Marissa countered, hoping to see a twinge of jealousy in her husband when she suggested such.

"Oh, okay...yeah, have him over for dinner sometime, hang-out, sure," Ray replied in enthusiastic agreement, eyes on the road.

Ken Knight

That was not what she wanted to hear. Giles flirted with her and Ray didn't care?!

"Hmmm...I'm surprised a man like that is single, heenh-heeh," she added to try and provoke a jealous response form Ray.

"Hunh, some guys stay single, Marissa, no big deal," he sighed casually.

No such luck.

No big deal, he said. Something was funny here and she couldn't put a finger on it.

September 10th:

This was too surreal in scope to be a simple nightmare. No, it sounded more like a conspiracy-on-rye! Ray had been on the phone to his credit card company and the bank for the past five days, trying to iron out this financial problem which seems to be growing worse for his name!

The bank he had a savings account with claims to have no computer record of his account balance and his Social-Security-number isn't in their master computer file, either!

His credit rating is non-0existent and his credit card company have no record of him even applying for a card two years ago!

It was as if he has been "erased" on financial record. No bank account, no credit, no social security number?!

He just got off the phone with the Social Security Office in Charleston, and some bureaucrat there told him that the database was showing his Social Security number belonging to a deceased man named Gomez in Florida! This was unreal.

At least the Social Security Office promised to investigate; if they do, he'll be surprised.

Sitting in the den of the house on the second floor, Ray relaxed in the recliner with Marissa's cell-phone in one hand, a beer in the other. He had already smoked one pack of cigarettes

One Minute After Midnight

and considered another as he sat there in his jeans, aching with worry over this mess.

How much worse could it get for him? Rex dead, Marissa his jailer, bankruptcy and financial non-existence.

This couldn't' be happening, and the more he thought about it, the more he wondered about Marissa. Could she, somehow, ruin his credit, sabotage his SS number? How? Why? The possibilities ran through his mind endlessly as he sat there in the quiet, dimly-lit den of the huge home, alone with his horrors.

Maybe I deserve this. Maybe this is justice for what I did to Rex. Rex, a retarded kid with no other cause in life but to exist in his simple world, and I killed him! Instead of prison, Marissa Borders holds him incarcerated in this museum-like house of hers not far from the crime scene.

Maybe I deserve this, to be ruined as if I was sentenced to 20 years in prison; no money, no self-esteem, a job other men of pride refuse to do, and having to sleep with my executioner!

Maybe Marissa planned it all…my god, what was she doing out jogging in that rainstorm on June 4th? She's a work-out nut, yes, buy why in a storm? Was it coincidence when he didn't remember driving past a jogger along that road prior to hitting Rex on his Moped?

It all sailed through his tormented mind as he sat there, self-paralyzed in fear and loathing.

Never did he for once imagine being married to a shapely woman like her only to be so miserable, held against this will!

Prison can't be so bad compared to this nightmare. No record of his credit, no Social Security number, he was financially inequitable! Could he still hold a job with such a problem? He wondered.

The thought of turning himself in to the police and confessing his crime was beginning to appear less heavy than the burden he now had as Marissa's footstool.

Maybe this was "justice". It has a way of finding you, he had been told once.

Maybe this was hell, his very own piece of hell where he was sentenced to something more torturous than flames of sulfur and chains of ice.

Marissa had to have an answer to one thing in this financial mess, one due at least, and so he waited impatiently for her to return home from her nursing job this afternoon.

Waiting was another torture.

No. Maybe he shouldn't say anything to Marissa, especially if she does have a hand in it somehow? It seemed impossible yet logical since control over one's financial status is one way to control him form within.

The conspiracy theory sounded crazy, and there was no way he could come out and blame her without proof. Marissa was a she-devil when she was pissed-off. She broke her mother's wedding gift the last argument they had by throwing it across at him.

She could throw a ceramic cookie-jar at his head but if he ever physically hit her, she promised that she would have him locked up for it. He took her seriously on that kind of threat, like he did when he agreed to marry her three months ago.

Getting to know his wife more-and-more now, Ray distrusted and feared her a little more. Most women in their early 20s have a circle of girlfriends they hang out with, and gossip, party, etc. But not Marissa' not one of her friends have come around since the wedding, as if they weren't really her "friends" at all. Most of all, his friends of past years were gone off to college, careers or families outside of rural South Carolina. He yearned to have buddies again, but like youth, friends don't last forever.

Marissa was different, though; it was as if she didn't need friends, or a t lest a lot of them as others do, to succeed or get what she wants. She doesn't need to be "accepted" by peers because she is arrogantly self-satisfying.

An only child, she fends for herself and does for herself very well and is used to being alone, whereas Ray wishes he wasn't as "alone" in this debacle as he felt right now.

"Powerless is a bitch, and she's back in heat."

It's bad enough he's broke with no credit, but to feel this guilt and have your wife standing over with an ax...able to end your freedom on-a-whim!

Powerlessness, like a disease invading his mind, a stress unlike any other. Ray chuckled when he thought about it: This is prison!

Only difference is, the food is better, the bed is real, and nobody named Bubba is trying to stick him up the ass.

He took a sip of his beer, thinking of his wife more, trying to put aside the fact that he was financially ruined. Marissa had told him countless times how much she "loves" him, and that what she had done to shield him from the police in Rex's death was out of love. Blackmailing one into marriage is hard to reciprocate love.

The skinny little girl with braces back in high school now had him by-the-balls, and professed an obsessive love. The job she got him pays decent but is demeaning, except for his co-worker and fellow clown, Rosemary Jones. Now, that is a woman he would love to have instead of Marissa! Sweet, sweet Rosemary AKA "Jiggles The Clown", what a fox.

He hadn't seen her at work much lately, because she had been performing at night-time bachelor parties for two weeks now. Men getting married to a woman they want and love, paying to see a busty clown called "Jiggles" dance around naked and act silly fro 30 minutes. Go figure. Hell, if Marissa found out what Rosemary looks like, she'd become insanely jealous, at least!

He guzzled more of his beer as he sat there in day-dreaming paralysis. Marissa liked sex, that was for sure, and he did enjoy her in that way. God knows he wasn't getting-any before she hooked him three months ago!

She didn't strike him as the type who would cut-him-off, either, because she liked intercourse unlike so many of these frigid young women nowadays who think of "cybersex" of foreplay-only.

Ken Knight

She didn't want to have children, so none of that 9 months of pain and suspicions that the kid isn't yours; not-to-mention the current social trend of young women getting knocked-up by their husbands who they soon divorce to fuck around with some other guy, with your kid in tow, and you paying her half your paycheck! At least, he didn't have to deal with that, Ray thought in gratitude.

Still, he had to get out of this arrangement, on his own, even if he goes unemployed and homeless. Marissa leaving him for another man sounded so good right now, so easy compared to the alternatives.

Later that night:

Marissa snuggled close to Ray in their king-sized marital bed beneath her silk sheets and fur comforter. They had discussed his financial mess and she only told him that she will try to straighten it out herself and not-to-worry. Holding her into him, he smelled her musk scent and her hair-spray as she lay her head on his chest, relaxing.

Even when they didn't romp in bed, she slept naked and wanted him to do the same, except Ray hose to wear boxers often to bed.

He didn't want to sleep, but knew he had work tomorrow at 7:00 sharp. An office gag-party at 9:00, then another kid's party at 10:30. Wow, what a work-day!

Marissa groaned slightly and moved her entire body over onto his now and he just held her loosely, listening to her breathe.

October 21st:

Marissa watched intently as the petite, buxom blonde female exited the front entrance of "Pop-N-Rock Entertainment" here in the shopping center.

Dressed in her clown suit and make-up, Rosemary Jones strolled to her car, and Marissa had to laugh at the sight of the tiny automobile. A new generation Volkswagen "Bug" orange in color with funny-looking wheels and a personalized license plate which read "Jiggles".

"So, that's Rosemary...who Ray mentioned he worked with, hmmm..." she said to herself as she sat in her own car in the parking lot of the shopping center.

Rosemary pulled out of her space and drove toward the highway in her tiny car, passing by the red BMW where Ray's wife sat watching. Marissa watched the girl clown drive out onto Rt. 501 hurriedly, proceeding toward her next "gig".

Picking up her cell-phone, Marissa dialed a memorized number and listened to the ringing on the other end, once, twice, six rings before the male voice answered on that end.

"Spaz...what took you so long?" she snapped in response.

"Marissa, hey, I was busy on the computa...uhh, what's up?" answered the young hacker nervously, his voice lowered.

"The name's Rosemary Jones...license plate J.I.G.G.L.E.S....hack into the DMV computer and get me her residence address, and my other info you can," she commanded coldly over the phone.

"Shouldn't be a problem, Marissa, 'cuz DMV is a piece of cake," McCracken replied softly, static sounding over the line as soon as he spoke.

"Make it happen, Spaz...it's important," she said next.

"Yes, ma'am," McCracken concluded.

Marissa killed the phone and replaced it in its holder on the dashboard. Keying the ignition, she listened to her new car's engine roar to life again.

Ken Knight

6:00 p.m.
Same day:

The Diamond Back Restaurant was unusually "dead" for a Thursday night, but Ray Torelli knew one of the "regulars" would be at the bar and he was right. Giles sat on the corner stool with a mug of draft brew and a cowboy hat on his head. A black cowboy brother sitting alone in the country-western joint.

"Giles, what's up, man?" Ray spoke amicably as he stepped up to him at the bar.

"Hey, Ray, what-it-be-like, my friend...buy you a beer?" Giles said in greeting, shaking his hand.

Ray took a stool next to the only brother in the place, and the small talk began. All day at work today, Ray was thinking about his idea, bettering it actually.

Marissa said that she thought Giles was cool when she met him a month ago. He took that as a good sign.

Ray and Giles talked and talked past 6:30, jovial and humorous in a conversation.

Ray sipped his beer, contemplating how he could get this Simple Simon's cooperation in a scheme he wasn't so sure of himself. Giles thought Marissa was pretty, sexy, and told Ray he was lucky to have her.

"What if I told you that you can have her yourself?" Ray asked up front. He was surprised he even said that.

"Hunh...what do you mean?" Giles retorted with a boyish expression of confusion.

"I want to get a divorce...and if Marissa has an affair, I could get that...I know she likes you," Ray said hesitantly.

"You're crazy," Giles said in response, staring at the man in surprise.

"No, I'm serious and you can help me and tag Marissa at the same time," Ray offered in a more bolder tone.

"Man, that's your wife," Giles snapped.

"Yeah, but I don't want her anymore," Ray chimed, then downed the rest of his beer.

"You're crazy," Giles repeated.

"You're crazy if you refuse," Ray added with a laugh.

"C'mon, Giles…I thought all you brothas like white chicks like Marissa…." Ray said in patronizing humor.

"Hunh, you're kidding me, right?" Giles replied meekly.

"No joke, man, help me get a divorce and I'll make it worthwhile," Ray said softly with a grin, running a hand through his short, dark hair.

"You want me to try to…uhh…seduce ya wife, so she'll divorce you?" Giles asked nervously.

"Bingo, my man's got it now," Ray said in response, laughing in spite of himself.

"I still say you're either crazy…or a pervert who likes other guys to pork his wife," Giles said under-his-breath.

"Neither, 'cuz I want to get rid of her, legally," Ray snickered, patting the broad-shouldered man on the back.

"Ask her for a divorce," Giles suggested.

"She won't go for it," Ray answered flatly.

"What makes ya think she uhh…." Giles stammered.

"If she takes-a-liking to another man," Ray answered him eagerly.

Marissa left the bedroom after Ray had fallen asleep around ten o'clock, slinking down to the kitchen in only a flannel shirt. Grabbing a bottle of juice from the fridge, she strolled to the rear sliding-glass door in silent contemplation.

Ray was getting kind of "stand-offish" lately, and he didn't want to make love for the past two weeks or more. Ray didn't love her, true, but he was always horny and willing to fuck her whenever she even suggested sex.

Another woman? She thought. Maybe that dizzy little blonde clown he worked with? If so, it was about to end. She doubted it, though, because Ray was so goddamn affable and personally broke that no woman in her right mind would hitch her wagon to Ray. Then, again, some people are foolish, including her husband.

Ken Knight

Ray was still frightened about what she could do to him, no doubt about it.

She opened the sliding-glass door and stepped out onto the wooden sun-deck in back of the huge home she cloned, feeling the cool breeze on her skin.

Fishing a cigarette from the pack in the flannel shirt pocket as well as the matches, she lit a cnacer-stick, her first in two days. Marissa never smokes much, being a jogger and all.

Standing out on the deck in the breeze, she looked out at the darkness around her home, hearing only distant sounds of the highway and the wind itself.

She took a long drag on the cigarette, inhaling deeply as she thought about her life up to this point. Damn Ray and his dislike of her all these years.

She had won him in her own way, but she was feeling like he was going to shut her off like her father had her mother long ago. You can't make someone love you, that was a ace, but you can love that someone regardless.

Marissa had collared the men she had loved since high school, and she wasn't about to lose him in any way.

Marissa stepped to the end of the sun-deck, leaning on the railing there to stare up at the trees behind the house.

"Some things you get in life, you've got to protect," she said to the wind, smiling in spite of herself. She blew smoke into the breeze and watched it vanish.

The cool sensation of the wind on her bare skin beneath the unbuttoned flannel shirt felt good to her, so she just stood there in solitude, enjoying the moment.

To protect what she had in life so far, perhaps she had to eliminate a few threatening factors, kind of like Ray's credit rating.

Tossing the cigarette butt away, she walked over to the step-down of the deck and walked out onto the freshly-cut grass of her back yard, her bare feet cold against the ground. "I've got what I want in life now, and no one's gonna screw it up, not even you, Ray, 'cuz I'll see you in hell first," she said to herself in a chuckle.

She walked further out into the yard, and lit another cigarette.

Marissa remembered growing up an only child, and possessing her independent soul that few others understood! Never "popular" with peers, she got whatever she wanted on her own steam, on her own terms.

Her grandmother's inheritance money helped but Marissa was on-her-own as always. Money buys a life, and the loyalty of others, sometimes, but it hadn't bought Ray Torelli. He came in lieu of an accident and the chance that Marissa saw it, deciding to threaten him into marrying her. Money didn't impress him, nor did her shapely physique, only the danger of going to jail.

Damn, it hurt to love someone who failed to reciprocate that love, actually refused to love her in return! Maybe, in time, she told herself as she strolled half-naked in her backyard tonight. Maybe in time, he will either love her or leave her, both were possible, but the latter was more so, and she knew it.

She couldn't hold Rex over his head for much longer, and she knew it.

Protect what is yours, she thought, turning to stroll back to the sun-deck, to the backdoor of her posh abode.

November 2nd:

"This lobster's real good, Marissa...." Spoke Giles with a boyish grin at the woman across the table from him. Ray nodded in agreement, seated next to his wife.

"Thank you, I try," she answered the dinner guest politely with a smile, glancing at Ray as she raised her wineglass to her lips.

Why Ray insisted on inviting his new friend, Giles, to dinner tonight was a wonder to her, but Marissa allowed it. This guy, Giles, wasn't like most Blacks she knew of, talking, acting and

Ken Knight

dressing "White", and he wasn't someone she thought Ray would be hanging around.

Giles ate mechanically, nervous, and Marissa noticed it. Ray sat on her left at the table, eating calmly, drinking beer instead of the iced tea Giles had downed three glasses of so far.

"Giles...you like horror movies?" Marissa asked softly.

"Uhh...yeah, some of them," he replied, glancing at Ray.

"Then do stay after dinner, because I rented the classic Frankenstein movie for tonight. It's a movie you can watch over-and-over," Marissa offered softly with a wink.

"Uhh, okay, Marissa," Giles responded hesitantly. She noticed the man look at Ray as if to get his approval to her request. Was this guy a pansy, or just insecure? She wondered.

The three of them finished their lobster meals minutes later, and Marissa offered a dessert which Giles took gratefully.

Ray sat there at the table, drinking another glass of beer in silent contemplation. Marissa thought strange of that, also. If Giles was his "buddy", then why wasn't he talking with him more?

The whole thing felt strange, as if something was going on, which, so far, eluded her. She was missing something, and she hoped she'd find it before Giles leaves, which is why she invited the guest to stay for a movie.

Ray was preoccupied, and this idiot named Giles lounged next to her to watch the 1931 Universal Film "Frankenstein". What a "non-brother-brother", she thought with a grin of humor.

She touched the remote, beginning the movie on the 57" screen. Ray turned the ceiling light out and just stood there with his arms folded, eyes glaring zombie-like over to the screen.

"These old movies really are creepy with the lights out, aren't they?" Giles whispered to Marissa. She nodded and chuckled in contempt.

"Honey...I'm gonna run to the post office and maybe the store...be back shortly....See ya when I get back," Ray said.

"That movie's just a little over an hour-long," Ray spoke up suddenly, surprising his wife.

One Minute After Midnight

"Ray…shit, all right," she chimed as she heard him open the front door to leave. Arguing was moot now, but she wondered why he was going to the post office at 8:30 p.m.?

Her first thought was maybe he was really going to meet somebody now? Rosemary? No way he'd be this obvious, she thought as she laid back on the sofa cushions next to her guest.

"Mind if I grab a beer?" Giles asked politely.

"Help yourself," she said as she thought over Ray's sudden exit leaving her herewith his "buddy" who didn't seem to be that much of a buddy anyway.

Giles returned seconds later with a bottle, walking to the black sofa, closer to Marissa now. He felt the vibes, and remember what her husband told him. Marissa is a "freak".

Watching the black-n-white film in the dark room was eerily intoxicating, making Marissa feel sleepy already.

She wasn't alarmed by Giles' slow advance closer to her, not seeing him as any threat.

"Man, this is a classic," she sighed as she watched the first castle-scene of the movie, when the monster is rapidly brought to life.

"Sure is, and so are you, Marissa," Giles said softly, as he nudged up to her, leaning in to her pretty, alluring face.

Before she could move or speak in protest, Giles' mouth met hers in a kiss, long and deep, his body momentarily pinning her. When he let up, Marissa jumped to her feet in defensive stances, looking down at her suitor angrily.

"What was that?"! she snapped in surprise, completely unexpecting such a move from him. She guessed that she should have seen it coming.

"Whoah, Marissa, baby…it's just a kiss," Giles retorted nervously, gesturing with his hands as he sat there.

"My husband steps out for a few minutes and you put the moves on me?" she asked angrily, fists clenched at her sides.

Giles stared up at the young woman in the black dress and felt confident enough to say what he wanted to say.

Ken Knight

"It's okay, sweetheart...Ray won't be mad trust me....We can have fun 'till he comes back," he continued, sitting up straight.

"I'm not your fuckin' sweetheart, asshole...now, get out!" Marissa chortled out loud, turning on the lights once again.

"Marissa, it's okay...Ray won't mind," Giles added with his boyish smile, standing up now.

"Ray...he...he...that motherfucker, he told you you could come-on to me?!" Marissa roared in realization of his intent.

Giles nodded, unbuttoning his western-style shirt as they faced off.

"No, get out or I call the cops," Marissa said as she backed up into the kitchen now, going for the portable phone on the wall.

"No need for that, honey cheeks...." Giles said as he turned from the living room as if to go for the front door 20 feet away. Marissa stood in the kitchen, phone-in-hand, thinking in boiling anger.

"Ray, you son-of-a-bitch," she said to herself in a hot whisper. He had set her up with Giles to see if she'd cheat on him. Or, better yet, catch her cheating?! Was there a hidden camera somewhere in the living room? She wondered. Stepping back through the dining room into the living room, Marissa looked around, the heard footfalls from the hallway leading to the front door.

"Ray...." She snarled aggressively.

"Better than Ray, baby," spoke Giles as he sauntered back into her living room wearing only his green boxer shorts now, flexing his 18" biceps in vain-attempt to impress her.

"Giles, goddamnit, get the fuck outta my house or I'm gonna shoot you!" Marissa screamed in response, pointing at him hatefully.

"But you kissed me back...." Giles chuckled, stopping six feet from her. He wasn't going to force himself on her, thinking that she would eventually "give-in". He really wanted her now; that figure of hers so appealing!

Her face contorted with anger, though, and Giles knew he was wrong to try this.

"I did no-such-thing, you fuckin' nigger ape...get out before I kill you!" she sneered aloud in disgusted ardor, pointing to him threateningly.

"Marissa, why you goin' there, sayin' such things to me?" Giles asked in surprise, hands-on-hips.

"Because you are a worthless fucking Nigger, Giles. Now, get the fuck out or I'm gonna put a bullet in your sorry black ass!" she quipped in anger, stomping into the kitchen.

"Marissa, c'mon, baby..let's play fo' just a little while, sweetness," Giles added boyishly.

"He paid me two-grand to come fuck his wife and make her mine," Giles said as he stepped to the kitchen's threshold.

"Motherfucker!" Marissa roared in white hot anger suddenly, stepping back toward him now with a handgun in her right fist, leveled at her target.

"Jeezus," Giles sighed in stark surprise, fear chilling his ardor quickly as he faced the black handgun pointing at his face.

"Run...you fuck...run or I will kill you!" she sneered in hatred as she leveled her gun down to his groin area. That convicted Giles to turn and head to the sliding-glass door, exiting as fast as he could, wearing only his boxer shorts, into the cold wind.

He ran across the lawn into the night, crying. Marissa had insulted him in a way he never imagined happening, and Giles broke into fervent crying as he ran into the woods in only his boxer-shorts.

Marissa walked out onto the sun-deck, boiling in anger now after what just happened. Ray paid Giles the $2,000 she gave him to pay off his credit card, to set her up?! Damn him!

A tear trickled down her left cheek as she stood there in the chill breeze, still holding her handgun. Ray betrayed her again, so she would have to retaliate in some way.

"I should kill him...bastard, I should gut him like a pig," she groaned in furious ardor, looking up at the night sky.

Ken Knight

10:00 p.m.:

Ray walked up to the front door of the expensive home rather nervously now, having returned after an hour of just driving around to kill time and let nature take its course back here. Gile's truck was gone already, so it wouldn't have worked out, and he wondered what Marissa was going to say when he opens this door.

Grabbing the knob and turning, Ray opened the front door and stepped inside quickly, shivering slightly from the outdoors' cold wind.

The house was dark except for the living room, eerily-quiet and sterile. Marissa was home, because her perfume was on the air as usual. Walking into the lit room, he found his wife leaning up against the fireplace mantle, smoking a cigarette.

When those dark eyes met his, he knew. The fury he saw in those onyx eyes of hers at that moment made him shiver again.

"How dare you…Raymond Torelli…set me up like that, you fucking faggot…how dare you?!" she sneered in rolling contempt, her voice calm, yet enflamed. She straightened up and took a step forward, facing the man boldly, cigarette in her lips as she spoke.

"Marissa…I…." He stammered nervously.

"Don't even consider denying it, Raymond. I'm not as stupid as you are and …your ploy didn't work," she snarled with clenched fists.

"Giles?" he muttered.

"Went home with his tail between his legs like a bitch, and he told me everything, even that you paid him the two-grand I gave you to coax me into fucking him…hoping I'd leave you," she continued, crushing the cigarette out on the ashtray by the sofa.

She circled the room like a cat, her body stiff in tension now.

Ray didn't know what to say. His plan had backfired and it felt like shit. Damn Giles for letting it out like that, and for failing to tag Marissa!

"You worthless turd...you don't know how good you've got it with me and you try to undermine my marriage to you...in a half-ass scheme involving that ape!" Marissa ranted indignantly, pacing the room.

"I want out, Marissa, you bitch....You've ruined me and made me play footstool too long....Let me go, you castrating bitch," Ray said in tense anger, shaking a finger at her in protest.

Her eyes beamed sheer rage, burning into him like hot coals, and Ray froze where he stood. He failed to move when she picked up an open beer bottle and threw it; the glass container glancing off his skull in shattering melee.

The pain of the blow forced him to move and he went down to one knee at the dormant fireplace, feeling his head where the bottle struck. Blood was sticky to his fingers, searing pain.

"Bitch!" he growled in response as she moved around him, cursing her husband in a manner he never heard before now.

She was pissed-off far more than he could be at this point.

"Look what I am giving you...and you shit on me in return, Raymond? Who'd you go see earlier...that bimbo-bitch, Rosemary, your work with?!" she raged, knocking over the dining table now, plates and all.

"You fucking her?!" she wailed out loud in a fit of angry blood lust.

"No, and I wish I never slept with you....God damn, I hate you, Marissa, you fuckin' ruined me...you had my credit flushed didn't you?" Ray retorted as blood trickled down his forehead into his left eye.

"I am takin' care of you, you ungrateful prick...and you are my husband, like it or not...I fuckin' own you!" she roared, standing on the overturned table shaking her arms and fists violently.

"You don't own me!" Ray snapped as he stood up slowly.

"Remember Rex and what I can tell the police, Raymond; force my hand and you'll be in prison by the end of this week!" she said in a suddenly calmer voice of meanness.

"Maybe it's better than being your prisoner here, bitch!" Ray snipped self-righteously as he approached her. As soon as he was close enough, Marissa swung out a fist square to his jaw. The impact was forceful enough to blow him backward and off balance to the rug below.

Marissa followed-through with a quick kick to his groin as she stepped forward with a push. The pain racked through his system like lightning through steel. Doubling up beside the coffee table, Ray was wounded and helpless.

Marissa stood over him for a few seconds, breathing heavy as he lay there, groaning in paralyzing pain. Ray roared out in cursing protest of her attack, angered mostly by his slow reaction to her assault. "Motherfucker...cocksucker!" Marissa shouted down to the injured man she felled.

"You make me want to hate you, Raymond, but I still love you, ya know," she sneered in a quaking voice. As she turned, Ray reached out and grabbed her foot, tripping her. Marissa cursed as she fell to the floor across from him now.

Ray lay in the fetal position, groaning in pain. A kick to-the-balls was something he hadn't suffered, until now. Marissa sat up against the rock wall of the fireplace, facing her husband again, just sitting there with her icy stare.

"I should've put a knife in you years ago, Raymond Torelli...hunh, as many times as you spurned me and humiliated me in front of our peers, you fuck," she said in a low voice of contempt.

"I...didn't want you," he managed to say, despite the pain, blood running into his eyes from the gash on his head.

"Doesn't matter, honey, 'cuz I wanted you so bad, and I'd done anything back then," she added meekly. "However, I wanted several years to finally catch my man in a compromising situation I could use."

Ray just moaned in painful retort, beginning to cry now in hopelessness. This was hell and his wife was the devil.

"You just don't understand, Ray....I loved you since we first met...a woman can love someone forever sometimes, even if it's

One Minute After Midnight

not returned," she continued as she sat against the empty fireplace, legs out as she stared at him curled up under the coffee table now. "That kind of attraction I can't really explain, but I chose you, and you still curse me even now, when I offer you a good life," she said in a calmer tone.

"Hmmhh...I chose you, Ray, and you told me to fuck off, then you splashed toilet water on my prom dress, remember?" she asked him coldly. Ray just laid there, listening.

"I was the only girl at that prom without someone, and you...you still humiliated me on the night when I would've done anything for you," she spoke in her soothing, comfortable voice now.

"Yeah, that's years-ago, I know, but I'll never forget that prom night...and neither will you," she snickered next.

"I'm attractive, fit, wealthy, and don't have another man's kids; where else would you find such a great female catch, hunh?" she chuckled in spite of herself.

Ray didn't speak, just listening to her speech in hopeless felling of guilt. Maybe he deserved this, he thought again.

"I can't seem to buy you, either, shit; that dirty ape friend of yours would take me for sure, if I offered half of what I offer you, Ray," she continued in more polite terms. Sorry, honey, but I'm not in to black guys, and I should cut your balls off for trying that shit on me," Marissa said impishly, rubbing it in more.

"And you're a racist to-boot," he managed to say through gritted teeth.

"So...least I fell in love with an unemployed wap like you?" she snickered in coy response. Ray just closed his eyes, staying on the floor beneath the coffee table.

"You belong to me, honey, just face it, and if you try to weasel-out from under me again, I swear...I'll kill you, and probably get away with it," she said as she slowly stood up.

"And you can quit your clown job now; I'll put some money in your checking account to hold ya over awhile," she added softly.

125

"That's okay, I'll keep my job," Ray retorted quickly, making her laugh in turn.

"Hah, because you like that bimbo clown named Rosemary, don't you?" Marissa replied coyly, walking into the dining room again.

Ray didn't answer any further, part of him wanting to smash her skull in for assaulting him like this.

"Fuck another woman and I'll know it, you asshole," Marissa chimed as she headed for the stairs.

"Sleep on the couch," she concluded as she walked up the carpeted stairwell now.

Ray sighed in relief of pain as he lay there in anger and numbing frustration. "Gladly," he silently answered her.

Chapter 10

Ray walked into the personnel-room in the rear of the "Pop n' Rock" offices, returning from two gigs this afternoon. Rosemary was there, applying fresh clown-face in the mirror.

"Hey, guy...you cool?" Rosemary asked as soon as she saw him enter.

"Guess so, goddamn kids are a pain in the ass," he chuckled as he strolled up behind her, seeing his make-up smeared on his face,

"that's why I don't do gigs like those unless I have to," she laughed in reply, smiling up at him.

Ray began to remove his clown outfit, pacing the room in simmering anger.

"Ray...don't sweat it, honey, it's better than working ya ass off in a factory or worse, and ...it's steady," she told him with a grin.

"Hmmph, maybe, but I can do other things," ray added as he began wiping off his face.

"Use the Noxema, Ray, removes the makeup faster," Rosemary said as she turned to toss him a can of the cream-cleaner.

"Make-up," he laughed in contempt as he caught it.

"Consider it art...in a way, and you are an entertainer. Hell, I can do other jobs, too, but this one is fun and that faggot boss of ours lets us do nearly whatever we want within-reason," she spoke softly.

"Yeah, but now even my wife has asked me to quit and help her open a business of some kin," Ray sneered in contempt, cleaning the white paint off his face, using the big mirror.

Rosemary perked up in interest, looking to him with a slight scowl.

"Do what?" she snapped.

"Yeah, she wants me to quit the job she told me to take in the first place," he chuckled as he took off his big clown shoes.

Ken Knight

She glanced at him with a patronizing grin, feeling sorry that he had a wife at all.

"No shit," she sighed as she stood up, listening to her co-worker.

"She saw you, that's why....She doesn't want me working with a gorgeous woman like this; pure jealousy," he answered as he wiped his face with tissues.

"Hmmm...really," Rosemary chimed in interest, brushing her blonde hair now, sitting back down in front of the mirror.

Rosemary's tone of voice just then told Ray that she thought it was humorous. Damn, why can't I have a knockout blonde like Rosemary Jones? He asked himself again in silence.

Marissa is pleasant physically, but that certain "attractant" isn't there for him when it comes to her. Rosemary, on the other hand, can blackmail him into marriage any day! "I've gotten to the point where I hate going home now...." He added, feeling like he could tell the lady clown anything. They had really bonded as co-workers over the past month or so.

He knew she like him in that certain way, and oh how he wanted to sleep with Rosemary, if the opportunity ever came.

"Sounds like ya wife's a real ball-buster," Rosemary said with an impish grin.

"Pretty much, and she has ruined my credit-rating somehow...just can't prove it," he added, pacing the aimlessly now.

"Leave her ass, since you don't have any kids," Rosemary suggested casually, watching the man's response. She found the credit theory of his to be improbable.

"Wish it were that simple, Jiggles, I really do," he said in a lowered voice.

"Why isn't it?" she asked hesitantly, watching him in the mirror.

"She's got me over-a-barrel in a way I can't discuss...and I'm stuck," Ray answered cryptically.

Rosemary's interest was peeked now, and she just had to find out what Ray was taking about, somehow. He was a good-looking guy, married to someone he didn't love. What a soap opera! She thought as she sat there in her clown suit.

"You're stuck, hunh?" she cooed girlishly, then honked her obnoxious clown horn at him.

"Stuck-like-chuck," he said in a chuckle.

11:30
That night:

Waking in a sweat, Ray sat up in the bed slowly, yawning. Damn, he thought as he glanced over at the electronic clock on the wall, seeing that he had been asleep only three hours. Damn!

Marissa stirred slightly next to him, but was otherwise sound asleep, naked beneath the silk sheet. Ray swung his legs over, feet touching the floor below. He sighed, then stretched and yawned, doubting his ability to return to sleep for awhile.

Maybe a glass of wine and some music would help, eh thought as he stood up slowly, sauntering across the darkened bedroom for the door. Not bothering to put his robe on, he walked down the spiral stairs naked, weary from sleep.

He stumbled into the living room, turning on the light. He stepped up to the large entertainment center against the wall, beside the wide screen TV, reaching for the stereo system perched there. Pushing the "power" knob, he then lowered his left hand to grab the stainless-steel shelf-bar which held the big stereo/CD player.

Before he could locate the country music station he favored on the dial, he felt it. Like a bolt of soul-burning lightning streaking up his left arm, impacting inside his chest; a continuous thread of searing pain, and he couldn't let go of the steel shelf!

Ray let out a howl of painful bellow, the electric current flowing into his bare body in steady assault as he stood there on his tip-toes, quivering in electrocution, unable to escape its onslaught.

"MARRRISSSAA!" he screamed out loud ardently, panic consuming him now.

His young wife heard him loud and clear, because she had been standing at the top of the stairs ever since he left the bedroom two minutes ago. She had been expecting this to happen, and a smile crossed her face when her husband screamed her name just now. Damn, it felt good!

She hurried down the stairs, eager to find her husband being mildly electrocuted by the little "prank" she set earlier. AC/DC to the steel shelf makes for a surprise!

There was Ray, standing there in front of the stereo, gripping the shelf and shaking like a leaf, body stiff and helpless to release from the current. He also had an erection due to the electrocution, and she had to laugh as she watched from the dark hallway by the stairs.

Ray screamed again, and managed to finally let go of the steel shelf, his jolted body collapsing to the floor below. The stereo system went dead, the breaker blown.

"Ray...omigod!" Marissa exclaimed in faked excitement as she ran into the room in her bathrobe, gawking down at her quivering mate on the rug. Ray curled into the fetal position, muscles stiffening from the electric shock.

Marissa knelt beside him, managing a tear actually, touching his face and arms in a frantic check of his vitals. The nurse in her took over.

"Ray...you get shocked...jeezus, baby?" she whined ardently, feeling his heartbeat.

"Yeah...yeah...goddamn stereo, it shocked me, jeezus-christ!" he answered her as he straightened out, lying on his back. Marissa looked him over, appearing concerned for him now, convincing Ray that she was.

"Honey...you feel faint or numb?" she asked next.

"No, I'm okay, Marissa, damn that hurt!" he sneered as he raised up onto his elbows.

"Saw my life flash before me," he added as she kissed his face, then hugged him close. The smell of her perfume made him feel better already.

"You'll be okay, honey, you'll be okay," Marissa cooed in a consoling tone, hugging him lovingly now. Ray then struggled to stand but his legs were weak, so he landed on the plush sofa instead, looking up at his wife.

This was strange, since he had installed that stereo himself and hadn't been shocked before tonight by it. Shaking a little still, he just sat there, cocked to his left in stunned silence.

"You're lucky it didn't send you into cardiac arrest, honey," she said with hands-on-hips.

"Yeah, man-that-hurt," he sighed as he looked over at the stereo, perplexed.

"I bet...can I fix you a drink?" she chimed as she strolled over toward the kitchen area now, eyes still on him.

"Yeah, a bourbon...straight," he sighed, desiring strong alcohol now.

Marissa went to fix the drink, happy as a clam that her little prank had worked exactly as she planned. It wasn't strong enough current to kill him and very few amps, so she didn't expect it to. Ray sat there in helpless surrender, obviously contemplating his actions, she thought.

This might plant in his brain the notion that he should be grateful for what he has. Losing one's life to trivial accidents is such a shame, after all.

Ray's first thoughts were focused on the accident theory, but as soon as Marissa walked back into the living room with his glass of bourbon, he guessed differently.

Maybe she rigged his stereo to electrocute him like that, buy why? It could have killed him. Damn, such a thought of Marissa doing that made him shiver again.

"Here you go, love," she said gingerly as she handed him his drink. He sipped the tangy liquid, then put it down on the coffee table there, looking up at Marissa as she just stood there.

Ray still had a rock-hard erection, thanks to the electric jolt earlier and it began to hurt a little staying so turgid like that, the head pressing against his belly-button as he sat there.

"Hmmm...no sense letting that go to waste," Marissa cooed with her cat-like grin, untying her robe in front.

Ray watched her loose the robe, then kneel before him naked with that look of a predator. She wants to fuck, after he nearly got electrocuted to death? He wondered as she moved in for a kiss.

"Feeling better, big guy?" she whispered softly, left hand caressing his rock-hard erection, then she kissed him again.

"A little," he said, peering into her dark eyes in wonder for a moment. Could she have rigged the stereo and shelf to shock him?

She smiled impishly, then lowered herself between his thighs, facing his turgid cock.

"Hmmm...you could've been a porn star, honey...with this tool," Marissa snickered, then licked the thick, purple head in delight.

"Hunh, bigger than some," he said in agreement. Too bad other women didn't get to it before Marissa did!

"Mmmhh...yeah, baby, you got a big ol' dick and I'm gonna enjoy it if you don't mind?" she teased him girlishly, then lowered her head to take him in her eager mouth.

"Not at all," he said in spite of himself, watching his wife literally devour his organ, snaking her hands up his bare, hairy chest. What man in his right mind would protest a woman worshipping his cock?

He didn't have this a year ago, even six months ago! No, back then every woman he asked-out told him no. They all had boyfriends, husbands, fiancée's and one a lesbian lover.

Now, he had a wealthy young wife who professed to love him, even though he didn't love her back, and she blackmailed him into marriage. Rex Matthewson was dead because of his carelessness. He deserved punishment and he knew it, and now, he began to think that Marissa wasn't all bad. She quite literally owned him and that ate at his gut like a cancer. Being "owned" in this way, by a domineering bitch who won't take no for an answer. Her kicking him in the balls the other night was icing on the cake. She was capable of violence, qualifying him as a "battered spouse".

But who would he tell, the police? The cops would learn of the driver's identity in the hit-n-run death of one Rex Matthewson soon after.

Marissa's head bobbed up-and-down, up-and-down, slurping on his organ greedily. He swore that mouth of hers was possessed! A life of its own, and it felt so good.

She gripped his tool at its base firmly, and raised off it for a moment to glance up at Ray as he laid against the back cushion. "I am sorry I kicked you the other night," she cooed, then kissed the sensitive head again.

He shivered slightly at that, then Marissa went down on him again, sucking his love muscle in expert fellatio.

"Ooaah, apology accepted...." He groaned in reply, running a hand through her short hair.

Seconds later, Ray was on his back across the huge sofa, relaxed and coerced while Marissa straddled his hips, riding on him in fluid motion, hands grasping his torso.

She rode him up-and-down, his manhood burrowing deep inside of her wet, warm canal, and the look on her face was one of sheer pleasure, mouth open wide in the reception of him.

Ray couldn't remember Marissa being so loud or passionate as this before, groaning in steady rhythm of lust. It was as if she enjoyed not just hid dick right now, but the electrical incident as well!

Maybe not, he thought as he lay there beneath his grinding wife, watching her breasts bounce wildly with her movement on him.

"Oh, Ray...oh, Ray...Ray baby, fuck me so good, baby...oooaannhh!" she cried out in delight, nearing orgasm. He reached up and squeezed her tits roughly and she came at that instant, letting out a wail of delight, riding his cock faster.

Ken Knight

Marissa raised off him just as Ray was about climax himself, and he swore under his breath as he did so; shooting his hot release out onto her belly some, then the rest just ran down his organ's shaft. Marissa giggled as she watched, then leaned over and took him into her mouth again.

Damn, what a freak, he thought.

"You can't complain about the sex, can you honey?" she asked as she raised up to her feet, standing by the sofa while he just lay there.

"No, ma'am, you're great, Marissa," he said with a smile of satisfaction.

"Really...." She sighed, faking doubt.

"Yeah, you're the best fuck I ever had," he told her with a smile and a wink.

"hmmm...and the last, too," she snickered as she strolled passed him slowly. Ray turned his head to watch her saunter into the dark kitchen again, her bare ass check jiggling slightly as she walked. He loved that about her, too. Now, exactly what she meant by "the last" made him wonder. The worst she could do is kill me, right? He asked silently.

2400 Seabreeze Road
Myrtle Beach
December 3rd:

The birthday party was for a 4-year-old boy named "Stevie", and "Bo-Bo The Clown" had been hired to entertain little Stevie and his cluster of little friends named Joey, Chuckie, Frankie, and Johnny.

Bo-Bo The Clown treated the kids to pin-the-tail-on-the-donkey, and Twister, plus he favored little Stevie to a toy-soldier doll and a big of fake money which made all the kids laugh.

Ray hated this, but had gotten used to it, even getting a raise this month to $12 per hour. The momma who run this household had the heat cranked up so he was sweating his ass off in the baggy clown suit and funny hat.

Now came the birthday cake and the present-opening by the birthday-boy, little loud-ass brat that he was.

Ah, at last little Stevie got the one toy he wanted out of all of them: the "bumble-bee beany-baby". Like most kids, he was happiest with the one toy he wanted as opposed to clothes and school shit his babbling mother gave him. Little ingrate even shoved one toy his friend Johnny gave him to the floor, and Ray nearly stepped on it.

He couldn't wait to get out of this gig but Ray kept smiling with his clown face, honking his finger-horn and circling the table of kids saying moronic stuff like: "Happy-birthday, Stevie-boy," and "How old are you now," Stevie...four, five, six-and-a-half?"

Little Stevie was clearly annoyed by Bo-Bo after an hour more of his antics, and Ray couldn't wait for the mother to cue him to leave.

Rosemary was supposed to pick him up in twenty minutes because hi struck was in the shop getting detailed. He couldn't wait to talk with her again, as usual. Rosemary was the only reason he kept good spirits in this job.

Ray glanced over at the soccer-mom with the thunder-thighs and she nodded to him, signaling him to leave now as planned.

"Bye, kids!" Ray spoke in conclusion, waiving to the circle of 5-year-olds he had entertained for 2 hours.

"Bye-bye, Boo-Boo!" little Stevie shouted up at Ray as he headed for the front door. He waived back in clown fashion.

That's Bo-bo you little toe-cheese, he thought sarcastically as he exited the house into the brisk autumn day outside. It was still just 3:45 p.m., fifteen minutes to wait for Rosemary to pick him up. Maybe she'll be early, he hoped.

Standing in the walkway leading up to the house, Ray glanced off to his right, seeing the garage door open there and little Stevie's father in there, working on something. Another

Ken Knight

one of those guys who toil in their tiny garage as if to actually do something "constructive".

Like his father used to badger him when he was a kid: "Do anything constructive today, son?!" And he asked that with liquor on his breath.

The old man of Stevie's couldn't be too much older than me, Ray told himself as the man walked to the open doorway of his house-garage/carport, looking at the clown.

"How ya doing?" Ray spoke to the father who was too macho to attend his son's birthday party today.

"Better than you…what do ya call yaself…Bo-Bo?" the disheveled man in the green coveralls retorted with malice.

"Yeah," Ray replied in disappointment, just trying to be friendly.

"Tell me, Bo-Bo, how does a man become a clown like you…how does a man lose his self-respect to do the clown thing?" the father asked from the threshold of the car-port garage.

"Hey, it's easy work, and I made your son laugh," he answered stoically.

"Yeah, reckon so, but you're still a goofball for doing it, why don't you get a real man's job?" the man rambled, not moving toward him.

"Like what exactly?" asked Ray, patronizing the ass-hole.

"Like construction, factory, or fire-fighter like me," the man retorted in self-righteous tone, hands on his hips.

Ray just glared at him contempt, feeling his face-paint beginning to melt in the sunlight, despite it only being 50° outside.

"Hunh, you candy ass," the man said as he looked across the yard at Ray. Just then, Ray saw the orange Volkswagen Bug roar up to the driveway with his fellow clown behind the wheel.

Rosemary was early after all, and he walked proudly to the car's passenger side, not giving the kid's father another thought now that the sunny Rosemary Jones was here.

"Hey, buddy, ready to go?" Rosemary spoke in bubbly fashion, watching him get in.

Ray smiled at the suited-up clown-faced "Jiggles" and nodded, slamming the door behind himself. She backed out of the driveway and onto the road leading out of the subdivision.

"Mary," the father chuckled to himself in contempt.

"How'd it go back there?" Rosemary asked as she drove onto Rt. 17, heading south.

"As usual, but the father was an ass-hole...how 'bout your gig?" Ray replied as he tried to get comfortable in her cramped little car.

"Oh, two office-gags where I flashed my tits at the boss and danced around like a clown...more than they guessed I would do," she answered happily.

"Bet they were pleased," Ray laughed, feeling better now as he relaxed next to her.

He always felt better around Rosemary; just her presence itself was pleasant. Not one negative vibe came from her sweet, sensuous form. Funny how one woman can enter your life and light up the sky, making a man desire her greatly, like a heavenly narcotic that makes him feel so good it seems, ad Ray was happy to know her.

Just riding with her made him forget the bad for a time, even his wife and the deed which forced them together.

"You wanna get a bite to eat?" she asked next.

"What about the Berryman party we're supposed to work at six?" he replied meekly.

"Canceled...they called the office an hour ago and the boss called me on my cell-phone," Rosemary answered with a snicker.

"All right, but no tips," Ray chimed in slight disappointment.

"Maybe next time, but how about you and I go for seafood here in town?" she added as she changed lanes, driving toward the Rt. 501 junction.

"Cool," he responded boyishly, more than happy to go eat with her, even if it had to be in this silly outfit and make-up. It didn't matter with her at his side, because her presence was intoxicating.

She piloted her little car leisurely thought the Myrtle Beach traffic, and he relished every second with her, listening to her sweet, southern voice.

They chose the "Calabash" Seafood House off of Rt. 17 southbound, and were lucky enough to be seated quick, off in a corner booth alone with platefuls of seafood from the all-you-can-eat buffet.

Ray was happy, despite the stares from other customers here and the slowly-smearing make-up on his face, he was eating dinner with Rosemary now!

They talked and ate, ate, and talked. Rosemary spoke of her strip-club nights and year-long affair with a rich-and-married tycoon in Atlanta. Of her strict Catholic parents whom she refuses to speak to again, and of the one man she said, "I love you" to, but lost to another woman. Ray listened intently as he ate slowly.

Other patrons kept gawking at the two clowns seated in that booth, but Ray ignored them, his full attention given to the buxom female clown in front of him.

Rosemary spoke of her intentions to "buy" "Pop n' Rock" Entertainment from its current owner, and she offered to make him a partner in the deal if he wanted.

7:00
That night:

Ray walked into the home he reluctantly resided in and headed for the kitchen for a cold beer in the fridge.

"Hey, honey, how'd it go today?" Marissa spoke up out of nowhere as soon as he turned on the kitchen light. Ray looked around and found her standing there by the dining table in her gray cotton jogging sweats with radio-headphones on her ears.

"Hey, Marissa, had a long day, how about you?" he answered softly, opening the refrigerator.

"I gotta work the midnight shift at the hospital tonight, so I'm gonna run my three miles now," she answered him as she started toward the front door, eyes glued on him.

"See ya," Ray said as he plucked a beer from the fridge, popping its cap with a bottle opener on the counter.

The front door slammed shut, signaling his wife's exit, and hew was glad to see her go running instead of talking his ears-off as usual. She was gonna work the midnight-shift. That was unusual for her, but good for him because he'd have the bed all to himself tonight. Taking a sip of his beer, he thought about Rosemary Jones again, wishing she shared his bed instead of Marissa.

Too bad Marissa couldn't encounter a serial rapist-murderer on her nightly jogs. No, not here in rural South Carolina! Here, she witnesses him accidentally kill a man and then, blackmailed him into marrying her. What a lurid talk-show topic, he thought. Too bad it was too oppressively fateful to tell anybody.

Telling someone else might help him deal with this continuing dilemma better, but it was risky. Admitting to a crime like what he did to Rex Matthewson would cancel Christmas, and he knew it. Marissa knew it as well, holding the ax over his head rather spitefully now.

As he walked into the living room to watch TV, he noticed her purse on the coffee-table. Funny, since his wife usually guarded her purse almost zealously, as if hiding something.

He sat down on the sofa and opened the soft-leather purse in anxious interest, eager to carefully go through Marissa's personal effects. Besides her unnecessary amount of make-up, squirt perfume, various keys, and her sunglasses and cell-hone, he found her checkbook.

Ray opened the neat little check register and was not too surprised to find a current balance of $102,000. Marissa kept her money well, because most women would be out there raiding a car dealership or a realty office with a bankbook like this!

The most recent expenditures were groceries for the month, a detail-job on her new BMW, and a check made out to cash for

Ken Knight

$6,000. No way she'd carry that much cash on herself, unless she paid someone in cash?! Interesting.

Looking back at her check listing, he found the vaguely scribbled name "McCracken" below the amount and check #.

"Who the hell's McCracken?" he asked himself softly, returning the checkbook to its exact location in the purse.

An unknown name like that was worth investigating, considering Marissa's penchant for subterfuge.

Ray was in bed by 10 p.m. and pretended to be asleep as Marissa came in to the dark bedroom to get dressed into her nurse's uniform. She was quiet about it, dressing in the dark as her husband lay there beneath the covers with a squinted eye watching her shadow in the moonlight coming through the window.

She was a fine-looking woman, despite her faults and what she had done to him. Ray closed his eyes completely as she walked up to the end of the bed fully-dressed now.

"Good night, Ray...I love you, honey," she spoke softly to the man she thought was sleeping. He didn't answer her, of course, but he felt a certain itch of guilt as soon as she said that.

Marissa turned and walked out of the bedroom, closing the door behind herself.

"Sometimes, Marissa...I wish I could say the same to you," Ray whispered to himself, then buried his head in the pillows. Something told him that woman would be in his life in one way or another, even if he succeeded in divorcing her in the future.

December 20th:

Bill Torelli held his younger in contempt for what he was saying about the foxy young woman he married. Sitting at the kitchen table inside his trailer home, Bill faced his brother Ray, listening to him squawk over his marital woes.

"She's tight, rich, and fucks ya brains loose. What more could a guy want in a woman, shi...wanna trade-lives for awhile?" Bill chuckled, then took another sip of his beer as they sat across the table form one another.

"I need your help, Bill," Ray told his brother coldly. The look on his face made Bill cringe.

"With what?" he replied softly.

"Getting rid of her," Ray answered flatly.

"No way I'm gonna harm that girl, sorry...besides, she's one of those ass-kicking types anyway," Bill retorted in a laugh.

"I just need you to run some static for me, that's all," Ray sneered.

"Like what?" Bill asked in wonder.

"Find out anything-and-everything about the name 'McCracken' in this area. Shouldn't be too many assholes by that name," Ray suggested politely, standing up from the table now.

"All right. My boy, Tryone, is good about that stuff...he's a P.I. and owes me a few favors, but why...who is the McCracken?" Bill replied, watching is brother walk to the front door of the trailer.

"Don't ask, just find out who has that name in this area if ya can...it's probably nothing," Ray said as he started out the door to leave.

"Hey, little brother...why do you wanna divorce Marissa so badly, so soon?" Bill asked abruptly, following Ray to the doorway.

"Don't ask," Ray sighed as he left the trailer-home, walking out to his truck. He was off-work today but so was Marissa and she expected him to be home by 5:00 for dinner. She was a good cook even if she was possessive about this time.

It was now 4:35 p.m., plenty of time to drive "home".

December 22nd:

The "Diamond Back" was rather busy for a Monday night, probably because of the holiday coming up in 2 days. Ray sat on his usual perch at the bar, alone with his beer and thoughts. People danced on the dance floor to the beat of "boot-scoot" country music, people whom probably had this entire week off from work.

Ray had two parties to work tomorrow and one big one on Christmas Eve. This was supposed to be the season of Santa, not clowns at a party! He thought. Drinking his beer, he failed to notice the man sit next to him, until the man patted him on the back.

"Hey...Giles," Ray spoke in surprise, looking at the black man with the Stetson, jean jacket, jeans and snake-skin cowboy boots.

"Ray, your wife is a racist," Giles chuckled amicably, as he settled onto the stool beside him now.

"Among other things, and I'm sorry about all that," Ray answered in a sigh, looking at the bartender to order Giles a beer on him.

"It's cool, and here's your check back. Figured you'd stop payment on it anyway," Giles said as he handed Ray the check he had written him as payment.

"Marissa did, 'cuz her names on the account, too," Ray answered as he ripped it up, letting the pieces fall into the full ashtray.

"Buddy, she is a first-class bitch on wheels. Did she tell you that she pulled her gun on me, too?" Giles continued in friendly tone.

"Pulled a gun on ya...I didn't know she has a gun!" Ray snapped in surprise.

"Yeah, man, one of those Glocks, like she was itching to put ten rounds into my black ass," Giles snickered again as the bartender handed him a fresh mug of brew.

"Really, damn...I didn't know. Sorry about that, Giles," Ray added meekly.

"It's cool, I'm still alive and I guess she hates me just 'cuz of my color, but it was kinda fun just tryin' to get in her pants," Giles said softly, not looking at Ray.

One Minute After Midnight

Ray had to laugh at that remark, in spite of himself.

"I did kiss her, though, before she went buck-wild and threatened to shoot me," Giles continued in humorous tone.

"Really," Ray chimed in thought of Giles forcing a kiss on Marissa.

"Tell me, Ray, no bull-shit...why on earth do you wanna get rid of that sexy girl, even if she's a ball-bustin' bitch?" Giles chuckled in lowered tone, patting Ray on the back again.

"I told you, she black-mailed me into marrying her, and I have to convince her to divorce me, somehow...Besides, I don't love her," Ray answered reluctantly.

"Does she love you, though?" Giles asked.

"She says she does," Ray said casually, then swilled more of his beer.

"Man, I wish I had a woman like Marissa in my bed every night, especially one with her physical attributes," Giles said softly, looking down into his beer mug.

"Even if she kicks you in the balls?" Ray sneered in response.

"Hunh, yeah...'cuz it sucks bein' alone, ya know?" Giles snickered matter-of-factly.

"You have a girl, don't you?" Ray asked.

"No, not for a while now...but if I had a gorgeous white woman like your Marissa...I certainly wouldn't kick her out like you're tryin' to do," Giles replied with a shrug.

"Well, she's a monster, and even if she's good in bed and wealthy in the bank, there's not much more I can take," Ray said with a grin of avarice, eyes on the beer in his hands.

"Good luck, then," Giles said in conclusion, then downed the remainder of his beer and stepped off the barstool to leave the unhappy man alone in his depression. Some guys don't know how good they have it, he thought as he walked toward the exit now.

Ray just sat there, his mind blocking out the other patrons around him now. Marissa was working tonight which was good, so the house would be empty by the time he got home.

Ken Knight

He was surprised Giles was so damn friendly to him a minute ago, especially after how Marissa treated him.

So, she has a gun, too, wonderful!

11:30 that night:

The house was dark and eerily quiet when Marissa walked through the front door, locking it behind her. Damn Ray, she thought, for leaving the front door unlocked again. Walking into the kitchen, she found the light switch, then opened the refrigerator door, feeling like a beer right now.

She began to peel out of her white nurse's outfit as she strolled into the dark living room with her beer. How she hated wearing this white dress with two name badges. Scrubs were so much more comfortable, but not always allowed for her duties at the hospital.

Stripping down to her black lace bra and panties, Marissa opened the cap of her beer and drank greedily as she stood there in her dark living room.

Ray was obviously upstairs asleep, because she knew that he had work tomorrow morning. When she turned on the lamp light next to the sofa, she spotted his floppy clown hat lying on a cushion next to the armrest.

"Hah-hah, my husband the clown…a happy-happy clown to kids everywhere," she joked mockingly. She had told him that he could quit his clown job any time now, but he refused, saying that he "liked" it now.

Marissa knew better. No, Ray liked that blonde little-miss-big-tits who worked as a clown too, and he probably was already trying to fuck her by now. His genuine interest in me has waned already, she thought as she picked up the clown hat.

"Hmmm…Jiggles and Bo-Bo…clowns-on-the-make, hah-hah," she chuckled to herself mockingly, then downed more brew.

One Minute After Midnight

She then put the loose, floppy hat on her head ad pranced around the room in joking imitation of Ray. "Fuck 'em," she sneered, then threw the clown hat over onto the fireplace mantle in contempt. "Jiggles" was on borrowed time now, anyway.

Ten minutes later, Marissa walked quietly up the stairs, stopping at the bedroom door to look in on her sleeping husband. All she could see in the dark was the human-size lump under the comforter.

She chuckled and turned to walk into the bathroom suite for a shower, relishing the fact that she had the rest of the week off-work thanks to an acquaintance covering for her at the hospital. It pays to know People!

Losing her bra and panties, Marissa stepped beneath the hot shower spray, enjoying the warmth on her skin as always. Part of her wanted to hop in the Jacuzzi here in the big bathroom suite, but she was too tired. She and Ray had used the in-floor two-man Jacuzzi only once since they'd been married. It was then that she found out he didn't like to make love wet.

No one truly knows someone until they live together for a while. Marissa relaxed in the enthralling shower spray, washing herself thoroughly with a sponge.

After a 15-minute shower, she got out, dried-off and wore only a towel around her naked torso when she went back downstairs. Her hair was still damp despite towel-drying, but using the loud hairdryer might wake up Ray.

She sauntered down into the dining room and lit up a cigarette from the pack laying on the shelf of her hutch-cabinet. Never a habit-smoker, Marissa enjoyed tobacco every now-and-then. Taking a long drag on the cigarette, she stood facing the sliding-glass door, looking out at the dark backyard.

"Hmmm…what else am I going to have to procure to further insure your loyalty, Raymond…hmmmph," Marissa chortled to herself in sarcasm. Her first thought was "Jiggles" the clown, AKA Rosemary Jones, who was, indeed, a "threat" where Ray was concerned.

Ken Knight

"I know where you live, bitch, so don't even think of stealing my husband," she whispered to herself, thinking of Rosemary in jealous contempt.

Blowing smoke to the ceiling, she decided on one option in an instant.

Marissa finished her smoke and decided to light up one more before joining Ray up in the bed. She placed the cigarette between her lips and lit the end. The end of the cigarette "popped" in sudden eruption, making her drop it to the foyer below.

"Son-of-a-bitch," she sneered in shock, realizing that the cigarette had been rigged with one of those gag "poppers" in the tip. Ray had access to that kind of shit.

"Heenh, you're such a fool, Raymond," she laughed in spite of herself.

Marissa tossed the cigarette into the sink in the kitchen and walked to the stairwell again. Maybe he owed her at least that considering the electrical plank she rigged form him a couple weeks ago.

She let her towel fall to the rug as she strolled into the bedroom quietly, slipping into the cozy bed next to her sleeping man, not waking him.

Marissa lightly kissed his stubbled neck and nestled beside him comfortably.

December 24th:

Bo-Bo, the clown, was in rare form this morning, working the Christmas Eve office party in a Santa outfit mixed with clown-face and frilly hat. Ray was happy to do this little office party at the Software Company this morning because he had a partner-in-gag, Jiggles, The Clown.

Though she wasn't stripping off her attire, she was so pleasant to be around and Ray loved every chance to work with her.

"Ha-ha-ha-ha! Computer people are so funny....I'm Bo-Bo, The Clown, who really gets around and here's my friend, Jiggles!"

Secretaries and PC nerds. Everyone thought it was funny, particularly how Jiggles shook her covered breasts like a burlesque girl.

Ray gave Jiggles a piggy-back ride into the boss' office nearby, and Jiggles honked her obnoxious horn and laughed hysterically.

A mere 6 months ago, Ray wouldn't have even imagined himself doing this kind of foolish "work", even if it paid good. Marissa had coxed him into this and he was glad that Rosemary Jones was here, otherwise he'd quit like Marissa told him he could.

Rosemary had gotten closer to Ray in the past month, and he relished every moment of conversation with her, every minute of the hour in her presence.

He and she were clowns, making people laugh for a living, even if most of these people are laughing at them. Laughter was good and positive, Rosemary had said, even if its ridicule at the clown's expense.

Ridicule. Like what he used to throw at Marissa Borders back in high school, that brace-faced, gangly girl who fawned over him back then, even when he teased and taunted her; who now had him by the balls, literally.

His "clownage" was sweaty now, this office building in Horry County well-heated. Ray played off of Rosemary's movement and gags, going to each desk and worker in joking promenade.

"Jiggles, I love you!" bellowed one of the male employees over by the water-cooler jokingly. She waved at him and honked.

"Hey, bub, she's by girl," Bo-Bo retorted, playfully hugging Jiggles into him, making her laugh and honk that loud horn of hers again. The entire office audience laughed in unison, and both clowns felt good.

They made their exit, waving, laughing, and honking. Ha – ha – ha –ha. Honk – honk!

Ray and Rosemary got on the elevator going down to the 1st floor of the building, still laughing form their office gig they had been paid to present today before the place closes at noon.

"Wanna go to my place for lunch?" Rosemary asked him girlishly. Ray knew they had no more gigs today and he was hungry, not to mention it was an invitation to her home!

"Sure, why not," he answered her casually, smiling at her as the elevator descended.

"Great, I make a mean Italian, and homemade bread, too," she added impishly.

"Oh, baby," Ray chimed in humored response.

Rosemary's house was a two-floor A-frame with a rather posh interior and a regal décor. The young woman had taste and took pride in her abode.

The place smelled like peaches, the scent thoroughly sprayed around much like how Marissa sprays potpourri in their house every day.

"Make yaself cozy, Ray, and I'll start the spaghetti and clam sauce," Rosemary told him as she bolted into the kitchen. Ray wandered into the living room, removing his Santa coveralls and frilly hat.

He sat down on her sofa and relaxed, looking around in curious interest. This was a nice place, he thought, a cozy home indeed and unusually well-furnished for a single person.

Rosemary had style, and a terrific outlook on life as well as a decent-paying job to afford comfort, Ray felt good being here today, even if Marissa would kill him for it, if she found out.

He would gladly risk her wrath right now, to spend "quality time" with Rosemary here in her home, gladly! Even if Marissa kicks him in the balls again, or shoots him with her Glock, this was worth it.

Resting back on the sofa, Ray thought about how Marissa might react. Fuck her, he thought next, and her jealous mind, too. Life is too short to regret a goddamn thing, or to pass up golden opportunities. Yeah, golden like the hair on sweet Rosemary's head, and the golden snatch between her soft, smooth thighs.

Rosemary strolled out from her kitchen, letting the pasta and sauce start to simmer on the stove. She smiled at Ray intently, standing by her little fireplace as she removed her funny hat and shoes.

"You know we're getting paid up until four o'clock, right?" she spoke gingerly to her co-worker and guest.

"Yeah, I figured we would be, that's cool of the company to do that," Ray answered her softly, eyes on her hawkishly.

"Mmmhh...see, being a clown aint' so bad," she chimed sweetly with a wink.

Lunch was absolutely delicious, a homemade spaghetti with clam sauce and home-baked garlic bread served with iced tea and an expensive red wine. Rosemary knew how to make lunch, indeed.

The two entertainers, still in clown-face, sat at the dining table engaged in casual, interesting conversation while eating well. Rosemary was a grand cook and conversationalist, and Ray took full advantage of her personae, getting paid for it, too.

Spaghetti never tasted so good, so smooth and richly spicy with the warm clam sauce evenly mixed and thick to the taste. If Rosemary was trying to make an impression on him she was succeeding!

"Enjoy the meal, Bo-Bo?" Rosemary asked him after he finished off his plate.

"Yes, Jiggles, it was almost as good as your company," Ray answered her with a smile.

"I'll take ya word on it, handsome," she said as she stood up in conclusion, smiling ear-to-ear again with her perfectly-painted clown-face.

Walking back into the living room with his glass of wine, Ray followed Rosemary with his eyes, the house lit up by the sunlight beaming through the windows now. She had let her hair down and removed her jumpsuit, wearing only her pink string-bikini and clown-face now.

"Ray, tell me about your wife...why does she make you so unhappy?" she asked him hesitantly, circling the room like a cat.

"She blackmailed me into marrying her; she is the sole eyewitness to an accident I caused one night last June..and if I didn't marry her, she would've gone to the cops," Ray explained in a rush. He felt good now that he had told her.

"No shit," Rosemary managed to say, surprised and aroused by such a story.

"What did you do?" she asked naturally.

"I can't say, not now, anyway...besides, it's depressing," Ray answered with a smile.

"Cool, but you can tell me anything, I hope you know," Rosemary added with a grin of appeasement, hands-on-hips.

"I know, but it was a hit-n-run and I'm at fault...Marissa is the only person who can stick me for it," Ray told her reluctantly.

Rosemary nodded as she slowly approached the man. She decided to pry no further on the matter. With one hand, she untied her bikini-top and the thin garment fell from her plump breasts to the floor. Ray could only stare in awe of those tits of hers.

"Take off your clothes, Ray, it's time I shoed you the thrills of clown sex," Rosemary chimed in her sweet, intoxicating voice, touching a hand to her boobs.

"Oh, yes, clown sex," he uttered as he fiddled with his tie-dyed T-shirt, yanking it up and off his torso and arms.

He was going to get to make love to this glorious blonde bundle of womanhood, and by the sheer anticipation of her sweet flesh, his manmeat grew fully-engorged inside his pants even before she touched him.

Already a thrill, blinding him to the possibility of another set of eyes watching them now.

Marissa peered into the house through the living room's bay window, unhampered by the drawn curtains. She had just enough space through the window to view her husband with Rosemary now. The sight broke her heart as she crouched at that window, peering in. A flurry of emotions welled up inside of her all at once as Ray stripped of his clothes to join the naked Rosemary Jones.

She froze right there, this scene becoming almost surreal, too much to ponder rationally, so she just watched in angering horror at the betrayal before her eyes.

"No," she sighed in emotional disdain, watching the two lovers touch. She partially wished she had not followed them here to Rosemary's house in Horry County, but part of her wanted to see if Ray would cheat on her, and she had guessed correctly. The son-of-a-bitch goy bastard was gleefully proceeding to fuck that twinkie-blonde bitch, and on Christmas Eve!

Marissa watched through the opening tin the window's curtain, seeing all-too-well, unable to stop a tear streaming down her left cheek. Now, she had every reason to cry.

Ray moaned in approval as Rosemary touched his raging erection, then he laid back on the sofa there as she headed for fellatio. Taking Ray's cock in her mouth, she relaxed between his legs, sucking on the manmeat lovingly, smooth and steady.

"Ooaahh...Rosemary, you're so good to me," he said softly, touching a hand to her blonde head. Seeing her painted face going down on him was kinky, but her mouth was the real prize.

Rosemary raised up momentarily and grinned at him, then moved over him into the 69-position, lowering her crotch over his face, his arms around her thighs as she laid on him, taking his tool back in her eager mouth.

Ray mouthed her blonde muff ardently, his tongue finding her sweet spot while Rosemary enjoyed bobbing up-and-down on his turgid dick, slurping in fellatio.

Through the bay window, Marissa watched the lovers in increasing anger. Ray never did 69 with her, and here he was in lewd abandon with that clown bitch!

Marissa watched and thought, considering she could do, what she will do..."Damn you, Raymond...hmmph, I can't have nothing," Marissa said to herself as she watched them, tears streaming down her face.

"I'm gonna get that bitch, and Ray...I'll pay 'em both back," she sneered with a sob, watching still.

Now, Rosemary raised up again and turned around, descending on his erection as she straddled his hips on the sofa. Ray reached up and pawed her plump boobs as she absorbed his cock up inside of her snatch, slowly sitting on him to begin a "riding" intercourse.

She felt so good and firm, moving up-and-down on his tool, boobs bouncing in her motion, giggling girlishly with a continuous expression of delight on her white, pink, and blue clown-face.

"Oh, Jiggles," Ray sighed in desire, enthralled by the feel of her soft flesh, her sweet scent and the body of a valkyrie. She bounced up and down vibrantly, continuous in rhythmic motion.

Marissa cursed as she watched the buxom blond ride her husband in vibrant sex. Her mouth was wide open in moaning delight, eyes shut in passion's blinding grip, up-and-down on the married man's cock.

Marissa could hear very little, mostly just Rosemary's moaning voice as she fucked ray on the sofa.

Ray's head rested on the sofa's padded armrest, and Marissa could see him clearly, his mouth moving, eyes closed.

He was probably telling the blond bitch how he loved her, the bastard....Marissa told herself since she couldn't him.

"Oooh, I'm gonna get you, Ray...I'm gonna get you...my husband," Marissa whined in teary anger.

"Nnnggh...you can stick your dick in that blond slut all you want, Raymond, but you're still mine," Marissa sneered as she watched the two fucking more violently now.

"Heenh-heh, enjoy that pussy, Raymond, you penniless, unskilled prick...it's the last time...you ingrate," Marissa growled.

One Minute After Midnight

"Ooohh-ooonnh, Ray...I love it, oooaahh...Bo-Bo, my stud," Rosemary cooed in satisfied ardor, leaning back as she continued riding on him. She reached to the end table behind her and grabbed the clown horn there.

Jiggles honked the horn as she continued her intercourse n Ray, moaning in kinky excitement, enjoying the manhood penetrating her so well.

Marissa could see and hear still: honk-honk...ooohh, oooaahh! Honk-honk, ooooaahh! Rosemary was having a good time with another woman's husband.

Ray reached up to her jiggling boobs and squeezed them again, making her laugh and drop that obnoxious horn.

She collapsed to his hairy chest, laughing and wanting to kiss. Sweat was melting her clown face now, smearing a little on Ray as they kissed, then rolled over to go into a passionate missionary position.

Ray plunged into her lovingly, groaning in sheer delight of the moment. He loved her, this sweet woman of gentle demeanor, everything about Rosemary...like a rose.

Marissa cried, watching her husband joyously making love to his co-worker and fellow clown-entertainer, in callous defiance to his wife.

Ray felt so good with Rosemary, so right in carnal indulgence with her. She felt good, tasted good, and her body molded with his perfectly it seemed. Unlike Marissa, Rosemary was a woman who fit him mentally and physically, and he wished he was married to this gorgeous woman of heavenly demeanor, rather then the Jew bitch, Marissa, who had him by-the-balls still.

"Oonnh, so good...sooo good; I swear...I'm leaving my wife!" Ray chortled in the sensation, then hunched down to suckle her big breasts.

"Mmmhh, oh, Ray...yes, harder, baby...you know how to use your dick," Rosemary wailed out in mounting orgasm coming quick.

153

"Oh, Jiggles, oh, Jiggles...Jiggles!" he roared in sheer enjoyment of her tender flesh and exploratory hands, her legs wrapped around his thrusting backside.

They switched to another carnal posturing, with Rosemary up on all-fours, and Ray kneeling behind her, re-engaging the shapely young woman doggie-style.

Marissa watched in interest, strangely-aroused as well as angered by the sight.

Ray pumped into moist canal from behind her, hands gripping her buttocks gently as he pumped forward like a piston, steady and hard.

"Ooophh-yesss, I'm coming!" Rosemary bellowed in ecstasy, arms on the armrest as her lover pounded into her rapidly.

Marissa still watched, seeing the expression on Jiggles painted face, one of pure pleasure, with eyes closed and mouth wide open.

And Ray, with his fierce motion, fucking Jiggles in free abandon, as if nothing else mattered, putting his entire physique into it. She had never seen him in such a sexual frenzy, even with her! It was as if she were watching a different man, fucking that twinkie-blond whore, gorging her gooey-white center.

Rosemary was going-off in quaking orgasm, yelping out loud in delight of Ray's phallic onslaught.

Marissa felt an incredibly malignant hatred for Rosemary Jones now as she watched. Burning jealousy raged inside of her, and it reasoned itself well.

That was her husband with Rosemary, her penis going inside of that blond slut, her sperm shooting up in the womb of another woman! Marissa reasoned it well and made up her mind.

"Ooooh, I'm going to make you both pay for this...you worthless ingrates, motherfuckers," Marissa snarled as she wiped away tears, sobbing some more.

She envisioned chopping Rosemary's pretty head off with a meat cleaver and castrating Ray at the same time.

Marissa continued watching them, fantasizing about killing Ray and his whore in bloody melee. No, torture would be better for these two, she thought.

Ray climaxed in a whirlwind of erupting pleasure, unleashing inside of his ladylove in glorious release, groaning and calling out her name in triumph.

They collapsed to the sofa cushions together, embracing in warm conclusion, then their lips met feverishly.

"Oh, Ray, you amaze me," Rosemary cooed as she held him to her, feeling him kiss her breasts.

"Honey, I wish I was single, 'cuz I'd be all yours," he answered her, then kissed her neck lovingly, lying entwined with her on the big sofa.

Rosemary smiled and kissed his sweaty face, not answering that one.

She didn't want him for keeps, only as a "boyfriend" with no-strings-attached. Let him think this was love, she thought, not wanting to spoil the moment by telling him she only wanted him for sex.

"All the good men are married it seems," she cooed in his ear.

Ray laughed, kissing her tits again.

"Lover, let's go take a shower," Rosemary suggested, eyeballing him.

"Yes, Jiggles, I agree," he chimed, boyishly-happy.

They got up from the sofa, arms around each other as they headed toward the other end of the living room, to the hall where the bathroom was located.

Marissa watched them walk together across the room in there, eyeing their bare asses in particular, side-by-side in moving unison.

"Oh, I wanna drop you both in a meat grinder...make cube steak outta your fuckin' bodies...feed it all to a dog kennel," Marissa said to herself, watching the naked lovers disappear deeper inside Rosemary's household.

Ken Knight

Marissa stepped from the window, face tear-streaked from the pain of witnessing Ray and Rosemary together. She couldn't help but to cry, because this was an upsetting incident, a "pivotal" moment of threatening influx.

She thought about how she can "right" this situation and not lose Ray in the process. Not wanting to keep him just because she had something over him, she wanted Ray to decide to stay married to her and grow to love his wife. But another woman stood in the way now, and Marissa knew her stupid husband was probably falling for Rosemary now. Especially now.

Marissa walked to the edge of the yard an pulled out her cellular phone, dialing a number she happened to remember. Raising the phone to her ear, she looked back at the house where her husband was brazenly betraying her with that Bimbo sugar-tits, Rosemary Jones. Love was turning now, becoming something else.

A deep male voice answered the phone on the other end and Marissa paused for a second before speaking finally.

"Hi, this Marissa Torelli, and I owe you an apology" she spoke firmly,, eyes up at the sky overhead.

Chapter 11

December 25th
7:30 a.m.:

Ray awoke in a sweat and found himself alone in bed, the house silent and eerily peaceful. As he sat up in the bed and stretched, he glanced out the window to see flurries of snowfall. Ha! A white Christmas in South Carolina? Doubt it will be any more than a dusting, he thought.

Marissa had played Christmas music all last night on the stereo system, and he was surprised that he didn't hear any now. It was strange that she liked Christmas songs and tunes of Yuletide, he thought again. Marissa was Jewish, though not a "practicing" Jew.

He got up and put on his cut-off jean shorts to head downstairs now, where his wife obviously was. The images of Rosemary Jones danced in his head still, for he had dreamed of her all night, and he was happy.

Descending the spiral stairwell slowly, Ray could smell that goddamn potpourri scent his wife liked so much, even on Christmas day!

"Merry Christmas, honey," spoke Marissa in jubilance as soon as she saw Ray saunter into the living room toward her.

"Merry Christmas, Marissa...good morning," he replied softly with a forced smile. The bathrobe-clad Marissa walked up to him and ht embraced tenderly, kissing in spite of morning-dog-breath.

"Come open ya presents, big buy," she said softly as she bounced over to the medium-sized Christmas tree next to the dormant fireplace. Numerous wrapped gifts were under the tree neatly. Ray had gotten her a gold necklace and a whole box full of "Victoria's Secret" panties and bras, hoping she'll be pacified by them alone.

He just didn't have it in his heart to "splurge" on his unwanted wife for Christmas. Dan her for making him feel so guilty, anyway.

They sat down on the sofa together, and Marissa handed him a gift from her, of course, and he unwrapped it while she lovingly kissed his cheek and neck.

Despite seeing him fucking "Jiggles" yesterday, Marissa maintained her masquerade of nonchalance, acting as if she knew nothing of his infidelity. Deep down, she was wailing in pain and wanted revenge. She would have it on Rosemary first, the bitch who flagrantly violated their marital bond.

She kissed Ray again as he held up the silk shirt she bought him, accompanied by silver cufflinks. He liked it, so he kissed her back.

How dare you, Marissa thought with a poker face; how dare you kiss me after your lips were sucking on that blond whore's tits....No matter, because "Jiggles" will soon get hers, in-spades.

A Bulova wristwatch, another silk shirt, a cologne-package and a pair of black leather biker-style boots with silver buckles on the sides. Not bad, Ray thought to himself, hugging and kissing his wife in gratitude.

Marissa opened her gifts to find the gold necklace and the box full of lacy panties and multi-colored bras form "Victoria's Secret". She loved them, thanking Ray up-and-down. Cheap bastard, she thought to herself, considering what she spent!

"I've got something else for you, honey, but I'm saving it for later," she cooed as she walked into the kitchen to fix breakfast.

"Awh, Marissa...you've done enough, and I thank you, honey, really," Ray retorted amicably, smiling at her for once.

"Mmmhh...you're worth it, Ray, Merry Christmas, baby," she said in a purr as she turned on the stove to make french toast.

"Same to you, Marissa," he sighed, walking up to the kitchen's bar-counter, adjusting his new Bulova watch on his wrist now.

"Do you have to work tomorrow?" she asked him casually.

"Yep, three gigs to do, probably be gone until late," he answered her.

"I'll be at the hospital from ten-till-six tomorrow," she lied again, convincing Ray that she'll be at work tomorrow.

She turned and smiled at him sweetly with a wink. Things were starting to return in rotation, what came around in going around, back toward Ray Torelli. Glancing at her gold wedding band, she envisioned his sticking it to that blond slut back at Rosemary's house. Marissa put the frying pan down onto the stove top, and silently cussed her husband as he stood behind her, adjusting the watch she bought him. He was hers' her husband, her mate, and it was her penis he used on "Jiggles" yesterday. Thinking like that made Marissa want to take this hot frying pan across her husband's lying face, but she kept her cool.

Pouring the egg yolk, she silently fumed in anger. This called for a reckoning, she told herself as she grabbed the spatula with her free hand. This called for a settlement only she personally could meet, and no one could know about it but her.

Accidents happen, she thought, as ideas for revenge comforted her while she cooked his breakfast. Accidents happen to anyone, from firemen to taxi drivers, to retarded guys on Mopeds; even to a clown with big milky tits and errant husbands who don't know how good they have it!

All she has done for this man, this jobless, boring fuck who had nothing and would have surely gone to jail after running over Rex Mathewson on June 4th. All she has done for him, and he still want s to split up, going to the haven of a bitch who strips and dances for horny men at parties. What would she give Ray besides heartache and the clap? She told herself indignantly in her mind.

Flipping the French toast in the pan, she glanced over a shoulder at Ray, who had sat down at the dining table now. Smug bastard, she thought with a slight smirk, he is convinced that he got away with his little fling yesterday, that I'll never know!

Ken Knight

Marissa hated him even more for that indifferent face, that lying-ass demeanor where secrets were kept. Hell, he seemed rather "happy" this morning. Of course, he dipped his stinger in Rosemary's honey yesterday, probably laughing in thought of his wife the whole time.

He had shit on their arrangement, the marriage, and the cozy life Marissa offered him and she silently swore revenge.

In her mind, fucking Spaz McCracken was only a means of getting the geek to do what she wanted-albeit secretly. It wasn't a betrayal like when Ray copulated with that Rosemary chick yesterday. No, that was an attachment, a loving merger. It wasn't the same, she told herself.

After breakfast, Marissa pulled Ray to the garage port, telling him to close his eyes as he entered.

When he opened them, eh found himself standing in front of a parked motorcycle next to his truck. He instantly recognized the bike to be a Harley-Davidson "Sportster" with candy-apple-red paint job and a leather pan-seat.

"Here's the key, baby, it's all yours," Marissa said sweetly, handing him the key to the bike.

"Jeezus, Marissa...omigod, it's ...it's beautiful...you bought this for me?" Ray exclaimed in surprise, walking around the bike in glee.

"Yep, you said you'd always wanted a Harley, so there you go," Marissa said with a chuckle, fighting back the urge to cry out the fact that she knew about Rosemary. Insult-to-injury this was, and she wished she could shove this entire motorcycle up his hairy ass right now.

"Thank you, honey," he said ardently, hugging her close and planting a kiss on her cheek.

She then watched him inspect the bike, enthralled by its new appeal, something he couldn't have afforded on his own. Marissa wanted to laugh in the irony of this situation. Here she gets a department store necklace and a shit load of slinky panties and bras for Christmas, whereas she gave Ray a $10,000 motorcycle, a $300 watch and $175 worth of silk shirts, and he wants out of this relationship?

"Glad you like it, Ray. Ya see...I'm not so bad after all," she told him as she turned to go back up into the house, leaving him with his new machine.

He didn't answer her, imagining himself cruising along Rt. 501 with Rosemary at his back, arms around him tight, riding the wind...

Remembering what Rosemary told him about freedom and self-reliance, he reaffirmed his intentions of leaving Marissa somehow and soon. She was trying to "appease" him and he knew it, so to hell with her and her money. She gave him this bike as a gift, so legally it was now 100% his to keep, he told himself next, examining the bike.

The Conway Inn
Conway, SC
Next day:

Jimmy Groves had finally drifted off into much needed slumber even though it was just 1:30 in the afternoon. He had driven fifteen hours from New York on his way to Miami, and crashed here this afternoon at the "Conway Inn" near Myrtle Beach off Rt. 501. All he wanted when he paid for a day's lodging in this room was peaceful sleep.

As soon as he heard that distinctive sound coming through he wall, Jimmy knew that wasn't going to happen right away.

A moaning symphony in soprano, roaring loud-and-clear from room #208 next to his, distinctively a female wail of sexual delight. Some young lass was obviously being penetrated rather furiously in the next room and she voiced her satisfaction.

The 32-year-old Jimmy Groves sat up in the bed and cussed to himself in cynical tone.

"Figures, no rest for the wicked," he sighed in a chuckle, listening to the lusty moans and grunts sounding off in

Ken Knight

obnoxious vigor. The headboard of the lover's bed was slapping the wall as well, as the female wailed out in delight of intercourse.

She groaned out loud, long and furious all-of-a-sudden, and Jimmy laughed to himself, swinging his feet to the floor.

"Ride it hard, daddy-o," he chuckled in spite of himself, listening sleepily to the raunchy sex next door. Male grunts sounded, flowed by a woman's wail again. Some dude was driving-it-home good and hard, and Jimmy wished it were him tearing that pussy up right now.

Man, that chick was enjoying herself rather vocally, and Jimmy wondered what she looked like as loud as she was. Wow, what a nympho, he thought humorously as he stood up and put his ear to the wall. Listening closer now, he snickered in curiosity.

"Damn...." He whispered as he listened to the ravenous lovers next door. They were going at it like animals!

He listened to the woman closely, her sweet moans of ecstasy arousing him as well. In all the bestial wails and moaning excess, he heard her say "fuck me" in throaty repose, then resumed her symphony of orgasmic soprano.

"Feel so good," roared the baritone male voice and then a series of groans as the bed creaked beneath his onslaught.

"Ooohh, yes...yes...don't stop!" the woman's voice growled in hissing ardor, then continued moaning loudly. She was absolutely going-off! Jimmy couldn't believe what he was hearing; it sounded better than any porno flick he'd watched.

Jimmy continued listening to them through the wall, thrilled by their loud erotic ardor, wishing he had it so good. Minutes went by, and the sounds of wild love-making continued without interruption.

Jimmy sat back on the bed, listening to the lewd act next door in room #208.

He pressed his ear to the wall again as the female voice became really muffled suddenly, as if she had something in her mouth. Jimmy could only imagine.

One Minute After Midnight

It was pure carnal indulgence pulsing through he wall, and Jimmy was impressed by what he heard. Glancing at his watch, he saw it was 1:50 p.m. already. These two weren't stopping!

The woman cried out in sheer delight, her moans louder than ever as the bed's headboard slapped the wall violently.

"Oh-oh-oh-oh...." She wailed in animal ardor, making the man on the other side of the wall laugh in admiration.

It went on for minutes more, the couple fucking in lewd abandon for over a half-hour now. Jimmy was almost disappointed when they ceased at 2:15. He laid back down on his bed and thought about his Florida trip again, wishing his frigid girlfriend would have joined him on this trip. If she heard those two in #208, she'd give it up.

In room #208, body heat warmed the room and two exhausted souls lay beneath the covers no in monetary relaxation.

Marissa Torelli raised her head up from the sheet, breathing heavy still, sweaty from the "workout" she just participated in. "Unnoohh...yeah, that hit-the-spot," she cooed in a hot voice of satisfaction, slowly sitting up in the cheap motel bed.

The man's hand pulled her back down under the covers again and she giggled in response, kissing her lover again as he pulled her onto him.

"Mmmhh...gotta get washed up and roll out, big guy," Marissa spoke gingerly, then rolled out from the covers and up on her feet, stretching her naked physique upward.

"Yeah," the man groaned beneath the covers. Marissa stepped to the dresser-mirror, looking at herself. She smiled slinky at her bare reflection, glancing back at the man-sized lump in the bed. She chuckled at her one-hour lover. Isn't that just like a man? He comes once, then Wants to go to sleep! She thought in humor.

She ran a hand over her full bare breasts, then ran her other hand through her sweat-soaked hair, staring at her reflection in the mirror.

Ken Knight

"Remember what I told you to do, now I'm gonna take me a hot shower....Please be gone by the time I'm done," she spoke to the man beneath the covers as she walked to the bathroom now.

The man rose from the covers in time to see her bare backside going inside the bathroom, then the door slammed shut behind her. Giles chuckled to himself as he swung his legs over the bedside, feet to the rug below.

Marissa wants him to do a favor for her and in-turn, he asked her for a favor, namely her cute ass in bed with him just once! She agreed and they spent the past hour in this cheap motel room fucking like rabbits.

Now, he had to fulfill his end of the deal, thinking on it as he stood up and removed the condom from his penis, tossing the used rubber into the room's tiny plastic trash can. He then reached for his pants, happy to have at least gotten laid today, Marissa was one hell of a lover to say-the-least, despite the strange request she asked of him.

As he got dressed hurriedly, Giles heard the shower going in the bathroom, and he laughed in thought of her scrubbing that sweet physique of hers.

He then grabbed his keys and jacket, but stopped before going for the door to exit, finding Marissa's keys on the room's wooden dresser.

"Might come in handy," he snickered as he plucked her house key from the ring, shoving it in his pocket. He hoped she would simply think she lost her key.

He trotted toward his car in triumph, giddy over his tryst with Marissa Torelli, who called him every word in the book and threatened to kill him only weeks ago.

5:00 p.m.:

Rosemary Jones was glad her workday was over now. Two bachelor parties back-to-back in the daytime were unusual but the country boys of the Carolinas were often like that, no sense of cool timing!

She drove her orange Volkswagen Bug along Rt. 501 enroute to her home here in Horry County, her mind forcing thoughts of work tomorrow and on her new lover, Ray Torelli aka "Bo-Bo The Clown".

Working with him, sleeping with him, and the fact that he was married all fired bullets at any hope for a normal relationship with the handsome man.

Rosemary turned onto Raines Road off Rt. 501, only two miles from home now. The sun was setting fast and she always liked to get home before dark, when she could.

Driving along at a smooth 45 mph with lights on despite orangy sunlight still illuminating the road, Rosemary was a careful driver, so she always slowed down around the curve up ahead. She thought about Ray again as she took the turn, braking gently.

She felt no pressure, as if the brake wasn't engaging, so she pressed harder, still no pressure, and Rosemary's gut wrenched in sudden panic because her tiny car was taking the turn too fast!

"Omigod...no!" she screamed in shock as the car brushed the guardrail and left the road over the embankment, descending in a helpless spin, carrying it's lone driver into the woods.

Rosemary screamed in futile abandon, the horror of the crash so violently disorienting as she was tossed around the Bug's cabin like a rag doll, her face meeting the windshield in shattering thrust. The car landed against a big oak and belted under the crash force, and Rosemary's broken body was thrown free of the car to land violently against hardwoods, then to the wet ground in mind-wracking pain.

She screeched out in the searing pain, the ripping sounds of the crash fresh in her ears as she lay prone on the wet leafy ground, her back and both arms broken as well as her left knee. Blood streamed down her left cheek and she could feel it. Looking up in the dimly lit woods she lay in, she could not see out of her left eye!

But her right eye could see her left eyeball on the ground below her face now, hanging by a thin, bloody tether. My god, her eye had popped out and her back burned in absolute pain.

"No...no...not this, my...." Rosemary chortled before coughing up blood in violent heaves, as if her insides were coming up. She couldn't see the car that had stopped up at the road's guardrail, nor the female driver getting out and starting down the embankment toward the wreck she had witnessed.

When it became too painful to continue screaming, Rosemary heard footfalls coming up behind her now, but she couldn't move. She eventually could see a woman's boot in front of her head.

Marissa Torelli looked down at the bleeding, broken Rosemary Jones lying prone before her in perfect chaos. She couldn't' believe it; her blond mane was caked in blood and shattered glass from the car's windshield, her left eye popped out from its socket and the limbs looked broken like twigs.

It couldn't have happened better because no one else saw the wreck she was certain. Marissa had been following Rosemary and as luck would have it, no other traffic was on this back-road when the Volkswagen's brakes failed at the perfect moment!

She had rigged it that way, sabotaging the brakes of her rival's care with precision craftsmanship this morning while it was parked behind the "Pop-n-Rock" office in Aynor at 10 a.m. In fifteen minutes, while Giles distracted Rosemary inside the office with a phony bachelor party-order, Marissa rigged the brakes to fail gradually, a mechanical feat not well-known.

It worked out perfectly, this crash into the trees only a mile form the slut's home was bad enough to utterly ruin Jiggles The Clown for good. The brakes failed at such an opportune time, she couldn't believe it! Perfect.

"Look at what we have here...a blond bimbo home-wrecker," Marissa sneered in kinky demeanor, staring down at the severely injured young woman.

One Minute After Midnight

With her one good eye, Rosemary caught a view of the woman standing over her, realizing who it was. Everything started to grow darker all over; the woods, the air, her mind....

"Please, god-help-me," she managed to speak in horror.

"Bitch, this is what you get for fucking my husband and trying to take something of mine, you cunt!" Marissa bellowed to her victim in triumph.

"Nooo...." Rosemary groaned helplessly, realizing that Ray's young wife here must have caused the accident somehow. Somehow! But it hurt to just lay there, thinking, coughing violently again, spitting up more mouthfuls of blood.

Marissa laughed in sardonic response, uniquely thrilled by this scene, this horror she caused.

She looked over at the wrecked Volkswagen 10 feet away, seeing no sign of fire, only leaking hydraulics and the creaks of ruptured metal. The orange car now resembled more of a big crushed beer can.

"Oohh, that's an insurance claim that'll get you dropped for sure," Marissa laughed in spite.

She looked back down at the ravaged body of Rosemary, seeing her eye lying out in front of her quivering face by a bloody tether. Marissa couldn't resist raising her left foot and brought her boot down hard over the exposed eyeball, crushing it like a grape.

"Nooo...unooggh!" Rosemary cried in protest, seeing her eye crushed beyond repair. It was the least of the damage to her paralyzed carcass, as the blood continued to evacuate her ruptured body.

Marissa laughed as she crouched next to the dying woman, knowing that she didn't have much time now that shock set in.

No other cars were stopping up at the road; passers-by probably couldn't see the accident down in the woods. She wiped off her jeans and huddled her arms in her fur parka as she watched Rosemary die slowly.

"Hunh, no one screws up my life without payback...and not it appears that Jiggles The Clown is going out-of-business,"

Ken Knight

Marissa chimed cruelly. Rosemary sobbed as he broken body shivered in both cold and shock of the trauma. Internal injuries and the bleeding eye socket were bringing her closer and closer to death, and Nurse Marissa Torelli knew it.

She stayed with her victim to be sure. This was the first time she had killed to "protect" what she owned, and it didn't feel bad at all.

Remembering now how Ray made love to this woman the other day, how "happy" he looked while sticking it to Rosemary here. Never again, she thought, as Rosemary's good eye closed in final loss of consciousness. Marissa touched a hand to the dying girl's bloody hair, then touched a finger to her blood-slick throat, feeling for a pulse. Her heart no longer beat, and a smile crossed the killer's face there in the darkening woods.

"Bye-bye, Jiggles, stay away from me in the next life, bitch," she said to the corpse. Standing up slowly, Marissa looked around the darker woods and up at the road 25 yards away.

She felt very, very cold suddenly, and stood over the body of Rosemary, shivering in contemplation. It worked out, just like her plan to nab Ray into marriage had. Her luck was holding out so far. Instead of luck-of-the-Irish, it was luck-of-the-Jewish, and Marissa was thanking her stars all the way.

Marissa stepped over to the smashed little orange car and laughed again, then stepped on something metal. Looking down to see it, she found the object to be Rosemary's personalized license plate: J-I-G-G-L-E-S. She broke into girlish laughter again, picking it up and walking back to the hill, up to her car at the guardrail.

She got into her BMW quickly, pulling back onto the road heading south, leaving the accident scene unnoticed it would seem. Funny how things go in vicious circles, she thought as she drove toward Rosemary's house now.

"Man, this worked out perfectly, and now Ray needs to feel the burn, too...haah-haah," she chuckled to herself as she turned onto the horseshoe cul-de-sac where Rosemary's house was located.

168

One Minute After Midnight

Ray's truck was parked in her driveway and there he was, walking up to the front door, using the key he'd been given to open the door.

Marissa watched him in awestruck contempt. The bastard had his own key to the slut's house! She told herself.

She was going to set the house on fire but decided to keep going since her husband was here, waiting on his new girlfriend, who would never come home.

Ray returned home at 8:30 tonight, walking through the front door with a sullen look on his face that Marissa noticed as soon as she greeted him with a kiss. He was wondering where Rosemary had disappeared to, since she had no gigs tonight and told him to meet her at her place by 3:00.

"Everything all right, honey?" Marissa asked him as she prepped the dining table for the chicken teriyaki dinner she fixed an hour ago.

"Yeah, I'm just tired...long day," he told her meekly as he sat down at the table to eat.

"I'll be quiet if you want to go upstairs to bed early," she said softly as they began to eat across from one another.

"Think I will," we sighed, not looking at his wife even though she was staring daggers through him. Bastard was disappointed his Miss Twinkie-bunny-tits didn't show up at her place earlier. Fuck him, she thought as she watched him eat mechanically.

Ray went to bed early, shortly after 9:00 p.m., desiring to sleep all night and go to work in the morning and see Rosemary. She was all he cared to think about now, sweet lady love Rosemary Jones.

Laying down in the bed in his boxers, Ray relaxed with his arms at his sides, head on the pillow facing upward. He could smell Marissa's perfume lingering in the bed linen, and he thought about the motorcycle she bought him. Grateful yes, in love with his wife, no. Ray closed his eyes in the dark bedroom and waited to drift into sweet slumber.

Ken Knight

The phone rang from the nightstand next to the bed and Ray instinctively answered it.

The owner of Pop-n-Rock Entertainment was calling tonight with grave news. He wanted to notify all his employees of the unfortunate accidental death of one of their co-workers earlier today.

Ray's heart sank and he dropped the phone receiver when the boss said the name of the deceased employee. Rosemary Jones.

He sat up in the bed, shaking. This cant' be true, not her. Not in a goddamn car accident. The words of the man on the phone echoed in his head as he sat there in the dark.

Rosemary was dead, victim of a car accident on the road home today around 6:00 p.m. He was at her house shortly after six o'clock; he must have just missed her on the road there!

This can't be happening, he thought as his mind melted with despair in seconds of gut-wrenching anguish.

"Rosemary…jesus," he sighed in a sob. His left hand slipped under his pillow and he felt something metal there. "What tha…." He sighed in wonder, pulling the metal plate out from beneath his pillow. He could see it in the moonlight coming through the window, a license plate. J.I.G.G.L.E.S., Rosemary's personalized tag!

"Jeezus, what the hell?" he erupted in shock of the situation, holding up the dirty plate in stark realization. How this could have gotten here was a horror in itself.

Possibilities filled his mind, but only one person he knew could have gotten Rosemary's plate and put it under his pillow tonight, and that was Marissa, without a doubt.

"Marissa!" he roared with emotion, leaping from the bed toward the door. Nearly falling twice, Ray hurried down the spiral staircase post haste. Emotions took over as he envisioned the lovely Rosemary Jones ravaged in a car crash.

"Marissa…Marissa…you!" he bellowed with emotion, as he stumbled into the living room to find his wife sitting in the leather recliner. She was wearing her red silk bathrobe and in her right hand was a handgun.

"Take it easy, Raymond...." She spoke softly, holding her loaded Glock-17 on the armrest, barrel in his direction.

"Marissa, what the hell are you...you fucking bitch!" he roared in tears, holding up the personalized license plate she had placed under his pillow. The man broke out into tears now, standing before her in horror of the moment. He didn't even care if she shoots him at this point.

"I'm no the fucking bitch, Ray; the fucking bitch you betrayed me with on none-other-than Christmas Eve?" Marissa spoke assertively with a wicked smirk.

"Jeezus," he groaned as he sank to his knees on the floor, crying in sorrow over Rosemary's death.

"Bad things happen, Ray, and this time it happened to your little friend, Jiggles," she added coldly.

"Migod, Marissa, you did it, didn't you? You caused her to wreck yesterday?!" Ray whimpered in quaking emotion, a mixture of hate and sadness.

"Oh, about as much as you caused Rex's death," she answered cryptically, her poker-face expression on of malice.

"No, goddamnit, Marissa...she was so beautiful, so soft and...No, she did nothing wrong!" he quipped with shaking fists.

"Like I said, Ray, accidents happen, and I thought you might like a memento of hers to remember her by," she said in reference to the license plate.

Ray stared at his wife in pure hatred, wanting to break her neck with his bare hands.

Instead, Ray just collapsed on the living room rug in a ball, crying helplessly. If he did lash out at her, he guessed that she would shoot him and claim self-defense. Marissa would get away with it, just like she was getting away with Rosemary's "accident". She was too smart, and he knew it.

The idea of Rosemary dead ate at him ferociously and all he could do was cry.

Ken Knight

Marissa stood up from the recliner, still holding her gun, and walked passed her downed husband as he sobbed harshly.

"My sad...sad clown," she said softly, enjoying his emotional breakdown. "Sorry it had to be this way, Raymond, but I'm not going to share you with anyone and ...no one is going to upset my apple cart," she continued in spite, walking into the kitchen.

"Bitch...I swear on my life...you'll pay for all of this shit...you'll pay for killing my Rosemary!" Ray barked out loud as he rolled over on his back, face red with tears and anger.

Marissa laughed at that statement, then thought of a good reply.

"After all I've done for you, Raymond, all I've offered you and you go stick your dick in a stripper and fall in love....Besides, I didn't kill her, and you can't prove otherwise, so forget about it, asshole and focus on what you have!" Marissa spoke firmly.

He couldn't retort any further, his mouth dry and the sobs feeling like seizures.

"After all I've done for you, honey, and all I've done to keep you satisfied, look at how you repay your wife...cocksucker; if anyone is responsible for Rosemary, it's you," she continued cruelly from the kitchen.

"Fuck you, you murderin' bitch!" he managed in hated response from the floor.

"Hmmph, maybe I should cut your balls off, Raymond, so you can't fuck anyone else again, you ungrateful little man," she answered angrily. After all, she only called him Raymond when she was pissed-off.

"You belong to me, you pussy," Marissa chided him mockingly, then headed up the spiral stairwell.

"Just another blond slut who can't drive worth-a-shit, fuck her!" Marissa said as she climbed the stairs now, knowing Ray would hear it.

He laid there, seething in a whirlpool of anger and sorrow. Rosemary was dead, gone forever. Never again would he kiss those peach lips, touch that soft skin and embrace her shapely body, never….

She was gone and it hurt like hell. Only two days ago he had made love with Rosemary Jones, enthralled in her sweet charms and sweeter flesh. He fell in love on Christmas Eve, with that bubbly, life-loving young woman who shouldn't have died like she did. He couldn't do anything but cry right now.

Marissa walked into the upstairs bathroom and turned on the light overhead, looking at herself in the mirror. She placed her gun down on the vanity top next to the sink and smiled at her reflection.

Ray had said "My Rosemary" when referring to his mistress. Imagine that, she thought in contempt. The betrayal was complete because he had fallen for Rosemary like some horny schoolboy.

After more than 20 minutes of crying, Ray slowly composed himself enough to get up and walk grudgingly up the stairs to the top floor of the house. All was quiet again.

He stopped at their bedroom, standing in the doorway. Marissa was in bed and looked like she was sound-asleep, lying on her back, covered up to her neck. Ray could see her, thanks to the blue night-light in the wall socket by the window, glowing a bluish haze over the room. Damn her little bullshit quirks like potpourri, rabbit's foot key chains, and night lights! He thought as he stood there.

She looked so peaceful laying there, so damn solemn as if nothing bothered her and slumber was so very easy.

How can she live with herself so well after what she has done? He wondered. Part of him wanted to kill her tonight.

How dare that bitch lay there so peacefully as if nothing was wrong, he asked himself as he stared at the sleeping Marissa. She probably expected him to join her, he thought, fighting the urge to urn in and strangle her.

He waked to the bathroom, turned on the light and stood there in surprise again. Marissa's Glock-17 pistol lay on the vanity, left there by proxy, he guessed.

Ken Knight

Looking at the back plastic-polymer weapon, Ray considered something he hand' thought of until tonight. Playing it out in his imagination, he envisioned going into the bedroom with her gun and shooting her dead in the bed in cold-blood.

Maybe she left it here on purpose, to tempt me! He thought as he gently picked up the light-weight weapon, holding it in his right hand. Touching his right fore-finger to the plastic trigger, Ray knew he couldn't commit murder as easily as Marissa could but he would do so in a rage, muck like any man. The rage he felt tonight could coax him into such an act, even if he was slowly calming down.

"I should kill you, Marissa...for Rosemary," he sneered to the mirror, holding the gun up. He had no real proof that Marissa intentionally killed Rosemary, and she wouldn't admit to it directly, of course. Innuendo never prosecutes, but he knew she did it somehow.

Why God? He asked to the mirror. Why do I have to suffer under this evil, Jezebel-of-a-woman, and the beautiful, sweet Rosemary Jones who never hurt anyone in her young life, has to die?

Why is this happening to me? He asked in his mind, then left the bathroom to walk back to his bedroom, gun in hand. Standing at the threshold, he looked in on the sleeping woman in his bed, his wife and tormentor, Marissa Borders.

Ray gripped the Glock handgun firmly in his right hand, finger in the trigger guard. He wanted to just shoot her so she wouldn't wake up ever again, so he wouldn't have to look into those black devil eyes of hers ever again.

"I hate...you," he whispered softly in emotion, feeling tears again as he stood there, holding her handgun. Ki8lling Marissa would land him on death row, and prison was what he wanted to avoid when he agreed to marry her six months ago.

Ray walked on into the bedroom quietly, and gently laid the Glock on the pillow next to her, then returned to the bathroom to piss.

One Minute After Midnight

When he finished in the bathroom, Ray walked back into the master bedroom. He had thought about crashing in the guest room, but for some strange, ungodly reason, he wanted to sleep in his marital bed even after the phone call, the license plate, and Marissa's shadowy role in Rosemary's death.

He stepped around to his side of the bed and gently crawled beneath the covers next to a naked, sleeping Marissa.

Hatred would lay in wait now, no sense in bucking the tiger without ammo to use on her. Ray decided to play it cool and try to pin Rosemary's accident on his wife if he could.

If she forced him into marriage, maybe, in some obscure way, he could force her into divorce? Doubtful, but he had to try. Maybe an "accident" could happen to her sometime soon? He thought as he shoved the pistol under the pillow between them, and laid his head down, facing away from the woman in his bed. His head filled with angry ideas now.

An accident, he thought, or a random crime?

Chapter 12

> Rejoice, oh, young man
> In thy youth!
>
> --The Bible, Ecclesiastes

Lightening flashing in violent strikes all across the sky, and thunder of Thor, himself, boomed like a dozen atomic bombs. Sleep is never steady with dreams such as this, and Ray woke about six times tonight during a rapturous sleep of only 7 hours.

A sensation of flesh befell his senses, provoking his sleeping subconscious to protest into waking realization. Lying on his back, Ray raised his head and focused his blurry vision to see Marissa gently straddling his hips with his erection already up inside of her. As soon as she saw that he was awake, she began her piston movement.

"Marissa...jezuss, girl..." Ray groaned in protest as she rode up and down on him in sudden motion, laughing.

"Good morning, Ray," she chuckled girlishly, then laughed again when he gently pushed her off him to the bed.

"I'm not in the mood as you might imagine," he said softly, sliding off the bed to feebly stand up.

"Aww...c'mon, honey, let by-gones be by-gones, and let's make up...I'm willing to negotiate," Marissa spoke slinky, lying on the bed with legs open in lewd posture.

"Yeah, taking advantage of my morning hard-on isn't gonna make me forget about...." Ray said hoarsely as he sauntered out toward the bathroom. He couldn't even bring himself to mention Rosemary now.

He wanted to play it cool from now on, and get Marissa when she least expected it. Being her whipped-puppy was repulsive, but he had to eat-crow for now, so he could find an advantage over her later.

Marissa laid on the bedspread, giggling to herself in humor of the moment.

"Negotiate my ass, you fool," she sighed.

A half an hour later, Ray was downstairs seated at the dining table after fixing breakfast. Marissa joined him minutes later in her white nursing uniform, sitting down across from Ray with a pleasant look about her now.

"Delicious eggs, Ray," she said casually, eating slow and sipping at hr orange ju7ice.

He nodded, eating quickly himself.

"You killed Rosemary. I still can't believe it, Marissa...how?" he got up the nerve to say after another minute of stone silence between them.

"No, she wrecked her car on the way home yesterday, but I will admit that I was chasing her," she answered flatly.

"Chasing her?" he sneered in surprise.

"Yes, I was gonna kick her ass and she knew it, so she sped up and lost control," Marissa lied.

It made sense to him and he would have never guessed that Marissa knew hot to sabotage a car's brakes like she did. "You still killed her," he sighed in anger, trying to keep his cool, though.

"Whatever...don't throw stones, Ray, honey, considering what you did to Rex back in June, hmmh-hmmph...besides, Jiggles wrecked all by herself technically, and the cops already got my statement because I called none-one-one for her," Marissa lied again.

It made sense, so he didn't argue the point. Damn her, she's still responsible! Of course, he couldn't go tell the police on her for obvious reasons.

He shook his head and ate the rest of his eggs and bacon quickly. Marissa ate slowly, taking her time even though she had to be at the hospital soon for a 10-hour shift.

"You going to work today?" she asked him casually, her dark eyes staring at him intently.

"No, I'm going to quit, just like you suggested I should," Ray answered softly. There was no way he could return to work as a clown-for-hire with Rosemary gone, no damn way.

"Cool, because I wanna open up the business I've been planning soon, as you well know," she added.

"Hmmh, I don't care about any business venture of yours, really," Ray said as he got up from the table.

"You will if you stand to make a lot of money in the process, all for yaself," she said calmly.

"Working for you, I suppose," he said casually.

"Working for us, we're married after all," Marissa retorted with a grin.

"Don't remind me," he sneered, walking into the kitchen. That damn potpourri smell was gonna make him puke his eggs if he stayed in the dining room one moment longer!

"Awwh, don't be mad at me forever, baby. Forget the past and focus on our prosperous future," she responded in her disarming, cool tone of voice.

Ray dropped a glass in the sink and it broke into five shards in a loud crash.

"Ooops, you'll be okay, Ray...get over it and let's get on with our lives," she chuckled as she stood up from the table to get ready to leave.

Ray stood in the kitchen in silence until she got ready to leave for work. Marissa walked in, approaching Ray for a kiss.

"Bye, honey, see you tonight," she whispered, then kissed him on the lips even though he didn't kiss her back.

"I'm going to her funeral," Ray announced as Marissa walked toward the front door to exit.

"Fine-by-me, honey, but don't be surprised it it's closed-casket," she told him cruelly on her way out the door.

Ray cursed out loud in hatred of her slamming a fist against the refrigerator in anger.

Growing up, he hated his father, the drunk, tormented by his older brother, the pot-head as well. Now, his hatred focused on his wife because she was 3 times as malignant as a drunk in his life. For lack of an education at a college, and living in a poor state, he was poor. Because of a fateful accident six months ago, he was at Marissa's mercy.

To hell with her money and comforts, he voted for his freedom now; freedom from marriage to this bitch, who killed Rosemary. Anyway, she told him. He considered Marissa rightfully responsible for Rosemary.

Ray locked up the house and went out to his truck in the driveway, then decided to take his new motorcycle instead, even though he didn't have his motorcycle license yet.

When he kicked the engine to life, he gunned it in neutral just to listen to the Harley's loud, monstrous roar. This was one thing Marissa gave him that he liked, so he would enjoy its ride without a permit.

Half of him wanted to ride out onto Rt. 95 north and keep on going, but that was every biker's dream, and consequences kept it form coming true.

December 31st:

Arriving home from dinner and dancing, Ray and Marissa settled into their comfortable abode to watch "the ball" drop on TV. It was now 11:50 p.m., only ten minutes away from the year 2001.

Seated on the sofa with a cold beer and a deep dish of popcorn, Ray relaxed in temporary serenity, the funeral today, having saddened him further. Rosemary "had" to be cremated according to her father from Virginia. She was interred in a cemetery in Florence, S.C., not far from Dillon.

He just wanted to relax and welcome the New Year in here at home. Marissa was leaving him alone now, since he indulged her with going out earlier to a Myrtle Beach nightclub. Good, because he didn't want to talk with her anymore this evening.

As the minutes ticked away, Ray hoped the year 2001 would prove would prove to be his good year!

Ken Knight

Meanwhile, Marissa stood at the front door's little window, still in her evening dress from earlier. Peering out at the driveway where Ray had left his motorcycle out, she anxiously waited.

It was almost midnight and they hadn't shown yet. Three guys she vaguely knew were to come and quietly steal Ray's new motorcycle she gave him. She had paid the three redneck fools $200 each to rip off the bike from her driveway tonight.

When a beat-up old Ford pickup stopped in front of the house and began backing into the driveway, she breathed a sigh of relief. They were here, and they'd take Ray's bike and be gone without a trace.

Marissa chuckled and turned back toward the living room. The ball was dropping in New York City's Time Square, 3 – 2 – 1 ....

"Happy New Year, honey," she spoke up abruptly as Ray just sat there complacent.

"Same to you, Marissa," he answered her with a half-smile, then swilled more of his beer. She walked on through the dining room into the kitchen. By the time she made it back to the front door, her paid thieves were gone, and so was Ray's new motorcycle! They had stolen it without a noise, and she was happy. Money-well-spent for once.

"My Rosemary," Ray had said in reference to the dead clown lover of his. Yeah, Ray, my bike, she thought.

Fuck him and his ingrate attitude, she told herself. This theft would simply drive another nail into his coffin.

She'd get the insurance for the stolen motorcycle since it was purchased in her name, and Ray is paid back just a little more.

Marissa walked tot eh stairs and ascended in glee, her plans continuing perfectly with each passing stroke.

Walking upstairs to her "den" where she often sat in the bean-bag and watched movies on the other TV/VCR set up in there. Marissa just lit up a cigarette and laughed to herself.

"I still love you, Ray, you big idiot," she said out loud, pacing the quiet room in blissful solitude.

"One of these days, fool, you'll come around," she chortled in self-righteous ardor.

Downstairs, Ray downed the rest of his beer and decided to go out for a spin on his bike, even though he was still in his good clothes. Walking to the door with his helmet and keys, he opened it and stepped out onto the front stoop.

"What the...." He stammered in shocked surprise, looking at where he had parked his Harley in the driveway behind his truck. It wasn't there anymore...gone.

"No, omigod...no!" he barked as he ran to the spot, looking around in vain. Marissa had warned him to put it in the garage yesterday evening, because it could get stolen.

"My bike, it...it's been ripped off," he snarled in realization. This couldn't be happening, not now! He pleaded with the heavens. Bad luck doesn't plague one soul this heavily, no way in hell.

He looked up at the house, seeing the light on in the window of Marissa's upstairs den. He couldn't put it past her, but he doubted she would have someone steal it purposely.

Then, again....

January 7th:

Why on earth his brother insisted on meeting him here at the golf course in Horry County, in this weather, was beyond him! Ben Torelli wanted to just call his younger brother, Ray, over the phone and tell him this info, but no....

Parking his car next to Ray's Chevy 4X4 in the gravel parking lot of the Golf Range, Ben got out to greet his sibling in the chill wind that was at least 40°F now.

"Hey, man, why couldn't we just discuss this over the phone?" Ben spoke in greeting, looking at Ray in the flannel shirt and jeans.

"Sorry, don't trust my phone at home, 'cuz Marissa's spying on me," Ray said calmly, patting his brother on the arm.

"Well, bro, my P.I. friend came up with the one asshole named McCracken in all of Allen County, Aynor, and Florence," Bill said sharply, hands in his jean's pockets as they stood in the cold, face-to-face between their two vehicles.

"And?" Ray asked in wonder.

"And, Ray-Ray...he's an eighteen-year-old kid who is a computer-hacker, even convicted on it once, some kind of geek genius," Ben explained politely.

Ray hated it when Ben referred to him as "Ray-Ray", because it used to be one of those childhood names of ridicule between brothers.

"So, where does this kid live?" Ray asked in curious contemplation about why his wife would be paying a computer hacker anything?

He was handed a slip of paper with the address.

"No big deal, why do you think it's important?" responded Ben Torelli with a scowl, shivering slightly in the cold air.

"I'll let you know after the divorce," Ray chuckled with a nod of thanks, then turned to hop back into his truck.

"Man, you're crazy, ya know, so just keep me out of it," Ben laughed as he return to his car to leave as well.

"Jeezus, Marissa, what are you doing with a computer-hacker?" Ray asked himself out loud as he pulled out onto the road, driving without music on, so he can think.

"No, that's insane," he said to himself as soon as the one peculiar thought crossed his mind. A hacker could tap into a bank computer and dice one's credit rating!

Sure, he saw a TV show once about illegal hackers getting into confidential files and such, and wrecking havoc with other people's money, job status, etc.

She could have ruined his credit, thanks to this hacker she paid cash to last year. Why, though? To better cement his dependence on her, that's why. It was making sense, because

One Minute After Midnight

how could he leave her if he would be financially-ruined without her?"

Damn, Marissa was smart, he thought, someone he had underestimated for too long. Driving the speed limit along Rt. 501 now, he decided to look this address up and see where this McCracken character lived.

"I want answers," he said to himself again.

1:30 p.m.
Same day:

He hated hospitals, even the front lobby of one, always feeling "weak" whenever he walked into a place like this. Someone once told him that hospitals are the unhealthiest places to be when it really comes down to it. That explains why his sister came down with staph infections the two times she had operations.

Giles visor walked to the elevators and got on, hitting the button for the 5th floor. It was where she told him to go and deliver the package directly to her.

Marissa was a strange cat, he thought as he rode the elevator uninterrupted to the 5th floor of the hospital. She wanted him to get hold of an original Dillon County Sheriff's Dept. Incident Report from and bring it to her. She also asked him to keep an "eye on" the second house she owned in nearby Aynor for the next couple of weeks. Why? He could only guess, but Giles like being on her good-side now, and had accepted her profound apology for calling him racial names and pointing a gun at him back in November.

Doing her a favor or two wasn't bad. Besides, he was in-the-process of being hired by the Dillon County Sheriff's Dept. and had access to the office where he could swipe a blank Incident Report form like she requested.

Walking down the hallway toward the ICU wing, Giles knew that he shouldn't ask Marissa why she wanted a blank

Police Report form. He wanted to remain on her good side, so to hell with "why".

"Giles!" spoke a familiar voice from out of nowhere, making the casually-dressed black man turn to confront her. He smiled at Marissa nervously as she approached him from the adjacent hallway, wearing blue O.R. scrubs and her name badge.

"Hey, Marissa...got that item you wanted, here ya go," He spoke in greeting, handing her a manila envelope.

"Thanks, man, I appreciate it, really," she chimed amicably, taking the envelope. She smiled at him sweetly, touching his forearm.

"How are you, Giles?" she asked as the two of them walked back the way he came, toward the elevators.

"Cool, and I rode by that house of yours in Aynor...on Applegate Road, and it was secure, nothing amiss," he said softly.

"Good, 'cuz I'm selling it soon and I've already had kids try and fuck with the front door and windows, nothing serious...but I would like to know if you see anyone outside in the yard, et cetera," Marissa spoke in slow, easy tone as they walked together. She lied so easy to men.

"No problem," Giles added honestly.

"Also, if you could, make an anonymous phone call to this number and tell the guy who answers that if he comes out of his house, you're gonna kick his ass big-time, okay?" she continued, handing him a slip of paper.

Giles found that favor funny, but agreed to do it, of course. A prank call, what a juvenile thing, but it would be anonymous after all. They got on the elevator with another nurse going down.

"It's my lunch-break, so would you like to join me for a bite to eat down in the cafeteria?" she asked Giles next, touching a hand to his back.

She had fo8und that men were better coerced into agreement when she was touching them while talking.

One Minute After Midnight

"Sure, love to," Giles answered as he stared at her, feeling the elevator descending slowly.

They got off the elevator on the ground floor and walked down another long corridor toward the cafeteria, talking.

Marissa found it funny that Giles wore jeans, cowboy boots and a pleated brown work shirt with a ball cap on his head, not to mention the western-style belt buckle!

He dressed like a redneck, even talked like one most of the time. There was a kindness about him, though, a soft demeanor that she found she could take full advantage of.

Giles was idiot enough to fall for Marissa's half-assed scheme, then she could easily use him for her plan now. It was simple, appeal to his male senses, and she had him eating out of her hand.

They got their trays of food from the line and Marissa paid for it all, then they took a seat at a two-man table together.

"Thanks, Marissa," Giles said as he settled in to eat.

"You're welcome, honey, we're friends now, right?" she replied gingerly, then sipped her iced tea.

"Oh, at least that," he chimed with his stupid smile. She smiled at that remark. Indeed, he was easy to use.

Marissa watched Giles eat, finding him to be rather a slob at dining. The man couldn't eat with a fork, it seemed, dropping food nearly every time he raised it to his mouth.

"Last time I saw ya husband, he said he was going to get a divorce, ya know," Giles told her with a mouthful, not caring about Ray right now.

"Over his dead body," Marissa snickered, not surprised by that. Giles chuckled, spitting little of pieces of food as he did.

"Exactly what I mean, too…one of us is going to have to die first if he wants a divorce, hunh…fuck that," she added coldly.

"I told him he's crazy for wanting to divorce a fine young woman like you, anyway," Giles said in humored tone.

"Hmph, ungrateful wap bastard doesn't deserve me really, but I fell in love with the hairy dork," Marissa chimed in light laughter. Giles laughed again, a particle of food landing over on her cheek, so she casually wiped it off. Damn, he was a slob at the table! She thought.

"Why did he marry you if he doesn't love you?" Giles asked in contempt of her former "buddy".

"My money, I guess," she answered, lying again. Of course, Giles believed her, because he was enamored with Mrs. Torelli. Surely, he thought, if Ray does leave Marissa, then he could move in on her full-time, and have that sweet-sweet ass of hers all to himself one more time, anyway.

Giles kept thinking of that as he dealt with Marissa. It was good to have a goal! Then, there was the other factor.

Marissa, on the other hand, viewed the affable Giles Visor as a useful but expendable asset. Why else would she want him?

"I don't mind telling you, Marissa...if you were single, you'd be in trouble," he snickered boyishly to her.

"Really," she cooed, patronizing him.

"Yep, though we might never leave the bedroom if we were a couple," Giles spoke with a grin, leaning over the table slightly.

"Behave," she chuckled humorously, then winked at the man.

The music over the system in the cafeteria was often elevator-music, but now it played a tune humorously-familiar to Marissa and it made her smile as she heard it. "Send in the clowns" played over the cafeteria's PA system, and she found it suspicious to-say-the-least.

Bo-Bo The Clown, he really gets around...ingrate faggot bum who doesn't know how good he's got it, she sang in her mind as she heard that slow song, "Send In The Clowns". For the life of her, she couldn't recall who sang that old song.

Wait until Ray finds out that the business she plans on starting is actually going to be one that is already in business. She was going to buy Pop-n-Rock Entertainment. Bo-Bo lives!

One Minute After Midnight

That night:

Dreaming occurred all too often, making for some restless nights, because he would always wake-up after the dream ended. This night, Ray dreamt of himself running through the dark woods naked with only his clown hat on, chased by Marissa and her gun. When she opened fire on him, he woke up, sweating profusely.

He laid there under the covers, looking up at the ceiling, the glow of the night-light illuminating the bedroom in usual bluish tinge. Movement next to him signaled Marissa getting up, so he kept still, pretending to be asleep.

She slipped into her silk red bathrobe, tying it around herself as she slowly sauntered toward the door. Ray watched her well-endowed buttocks "shake" slightly as she walked forward, something he did like about her.

In brief moments like this, he sympathized with his young, well-meaning wife. Other times, he wanted to chop her head off medieval-style. Damn that night-light of hers!

The hacker named McCracken wasn't home today, but he would try again tomorrow now that he had quit his job at Pop-n-Rock Entertainment. That queer boss of his didn't know what to do now that his two feature clowns were gone.

Marissa was up to some evil shit and he was going to uproot it if it was the last thing he does. Being able to leave her became his prize goal for the near-future.

They had not made love in nearly two weeks now, and he was horny lying next to his wife because she sleeps naked, cuddled next to him. She hadn't offered since Christmas, morning after Rosemary's death.

He didn't want to make love to her either, out of anger over Rosemary and hatred of her hold on him. Rosemary was so sweet and enticing, one of those types of women whom make a man get hard as soon as he looks at her, and a woman who enjoyed her sexuality.

Ken Knight

Too many women are prudishly celibate nowadays, forgetting how enjoyable fun sex is.

Marissa strolled back into the bedroom, looking at her husband in the bed, guessing that he was asleep. Walking over to the window, she looked out at the woods behind the house and the darkness enveloping the tiny forest.

Thinking about Ray's stolen motorcycle, she remembered the police officer saying that it was unlikely it will be found in the same condition. She just hoped those three rednecks she paid to steal it weren't stupid enough to get caught with the machine before selling it off. If so, they'd give the cops her description and the fake name she gave them. She doubted it would go wrong.

Ray was pissed about his bike being stolen, ad he doesn't have a clue. All part of the overall plan, she told herself as she stared out the window for aimless seconds.

It's a goddamn shame I have to break this man just to let him see me in a better light, she thought in sullen mood now, glancing back at the bed.

A happy marriage seemed like a pipe-dream, but she consoled herself with the fact that at least she had the man she desired.

January 12th:

Ray had cased the little house where McCracken resided for close to a week now, and today was the day to confront the scrawny geek in his lair. Better now than later, because it appeared that Mr. McCracken was moving out.

Inside the tiny abode, "Spaz" McCracken was boxing up his possessions post-haste. He was moving the hell out of Dillon and far away from that evil bitch named Marissa. He found out about the fatal auto wreck one Rosemary Jones perished in on December 26th and his gut instinct told him that Marissa had something to do with it since she had him find Rosemary's address for her!

So, preoccupied with boxing his stuff up, he failed to hear someone open his unlocked front door and enter uninvited.

Ray Torelli was nervous coming into this house like this, but pissed off as well.

"McCracken!" he snapped harshly as soon as the four-eyed younger man came out of the back. Spaz froze in his tracks facing the bigger, mean-looking man in jeans and jean jacket, fists clenched.

"Who are you...whatta ya want?" the frightened hacker bellowed in surprise.

"Don't matter who I am, but you know who Marissa is, right?" ray quipped boldly, hands-on-hips.

"Th...that bitch is the reason I'm leaving the state!" Spaz sneered in defensive response, backing up two paces.

"I wanna know what she's got going on with you, McCracken...she's my wife and she paid you a lot of money awhile ago and I want an explanation, man-to-an," Ray spoke in a calmer voice, gesturing with his hands.

Spaz looked down to his floor in fearful regret. He should have left here sooner! This was her husband, the man she was systematically ruining with his help, now standing in the house Spaz was vacating.

What a day!

"Jeesuz...I don't need this shit, man, I just did a job for her....I should've known it would haunt me," Spaz rambled in frustrated ardor. He wondered if he could get passed this guy and out the open door to flee.

"Hey, guy...all right, just chill for a minute and tell me how my wife is connected to you, and I swear I won't tell a soul...not even the cops," Rays said in an even calmer voice.

Spaz relaxed in his stance, believing him for now. They guy didn't look too aggressive, anyway. Besides, Spaz decided he'd rather get his ass kicked by an irate husband than thrown back in prison by the Feds.

Ken Knight

"Hunh, if you're Marissa's husband...I'm surprised you haven't killed yourself yet," Spaz said with a hesitant smirk.

Ray frowned in response, feeling sick to his gut all of a sudden. Nothing this kid was going to say would be good news, and he knew it.

Spaz didn't care since he didn't plan on seeing Marissa ever again in this lifetime, so he began telling her husband everything.

The nervous, sweaty Spaz McCracken sat down on a box in the dusty house's living room and laid it all out for the man who barged-in minutes ago.

Ray stood against the wall in awestruck silence, listening to how Marissa approached McCracken this pas fall and paid him to hack into the computer of a funeral home and the local hospital to add a name to the lists of deceased. Then, she paid him again to hack into the state's Social Security database and delete Ray's Social Security number and make his credit utterly vanish.

That was difficult to do, but Spaz was the best in his illicit business, a hacker-artiste' with smarts-enough o hack virtually anyone.

Ray absorbed everything Spaz told him, his mind racing with possibilities. Why the funeral home and hospital? Was she getting him listed as dead on record long before she has him killed?

It made sense: She took out a $500,000 life insurance policy on Ray after they wed last year. But no, it didn't "fit" Marissa.

"Why the funeral home and the hospital...she trying to make it appear that I'm deceased?" Ray asked in wonder, sinking to his haunches at the floor now. He couldn't believe this, it was surreal, his worst conspiracy theories thought-up were coming true!

"Not you, someone else...Some name she wants falsely listed in the hospital and funeral home as DOA: dead," Spaz answered with nervous sweat pouring down his moon face.

Ray looked up at the younger man seated on a box and his eyes went wide in shock of realization. "What was the name...the name?!" he barked rudely, hoping he would be wrong.

"Uhh...Rex somebody...." Spaz stammered in remembering reply, squinting his eyes."

"Rex Matthewson?" Ray snapped in pusle-stopping shock.

"Yeah, that's it...she said the dude was someone she had to smear, make him look dead on paper, I guess...she didn't go into detail and I didn't ask," Spaz spoke matter-of-factly.

"You mean Rex Matthewson is alive?" Ray asked in earnest, standing up abruptly.

"I don't know, never met the guy. All Marissa gave me was the name to put on those computers as deceased," Spaz replied in angst.

Ray stepped toward the front door, feeling ill. Could Rex Matthewson be alive somehow? It couldn't be possible, and if he was, how could Marissa hold up her end of the blackmail when Rex would surely be accounted for?

He had parents surely, because a retarded man like him cannot live totally alone. There would be Rex, himself, telling the cops about the 4x4 truck that hit him and the man who drove away to leave him there in the road.

Marissa couldn't have "bought" his silence, because that was before she got her inheritance money! There would have been a reckoning if Rex had survived to tell the tale. They would have if he had been killed but it was nothing big about it in the press for some strange reason.

It was coming back to him now as he headed out the door, leaving McCracken without saying another word. When Marissa sent him to North Carolina for a month afterwards back then, it was to cover it all up without him seeing?

Could she have disposed of Rex's body after the accident? Yeah, she was that gruesome but she was jogging in the rain that night; no way she could have carried Rex any more than a few feet.

Walking back to his truck on weak legs now, Ray was focused on the impossible reality which was slowly unfolding.

This plot against him was becoming more and more of an evil scheme of destruction with each passing day.

If Rex was alive, then where the hell could he be? Marissa had said his parents were gone, so where could he be living? The newspapers didn't say anything about on on-going investigation into the hit-n-run, and Ray actively looked for such news.

"My god...Rex still alive?" Ray sighed as he got into his truck and keyed the ignition. It couldn't be, but if it was true, then Marissa had scammed him on a scale unfathomable.

Driving back onto Rt. 501, heading toward the Dillon business district, he was wrought with agonizing thoughts, realizing what could very well be real.

He couldn't confront Marissa about it without proof. McCracken could have been full-of-shit, but he did now the name! She has ruined his credit and financial fortitude for years-to-come, that is certain.

This news about Rex was more pressing than his credit and Social Security number right now, because he was the trump card Marissa held over Ray, and if she really didn't possess that, then Ray had her over-a-barrel.

Driving faster, he thought of how he might turn this to his favor if Rex was alive somewhere and....

Damn, he thought, I should have forced McCracken to come with me!

Chapter 13

The entire house was dark now, no illumination beamed except for the wide-screen TV set down in the living room where Marissa Torelli lounged on her sofa.

She was alone in the big house this evening because Ray hadn't come home yet, but she kind of expected that.

Her mood dimmed with the setting sun, and so to cheer herself up, she decided to watch the XXX-Rated Porn Film her friend, Patti, gave her as a gag-gift for Christmas.

It was entitled: "Bedroom Eyes", starring Jonny Faster and Christy Cannons. Watching this 1st rate porn flick, Marissa enjoyed the scenes between Jonny and Christy, both lovers looking great together.

She would give anything to have breasts like Christy but, Marissa thought, no man should have a dick as big as Jonny Faster's! He was huge, handsome, and Nordic-looking, and she wondered where they found a man like him?

"Certainly not in South Carolina," she said to herself, watching the porn film more.

Jonny Faster and Christy Cannons were out-of-this-world in their hot, animal lovemaking on the screen. Marissa watched in aw, sipping her bottle of beer in silence. Even as porn stars, they looked like they were in love as they gorged in carnal abandon.

This was a good adult film, she thought, and she'd have to thank Patti again for giving it to her. Marissa laid back on her sofa cushions, enjoying the sex on video better than any other movies she had on the shelf, that's for sure.

She told herself to look for another such flick with Jonny Faster and Christy Cannons init the next time she drives by one of those X-rated video stores in Myrtle Beach!

Marissa sighed as she thought about Ray again. Over on the dining table was the signed paperwork, making her the new owner of "Pop n' Rock Entertainment," purchased for a cool $88,000 from its elderly owner.

She put it out for Ray to see because if he would agree to manage the place he could sing-on as co-owner, split 50/50 with her. Not a bad deal, really.

She also thought about the second house she owned in Aynor, and her asking Giles to keep an eye on it for her. The last thing she needed was Ray snooping around that place, but as far as she knew, he considered the place empty and "For Sale", so why go check it out?

Ray was getting too curious, though, too intuitive for his own good, and she would have to do something about it soon. He was truly unhappy and blamed her for Rosemary's death. Yes, she caused it by fixing the Volkswagen's brakes to fail, but Ray just thought that she "scared" Rosemary off the road by chasing her.

Let him think that, let him hate me, she thought. It'll pass in time, and maybe turn to something else. Men grow complacent after awhile, and she hoped that her husband would get "comfortable" with her after awhile.

She looked back to the glowing TV screen and saw Jonny Faster giving it to Christy like a champ, doggie-style.

Marissa raised her beer bottle in toast of the porn stars on her big screen TV.

Downing more of her beer, she felt better. Watching two people fuck on video had made her cheer-up after all, and she hit the rewind-button to see Jonny and Christy once again.

Thoughts of Rex Matthewson came to her again, that stupid face of his and foolish grin. She had Rex to thank, though, because his bad luck landed her the man she wanted, too bad Ray wasn't playing the game.

She wondered how a retarded man like Rex made it through life with that handicap; that 200 laps-behind existence where he is in a man's body with a man's desires and instincts, but can't "win the prize" like a normal man of brains and brawn?

She wondered how someone like Rex could smile when condemned to the slow, oppressed life of the mentally retarded. Rex had foolishly tried to "swoon" her a year ago, asking her to the retard dance at the special school he attended. She remembered laughing in his face and telling him to go away. She had been nice to him in high school gym class and the idiot thought that she'd be nice to him as an adult. Ooops.

Marissa laughed in spite of both Rex and Ray, watching the porn film as Jonny and Christy continued their fucking in joyous, vocal ardor. She enjoyed watching those two get-it-on, thinking it too bad they weren't in-person right here in front of her.

When the video ended twenty minutes later, she didn't rewind, choosing instead to just sit there in the dark on her sofa, thinking.

"Hmmph, he wants to divorce me…ingrate prick," she sighed in reference to Ray. Lighting up a cigarette as she lay out on the sofa, Marissa took a long drag and exhaled. She'd been smoking more lately, thanks to him.

"Well, if I can't keep you, then no one else will either, Raymond Torelli; if you don't give-in soon, you might wake-up-dead one morning," she said to no one, a tear forming.

Marissa fell asleep easily, and two hours ticked by, allowing her peaceful slumber for awhile, until a noise awoke her abruptly. Someone coming through he front door.

"Ray?" she called out wearily, sitting up on the sofa as the hallway light came on around the corner.

Footfalls sounded, heavy and hard, boots on the foyer, two sets! She sprang to her feet as the two looming male figures stepped into sight. Before she could yell out in protest, they had her.

The first one belted her across the face with a gloved hand, knocking her off balance against the dining room table. Marissa fought to stay on her feet but she was overpowered easily, and the two intruders knew what they were doing.

Marissa was on her face on the rug by the sofa seconds later, and when she managed to let out a cry, one of the goons put a boot at the small of her back while the other one handcuffed her hands behind her back. What the hell was this? She wondered.

Ken Knight

Wearing only her bathrobe now, she guessed that she could expect rape from these two intruders. Were they burglars? She hoped they would just rob the house and not rape her ass.

"What the hell is this, you robbing me?" Marissa asked with her face to the rug.

"Shut up, bitch...or I'll give you pain unlike you've had before," snarled one of the black-clad masked men. She couldn't see them from where she lay in the dim living room now, but she heard them walking around the house, in the kitchen and dining room.

She obeyed and just laid there, angry and sore from the blow across the face, hoping Ray might come home soon and interrupt these two assholes. Maybe they'd kill him as they escaped and she'd get the million dollar life insurance policy she took out on him.

"Marissa Borders...this visit is complements of your only friend, you fuckin' bitch,'" sneered one of the goons as he lifted her to her feet suddenly, squeezing cuffs tight on her wrists.

"What?" she snapped before the gloved hand struck her jaw again, knocking her to the sofa in violent fall. This guy was strong.

They knew her name and the phrase "only friend" was something she hadn't heard in a few years, not since college! This cant' be, she thought in fearful wonder as she lay helpless on her sofa while both masked men home-in on her.

One grabbed by the hair at her scalp, the other untying her robe quickly. Were they going to rape her or beat her toe death? She asked herself now. Both were just as bad.

One of the men turned on the lamp next to the sofa so they could see better. Marissa gawked at her attackers in shock. Both were burly men in black ski-masks, but she didn't see any weapons yet. Her pistol was up in the bedroom, useless to her now.

They opened her robe and knocked her to the floor again, making her bellow in fear and pain of the blows. A heavy boot

One Minute After Midnight

kicked her bare buttocks in a glancing blow and he yelped in protest.

The other man turned the coffee table over and grabbed her by the hair again, pulling Marissa to her feet. Not being able to fight back was worse then the beating for her.

"What do you...want?!" she growled in earnest, facing the two masked intruders helplessly.

"Shut up, bitch" snapped the goon on her left, then he backhanded her hard across the cheek, knocking her back up against the fireplace. This was no simple home invasion/robbery, she thought as the other man belted her in the abdomen, doubling her over to the floor again.

With the wind knocked out of her, she just stayed on her knees doubled-up to try and resume breathing.

"Your only friend is worried about you and told us to tell you that you're an ungrateful cunt who forgets who truly loves her!" snapped one of the baritone male voices over her.

They could only mean one person, and Marissa didn't believe it. Not now, after two years of silence, why bother me now? She wondered in pain.

"This is merely a reminder, bitch...next time we come calling, you're a dead whore," sneered the man as he crouched beside her, holding something in his hand.

"Who sent you?" she whispered painfully.

The man held a tiny handcuff-key for her to see, then he chuckled and he slipped the key up into her cunt as she knelt there.

He then shoved a pink handkerchief in the pocket of her open robe and laughed again, standing up.

"Bye-bye, little bitch," one of the goons chuckled as the two of them made their exit out the back sliding door.

"Shit," Marissa snapped in frustration, slowly maneuvering her cuffed hands under her butt to bring them under her legs and to the front, then she could get the key and uncuff herself.

"I don't believe this crap...they must've had a key to the front door...goddamn," she said to herself as she uncuffed her wrists and tied her robe back around her. Walking to the front door, she found it unlocked but not "jimmied"! They did have a key. The key that was missing form her key chain?

She doubted it, thinking that Ray had to have something to do with this. Marissa took the pink hanky from her robe pocket and raised it to her nose. My god, that perfume was something she hadn't smelled in over 2 years, a rare and expensive fragrance imported at $800 per bottle from Barcelona, Spain.

It couldn't be, not after all this time and after college when she was certain she'd never see or hear from this person again.

"No fuckin' way," she sneered as she tossed the pink handkerchief into the trash can. Ray had to be involved in this since he wasn't home this late at night. Could he have found out about her college dalliance?

It was possible, because he was getting curious lately, asking about her college days and such at the dinner table and in bed. She never told him about the one "suitor" though.

Could Ray have hired two assholes to rough her up tonight, make her think it was her psycho college suitor?

She had given him $10,000 to have in his checking account, so it was possible. The man was getting rebellious and she knew he was plotting something tangible against her.

"Damn you, Raymond...I'll have your balls for this...all I've done for you," she sighed as she walked to the sliding-glass door again, looking out at the night sky. It was now 2:45 a.m.

4:00 a.m.
That morning:

Ray keyed the front door and slowly pushed it open, hoping that his wife would be sound asleep in bed by now. Locking the door behind himself, he quietly entered the grand house, offing his cat and hat at the wooden rack by the doorway.

The living room light and dining room light were on, and that indicated that Marissa was up and probably pissed off.

One Minute After Midnight

Wanting to get it over with, he walked into the dining room slowly. Marissa was seated at the dining table's head, clad in her red silk bathrobe ad a poker face.

"Marissa," he said hesitantly.

"Ray, honey...you're a tad late," she chimed softly with a slight smirk. He noticed that the left cheekbone of her face was bruised as id she'd been hit.

"What happened?" he asked her, pointing to his cheek.

"I bumped my jaw on the kitchen counter when I slipped in there earlier. Gonna have a bruise for awhile....Now, come sit down and look over my business purchase," she spoke smoothly, lying to him.

He stepped up to the table, sitting down next to her where paperwork lay. It was a purchase, all right. "Pop-n-Rock Entertainment" was now hers to run. Ray read the first page, knowing now what she had done.

For $88,000, the business was Marissa's. Parties, clowns, paraphernalia, party supplies, etc., all hers to make money on.

"You bought Pop-n-Rock," he sighed as he glanced at her, noticing her hair in slight disarray. She was usually a fanatic about brushing and curling it to stay straight, even at home.

"Yes, I did, and you can manage it as co-owner for fifty-percent of the net-profit margin, honey...Bo-Bo the Clown lives," she said softly with a forced smile.

She wasn't going to give him the satisfaction of knowing she'd been attacked earlier.

"You want me to mage it for fifty percent?" he asked her in surprise.

"Yes," she sighed, touching her hand to his.

"And if I say no?" he asked next, feeling emboldened all-of-a-sudden.

"Hmmm...foolish move, considering the opportunity, honey, since you know that business good enough now," Marissa spoke gingerly, slowly getting madder.

Ken Knight

"I know about your friend, McCracken. He told me about your sabotage of my Social Security and credit rating," Ray told her abruptly.

Marissa sat back in her chair, eyeballing the man with a cold gaze. Realizing what this meant, she decided not to erupt in a rage yet.

"You met Spaz, hunh...shit, figures that dork couldn't get out of town before you found him, hmmph," she snickered in regret, eyes on the table now.

"You've financially ruined me, Marissa," Ray sneered in contempt, eyeing her hard.

"A new beginning, Ray, right here," she said as she pointed to the paperwork.

"Sign it and you can make up for it," she added in polite tone of voice.

"McCracken also let it out-the-bag that he hacked into a hospital and funeral parlor computer to put Rex's name on a list of deceased persons...something like that, and Rex might be still alive?" Ray asked in hesitant demeanor.

Her dark eyes widened some as she stared daggers at him.

Marissa then reached for the papers on the bottom of the small stack in front of Ray and pulled it up to show Ray her next trick.

A Dillon County Sheriff's Office Incident Report. Ray read it slow and carefully, each word stinging him in rebuttal.

This was the police report on the hit-n-run death of Rex Matthewson on June 4, 2000. Suspect unknown, vehicle a full-size 4.4 black in color. Rex Matthewson D.O.A.

"How'd you get this police report?" he asked her, noticing it was an original, not a copy.

"A friend in the department," she said with a matter-of-fact smile.

Thinking hard on the matter, Ray surmised that if Marissa could conjure up a computer-hack job to "prove" Rex's death like that McCracken kid said so, then a hand-written police report was even easier. How did he know this cop's signature was real? Did this officer whose name was on this report even exist?

Now, he had doubt and it felt too good.

"Rex is alive somewhere, isn't he?" Ray asked her boldly, standing up abruptly.

"Even if he was, it doesn't change the facts, Ray. We're married now, in business together, independently-wealthy and you still committed a crime last June," Marissa replied politely, staying in her seat.

"He's alive, isn't he?" Ray snapped as eh circled the big table, pointing at her.

"No, but I did save you from the police investigation, so you are mine, Raymond...I've got you by the balls, so relax and enjoy the fringe-benefits...sign the fucking paper," she spoke in a low tone of contempt, fists clenched on the table.

Ray shook his head, walking into the kitchen to get a beer.

"Tell me what really happened to Rex, goddamnit," he sneered as he walked back into the dining room with an open bottle of brew.

"Fuck Rex...it's about you and me, Raymond Torelli, you and me, nobody else," Marissa said angrily, standing up now.

"Where is he, where's Rex?" Ray asked in doubt, pacing the room nervously.

"Six feet under, where an idiot like he belongs, wanna dig up the body?" Marissa quipped in sarcasm.

"You are such a bitch, Marissa, goddamnit, you are evil to-the-core," Ray snarled in anger, stepping up to the dormant fireplace.

"And what are you, good?" she snickered as she followed him slowly.

"No, I made a mistake on June fourth, and you took advantage of it to try and make me your footstool," Ray said next, hands on the marble mantle of the fireplace.

"Footstool...I love you, Ray, you know I do, otherwise I wouldn't have gone to all this trouble," Marissa crooned as she stood by the sofa now.

"You set me up, you bitch, and Rex is alive, isn't he?!" he bellowed as he turned to face his unwanted wife.

He had called her a bitch one-too-many times now.

"So what if he is still alive, what difference does it make now?!" she barked angrily, facing Ray in fighting posture.

It was an admission. Rex was alive, but where?

"I didn't kill him after all, I knew it," Ray said in a sigh of relief. Marissa was wounded now, the framework of her plan beginning to buckle under pressure now.

"So what, you stupid Wap, what would you be doing without me? Hunh?" she snapped indignantly.

"I'd be free," he said in cooler demeanor.

"Freedom costs money, fool, and you'd be broke if it weren't for me, and what kind of slimy trailer-park hose bag would you end up with if you weren't with me?" Marissa chimed in self-righteous fervor.

Ray shook his head vigorously, disagreeing with her entirely.

"Ingrate, I did what I did for you, not against you or to hurt you, it's all for you!" she yelled in retort, gesturing violently with her hands.

"Where's Rex?" he asked again, walking the perimeter of the living room.

"He's dead, a worthless retard who would've put you in jail…forget about him," she said with tears in her eyes.

"He's not dead," Ray said in confidence.

"You'll never find him, so forget him and sign the paper…let's start over, Ray honey, lovers and business partners," Marissa said in softer voice now, eyes ablaze.

"No, you'll probably kill me just like you killed Rosemary, you bitch, and I could never love you like I loved her," Ray said matter-of-factly.

"What…what…you fuck, how dare you say that to me, you fuck…." She snarled in sudden rage, picking up the lamp by the sofa and flinging it toward him.

Ray dodged it and the lamp crashed onto the fireplace mantle, its ceramic structure shattering violently.

Marissa screamed out in raging anger at her husband, shouting obscenities and cursing him with each ashtray, lamp, and sofa pillow she threw. "Damn you, cocksucking faggot!" she bellowed and then lunged at Ray as he tried to escape the living room to leave her.

Ray shrugged her off of him but she was nimble as hell and bounced back to kick him in the ass like a karate instructor.

"Motherfucker," she whined as she tried to punch him rapidly but Ray blocked her as he made his way to the stairs. He really didn't want to strike her, even now.

"Let go of me, Marissa, let me go, you bitch!" Ray bellowed as he fought to release her arms from around his neck and torso, hugging him from behind now.

He ended up shoving her backwards as she spun around on the spiral stairs. Marissa fell backward, landing hard at the bottom, rolling over like a rag doll.

Ray rocketed up the stairs toward the bedroom, decided to pack some of this things. Instead of sneaking-out on her later today, he thought, he'd leave right now.

He had glanced back and saw Marissa tumbled at the bottom of the stairs and, at that moment, he felt a quick, euphoric "kinky" feeling in his gut. Marissa had conned him on a scale unimaginable before, and it felt good to hurt her now.

In the bedroom, he managed to find one suitcase and began to quickly shove clothes into it, his mind racing. If she didn't have a dead Rex Matthewson to hold over him, then he could split and it would be her word-against-his. It has been too long, too much time since the tragedy to tell the cops she saw him run over Rex. And, a retarded man can't testify in court, he knew that much now.

"I'm outta here," he said as he finished stuffing clothes into the suitcase, closing it tight. Marissa wasn't yelling anymore, and that made him think. She hadn't come up the stairs, but was she going for her gun?

Ken Knight

"Wait a minute," he said as he walked to the head of the big bed and lifted the pillow she slept on. There it was, laying there loaded, her Glock-17 9mm automatic.

Ray palmed the lightweight weapon, looking at it in contemplation, losing himself in daydreams for a moment.

"Hey, baby," cooed the familiar, female voice from the door. Ray looked at a totally-naked Marissa in the doorway, smiling teary-eyed at her husband.

Marissa looked at Ray, then at the full suitcase on the bed, knowing what he wanted to do now.

"Don't leave, Ray, not yet," she sighed as she posed slinky in the doorway.

"Dammit," you don't own me, Marissa. I'm gonna leave for awhile, at least," he rambled in nervous reply, dropping the gun to the bed.

"You forgot that today is my birthday, didn't you?" she added matter-of-factly.

"Hunh, yeah,...so what?" he snickered with a shrug as she sauntered into the bedroom. Marissa fought the urge to curse him.

"Maybe you're right to hate me a little," she said as she moved up to him. Eyeing her shapely, nude physique, calmed him, so he just stood there.

"A little...you ruined my life," he sighed in retort, eyeballing her intently.

"I offered you a life, Ray, a life with me, and to hell with everyone else," she said quickly, then stopped!

"I want out, Marissa...I want out," he said as he turned to face her close. She touched a hand to his flannel shirt and forced a girlish smile.

"I want you, Ray; I want you because I love you and you were too ignorant to see it back in school, so I did what I did to show you how I love you," Marissa spoke slow and smooth, calmer now.

"Marissa, jeezus...you'll kill to have a man you want?" he asked as she leaned in to him, head against his chest.

One Minute After Midnight

"Oh, yes, ten-times-over, and you can't prove anything," she told him meekly.

"I don't want to, I just want out," he added in a whisper as she hugged his torso tightly.

Ray took a step back, around by her naked presence but didn't want to be.

"Let's make a deal, Ray," she said softly.

"No, Marissa, it's...." he stammered.

"Not over yet, just hear me out," she said quickly, cutting him off.

"Make love to me, one last time...and if you discover any feelings for me whatsoever, you sign the paper...and we remain husband-and-wife forever, but if not, I'll let you go," Marissa offered.

He couldn't believe that last statement: "I'll let you go." Never thought he'd hear that from Marissa, not this morning, certainly!

"What about Rex, where is he?" Ray asked hesitantly.

"Forget the retard, Ray; I'll make sure he never threatens either of us in any way," she said flatly. That "coldness" of hers always made him cringe.

She flashed that slinky, seductive grin at him, and he didn't know what else to say, he was so tired right now.

"C'mon, honey, fuck me on my birthday, please?" Marissa chimed girlishly, running a hand up his covered chest to touch his stubbled face. Her other hand went to his crotch and the zipper there.

He couldn't say no to her right now, his erection raging in his pants, demanding her flesh as she stood before him in pure lust.

Instincts gave in and Ray let her unbuckle his pants as he removed his flannel shirt. Before he knew it, she had him by the balls.

Ken Knight

3:30 p.m.
That day:

Ray awoke wearily to find himself alone in the bed, so he just laid there, his body coming out of slumber. His watch read 3:30 in the afternoon, and Ray remembered falling asleep after 7 a.m., sometime after he got done doing his wife one last time.

One last time: That sounded good, even though she was a great lay. Sex wasn't everything, but Marissa seemed to think that one more fuckfest might cause him to fall in love with her. He couldn't wait to tell her she was wrong, so he slowly forced himself up and out of the bed.

Looking around the posh, blue-walled bedroom, he didn't see his suitcase anywhere. Then, he thought of something, reaching his hand under Marissa's pillow. The gun was gone, nowhere in the room where she'd normally keep it. Marissa had her gun again, and that's not good.

Downstairs, Marissa had an early dinner prepared for herself and Ray whenever he'd come down. She checked on him about 30 seconds ago, and he was upstairs in the shower.

Next to his dinner plate was the contract papers for "Pop-N-Rock" entertainment, all he had to do was sign on the "X".

While she waited, the fully-dressed Marissa sipped on a glass of wine Chablis, thinking in a better mood now. New plans were coming to mind.

Even if Ray doesn't stick by her, she would keep the clown business, but change that silly name.

If Ray leaves out that door instead, his suitcase was on the front porch already, and she would let him go, with only the cash in his pocket.

Accounts with her name on them were canceled with a simple phone call by 5:00 this afternoon, and she had opened Ray's two accounts herself. So, guess what?

Ray won't need money where he's going.

Ray walked down the stairs five minutes later, clad in faded-jeans, biker boots, his "Myrtle Beach" sweatshirt and wet hair

One Minute After Midnight

from the shower. He smiled weakly at Marissa as he walked to the dining table where she sat.

She knew that look on his face was no sign of victory on her part.

"Dinner is served," she said sweetly with her smile.

"Thanks, Marissa, I could eat a horse," Ray chuckled as he sat down, not looking at the papers next to his plate.

"Mmmhh, I really enjoyed this morning's romp," she cooed impishly as she picks up her fork to dig-into the catfish meal.

"Me, too," he said.

"Really," she said with a smirk.

"Sex isn't everything," he sighed, looking at his food in wonder. Could she have poisoned it…maybe?

"Actually, two things rule the world, ya know: money and sex, so it isn't everything but it is certainly a priority," Marissa said softly, watching his reaction.

Ray ate quickly, wanting to get out of her before Marissa could cook up something else to ensnare him.

Part of him felt "attached" to his young wife because of the time spent with her so far, but life? No way, because he didn't feel that certain "vibe" like he did with Rosemary Jones, and he hated her for what she has done to him as well s to Rosemary.

God only knows what Marissa has done with poor Rex! He thought, stuffing his mouth with food.

She set him up, blackmailed and ruined him, and she wants him to love her? He asked in his mind.

Marissa looked directly at Ray as he polished off the remainder of his food.

"Moment-of-truth, honey…sign the paper and join me in the rest of our lives or…go out that door with what you've got in ya wallet, never to return," she spoke flatly.

He looked at her in surprise of her rancor. Marissa can be blunt when she wants to be.

He stared at her in gratuitous wonder. How can such a lovely, sexy, wealthy 24-year-old woman be so diabolical in her everyday life, so evil in her future plans?

Lives of others are rather insignificant to her, he thought, including his own!

Then, again, Ray had struck down an innocent handicapped person while driving drunk and sought to get away with it. He felt evil, too, for that, and for having the affair with Rosemary which caused Marissa to run her off the road in anger, killing Rosemary in the process.

I'm guilty in this tragic plot, too, he thought, but the guilty can always repent and recompense, right?

"Tell me what happened to Rex, please," Ray spoke gruffly, then took another swig of iced tea.

Marissa smiled as if expecting a repeat of that question.

"I told you, he's dead...gone," she said.

"No, you faked his death, didn't you?" Ray chortled in confident reply.

"Pretty much, so in all technicalities, he is dead and forgotten," she answered coldly.

"Not by me. If he's alive, I want to know," Ray added frankly.

"So, he can tell the cops who ran him over; so, maybe some obscure family member of his can sue you for the idiot's demise?" Marissa retorted in angst.

"You're a cold-hearted woman," Ray said flatly, putting his drink down.

"I can be, but I know what I want, Ray, and that is our marriage, period." She said with a sly scowl.

Hmmph, you can't own me like a dog or cat, Marissa, and how do you expect me to...what, forget what all has happened...Rex, Rosemary?" Ray retorted in frustration.

"Passing strangers, honey, they're all passing strangers in our years of life, easily forgotten," Marissa answered him.

"Damn, you are cold," he sighed, shaking his head as he wiped his mouth.

"Don't sweat it, big guy. Where else are you going to get laid whenever you want, go out to eat every night, live in luxury like we will if you sign-on to run the business?" she continued.

One Minute After Midnight

Ray thought about it more as he sat there with the paper next to his left hand on the table.

If there is no Rex Matthewson, then she cannot blackmail him any further, period.

"No, good-bye, Marissa; I want a divorce," he said as he stood up from the table slowly. Those coal-black eyes of hers went dead in sullen glare after he said that.

"Then, get out, Ray, you....Goddammit, I love you," she belted out loud in reaction, jumping to her feet.

"I can't say the same, Marissa, and I'd rather be home-less than live with you after what you did to me," he spoke with conviction, feeling a tear in one eye.

"Anything for love," she said with watery eyes now, just standing there.

"Yeah, right," he snorted as he slowly turned to walk toward the front door, fishing keys out of his pocket.

"Your suitcase is on the front porch, Ray," she added casually.

He just kept walking to the door, not caring that she was following him now. "Oh, I forgot to tell you, honey...heenh, I've been off the pill for a few days now and I'm ovulating!" Marissa said with a chipper voice.

He turned at the door, looking back at his wife in gut-wrenching anger. "You mean...." He sneered in realization.

"When you came inside me this morning, we probably conceived," Marissa answered him with a smile.

"Fucking bitch," he managed to say as he walked up to her, seething with contempt. Marissa just stood there, facing him boldly. Without thinking, Ray put his hand around her throat in violent gesture.

"I should kill you!" he yelled in her face, but she stood still in his grip.

"You're a cold-hearted man, Ray, wanting to kill your wife and child," she chimed softly to his face. He fought the urge to snap her neck like a twig, arms arching to do just that right now.

Applying some pressure around her throat as she just stood there felt too tempting, so he grudgingly released her and took a step back.

"Why?!" he snapped angrily.

"We're married, after all; pregnancy happens in marriage, besides...it's my choice," she spoke casually in rebuttal.

"If you are pregnant, abort it," he snapped, surprised that he said that.

"Oh, no, I'm feeling the nesting urge, honey," Marissa told him with a coy smile, staring daggers at her husband.

"I'm out of here," Ray sneered as he turned back to the front door, eager to step beyond it, out of this house and out of her life. This was surreal, a nightmare of horrid reality.

What hell am I consigned to? He asked himself as he cleared the threshold.

I want to be free! He told the wind as he grabbed his suitcase and ran for his parked truck in the driveway.

"I'll see you soon, Raymond, you won't go far," she said out loud, watching him leave.

"Now, plan-B," she said to herself s she watched Ray's truck spin tires out of the driveway.

She walked back into the dining room, retrieving the Glock pistol from beneath the chair where she sat to eat, and jacked the first round into the chamber.

"Hmmh, now to tie up some loose ends and wait for that ungrateful faggot to come crawling back to me," she said to no one, wiping her eyes with her free hand.

"I doubt he has enough money for a tank of gas," she chuckled in spite of herself, picking up the phone to call the bank and cancel Ray's accounts.

"Why did I ruin your credit, Ray?" she chuckled again in humorous rancor, listening to the phone ring on the other end. "Because I believe in insurance; I simply insured one of my valuables, namely one immature husband," she chimed to herself, then the bank answered the line.

One Minute After Midnight

She had to keep from laughing as she gave the pass-numbers to the bookkeeper over the phone, canceling Ray's accounts and transferring the funds to her checking account.

Dillon County Sheriff's Office
6:00 p.m.

Ray sat in his truck in the parking lot of the small Sheriff's Dept. here in downtown Dillon alone with burdensome thoughts.

Considering going to the cops here and filing a criminal complaint against Marissa seemed moot. How could he, without implicating himself in Rex Matthewson's hit-n-run case?

But was there a pending case of hit-n-run regarding Rex? That was the big fish which he could never seem to catch.

Marissa sacked his credit, his money, his Social Security rating, but how could he prove it now? That toad, McCracken, was long-gone by now for certain and Marissa was in a position to ruin him even further and play-dumb in the process!

Ray already guessed she has axed his account at the bank, that's a given.

Ah, the fucking guilt of that stormy night's accident 7 months ago. If he hand' been drinking-and-driving, he wouldn't have struck Rex and Marissa Borders would be fucking-over someone else!

But Rex: the mere possibility that he was alive clawed at his gut like a hungry lion demanding satisfaction.

Ray had to know for sure, somehow find Rex and make things right. The accident on June 4th was an accident, he didn't mean to do it, and if Rex was alive-and-well, then he could fix everything in his favor, maybe even make-it-up-to Rex somehow?

He had thought he had killed the kid up until he found "Spaz" McCracken. If what that computer hacker told him pans-out, then Marissa had expended a lot of resources just to cover it

Ken Knight

all in a gloomy do-or-die package to blackmail him into marrying her!

Ray felt better in a way, now that Rex was very possibly alive, but he can't tell the cops and he knows it.

Watching an off-duty deputy walking to his vehicle to leave for home, Ray thought about something Marissa had told him awhile back: "the more you see of other people, the better you like yourself."

Not really, he thought, because Ray had a tendency to covet the lives of other people namely because he never liked his own.

Wish I were him, Ray thought, working as a Sheriff's Deputy all day, then go home to an apartment at night...probably has a wife he loves, too!

Ray chuckled in spite of himself, then keyed the ignition, listening to his truck's engine roar to life.

Finding Rex, somehow, was now all he could think about. If Marissa could see to Rosemary's "accidental" death, then she could do the same to Rex if he's still around. Ray was afraid of what his wife could do, because she was so damn good at it.

Driving back onto the road, she sped up in anxious ardor.

Another thought popped in his head as he pulled out onto Rt. 501 again, heading east toward Aynor and Latte. Marissa mentioned something before he left that added mind-working "spice" to the mix: pregnancy.

She said she was ovulating, off-the-pill, and she seduced him one last time this morning...damn her!

Two things no man wants to hear from his woman: "Honey, I'm pregnant "and" Honey, I tested positive." Her telling him she had the fucking HIV would strike milder than a baby on-the-way, in Ray's mind.

This was an evil scheme from the get-go and he was mortified with each passing day this sick theater continued.

"I've got to find Rex, one way or another...the bitch can't own me forever...I'll kill her first," Ray spoke to himself as he drove.

One Minute After Midnight

When a police cruiser appeared in the dusky twilight behind his truck, he slowed down to 50 mph.

"Should've run Marissa over that night instead of Rex," he chuckled to himself, eye on his rearview mirror.

January 14th:
5:00 a.m.:

This was it. It had to be, since he had no money for a motel room and only a suitcase full of clothes, his truck and anew determination to leave his wife.

Ray had left a message on his brother Ben's answering machine, asking if he can come stay at his place for awhile. He drove along Rt. 501 in aimless wander, wasting gas and time, almost empty on both now.

Thinking about one thing took his full concentration: Rex Matthewson. The kid had to be alive and where was the big mystery? Driving along Myrtle Drive now, he turned onto the adjoining road to the house where he'd left. Something told him to go past it one more time.

Marissa's car was gone and the lights were out except for the porch light which signaled that the security alarm was activated.

Where could she be at 5 a.m. when she worked day-shift at the hospital now? Ray roared past the house and back onto Rt. 501, heading toward the town of Aynor.

Marissa's second house, the one she supposedly had up "For Sale" but no one ever called about it. He cursed himself for not thinking about it before! He had been there only once before but never went inside, thinking it to be empty.

Maybe it wasn't empty at all, perhaps that was where Marissa was at this early hour, and where she could be hiding Rex.

Ray was sweating as he drove, despite the cold air coming through the cracked-open window; nervous, pissed off and anxious. If he could find Rex, then maybe he could turn it around on Marissa and come out of this nightmare ahead of her. Damn, I'm so tired! He thought in angst.

Faster now that he was almost on empty. Ray headed for the house in Aynor that he'd considered empty all this time. Part of him hoped it was, indeed, still vacant.

Chapter 14

The house in Aynor was just a mile south of the town's business district, off Rt. 501 an perched in a cul-de-sac with one neighboring home to its left.

Marissa had held on to this piece of real estate for god reason, leading her husband to believe it was "For Sale" and empty. Stepping from her BMW in the gravel driveway, Marissa walked toward the front door, fiddling with her keys.

Raindrops began slapping her face as she approached her second house in the morning's darkness, and she remembered the forecast calling for morning thunder showers. At least, it was better than snowfall, she thought as she walked up to the front door, finding the right key finally.

Her parents had let her keep this place after her grandmother died, and she was glad they did because of how handy it came to be. She keyed the dead bolt lock and the knob-lock, opening the big door slowly.

She turned on the living room's ceiling light and took off her coat, hanging it on the rack on the wall. Not bothering to lock the door behind her, Marissa walked on into the barren living room, to the small kitchen of the 2-story household.

A noise sounded from upstairs and she heard the wooden floor creaking above her suddenly, making her chuckle to herself. He was awake, this early!

"Hey, big guy...it's just me, go back to bed," Marissa called out loud in response to the heavy footfalls upstairs.

He didn't answer, but that didn't bother her, since this was his last day here anyway.

"Hmmph, men...can't live with 'em, can't live without 'em...heenh, and I cant' have the one I want to keep," she said as she opened the knife drawer.

A stainless butcher knife was what she picked form the drawer, looking at its thin, razor-sharp blade in admiration.

Ken Knight

"Funny…you live a life decades-long, and one day a simple puncture can end your life, in seconds," she spoke to herself, imagining this knife plunging into Ray's chest.

Marissa heard a male voice call out her name from the top of the stairs, and she turned to walk out from the kitchen, butcher knife still in hand.

"Honey, I'll be up there in a minute, so chill…." She retorted aloud to the male "guest" upstairs now.

"Men," she sneered as she dropped her purse to the foot of the stairwell outside the kitchen, looking up to the top of the stairs. She smelled a scent of cedar in the air; this house was old enough to have such wood in its structure, she thought.

He must be back in the bedroom, she figured, not seeing him now.

"I'll be up there in a minute, honey…you animal," she spoke up with a laugh, gripping the knife tightly in her left fist.

It was all coming apart, it seemed, unhinging in slow, torturous melee. Marissa operated on the premise that nothing-lasts-forever, but his was ridiculous! After only seven months married to Ray Torelli, he was gone and her plan unfolding into chaos.

Now, she had a loose end to tie-up: the young man upstairs. He was a liability simply because he knew her too well, despite his usefulness with Ray.

Anger welled-up inside of her like a mercury thermometer, and she drove the butcher knife into the nearest wall, its blade buried deep due to her fit of rage.

"Fuck 'em all," she growled hatefully, walking in a circle at the bottom of the stairs.

A full-length wall-mirror was on the wall near where she stuck the knife, and she found herself staring at her reflection in angst. Wearing a blue sweater over a silk blouse and designer jeans enveloping her taut thighs and legs, Marissa wanted to cry. She was a good-looking woman with wealth, and here she knew only rejection!

One Minute After Midnight

Outside, Ray Torelli put his truck in-park right behind the BMW. She was here, and he decided to face Marissa and whatever this old house held, this morning, right now.

He jumped out of his truck and into the rain, hearing thunder off in the distant sky. It wasn't even beginning to lighten-up for dawn now, just dark and a miserable storm.

Ray stomped up to the front door, finding it unlocked. He then ran back to his truck and grabbed his wooden ball bat from behind the seat, feeling it necessary to be "armed" somehow.

Going back up to the front door, he pushed it open and entered unimpeded, finding an empty 1st floor to be lit but unoccupied. Cautiously, he walked to the kitchen, then around to the stairs, his boots making the floor creak as he went.

He looked at the butcher knife in the wall by the big mirror and guessed who might have done that!

Climbing the stairs slowly with ball bat in his right hand, the wet Ray Torelli grew even more apprehensive as he saw a light on at the top floor. He hoped for the element of surprise in his favor tonight.

At the top of the stairs, he looked tot eh door of the first bedroom, finding it cracked open and its light on. Ray crept up to the door ajar, his heart pounding furiously in his chest now.

Breathing heavy and sweating profusely, the 22-year-old husband peered through to find two people he was shocked to see in one room together!

My god, there he was, sitting on the ruffled bed in just a pair of jeans, with metal braces on his legs: Rex!

Marissa stepped into view completely naked, her back to the door as she slowly approached the bed where the leg-brace-wearing retarded man sat grinning boyishly.

"I told you, my little village-idiot, good things come to those who wait…now it's nooky-nooky time," Marissa spoke gingerly to her prey.

A rage flew into Ray as he saw his wife and Rex in there; seven months of agony, frustration, and anger hit boiling point at that moment.

Ken Knight

With his eyes on Marissa's bare ass, Ray shoved the door open violently, stomping into the bedroom with bat in hand.

"Marissaaa!" he bellowed in shock of the scene as she turned to face him defensively. She hadn't expected such an intrusion here, not now.

"Ray...migod, what are you...." She stammered before he yelled forth with bat in the air.

"You bitch, he's alive and you're fuckin' him!" Ray chortled, red in the face with rage.

Rex leaped from the bed haphazardly, stumbling to stand on his braced legs, eyes on Ray with fearful surprise.

"Ray, don't...this is the end of it, I promise...calm down!" she pleaded, defensively holding up her arms in expectation of an assault.

Ray didn't hear her though, his anger holding sway. Rex made a lunge toward him, his intention being to just escape into the hallway on his hobbled legs. Ray swung the bat with both hands, seeing Rex as an attacker instead.

The bat glanced off of Rex's skull with a sickening sound, like a ball being struck at the World Series. Without a word uttered or yelp of pain, Rex Matthewson simply flopped over against the wall and to the floor, like a rag doll.

Ray lowered his bat, staring at the fallen man off to his left in stunned silence. The bald head of the 20-year-old retarded man was bleeding from the blow and Rex lay completely idle. Dead? Now, by my hand, again? My god! Was all that went through Ray's mind at that icy moment.

He didn't even realize Marissa was beating fists on his back until seconds later.

"Now, you've done it...you've killed him!" she wailed with a face of hot contempt as Ray turned to her again.

"You...you did this to me; all this shit is on you, Marissa!" Ray snarled in hatred, watching the naked woman cross the bed in effort to escape another swing of his bat.

"Murderer!" she screamed as she bolted.

Ray swung in sloppy melee, missing her torso as she made it to the door in a sprint.

She was on the stairs before Ray could run out of the bedroom, fleeing down the stairwell in lithe stride, well ahead of her pursuer. Marissa was going too fast to grab her purse or any of her clothes, so she ran around to the back door while Ray descended the stairs, cursing her madly.

Jumping out into the grassy backyard, she stumbled and fell but rebounded quickly, still giving Ray two seconds of catch-up time.

When he ran out into the dark yard, he could see her in the faint morning light, running naked in the cascading thunderstorm.

A newfound energy pulsed through him, so he ran after his naked wife, ball bat in both hands, vengeance in his heart.

Marissa ran into the woods, barely able to see. She lucked out and landed on a pathway of mud without clutter to stop her urn. Ray followed in zealous fury, his only desire now to brain her with this ball bat just like he did to Rex back there.

Running barefoot, she still kept ahead of him; she was a jogger after all. "Damn you!" Ray shouted in frustration, between pants of breath. The thunder roared overhead as they ran doggedly through the woods, rainfall relentless in deluge, lightning in the sky.

Ray's ardor increased as he saw Marissa's buttocks violently shaking as she ran. He wanted to split her pretty head like the crack of that ass, so he tried running faster, getting closer to his prize.

Marissa was crying, rain pelting her face, stinging as she ran through it, and her heart changed as she fled her lover's wrath. In the storm, through these woods, love became hate.

She ran as hard and fast as her fit body would take her, through a cluster of hardwoods to the other end of the woods. Ray tripped and fell flat 20 yards behind her as she cleared the other end, running into a commuter parking lot that was dimly

Ken Knight

lit, and where it just-so-happened, a police car sat, scanning radar.

The police officer behind the wheel saw this naked female running toward the cruiser and he got out immediately to confront her.

"Miss...miss, stop!" the tall, lean cop said to Marissa as she ran toward him in slowing sprint.

"Shoot him...shoot him...shoot him!" she cried in emotional release, running toward the cop with arms up.

He didn't see anyone else behind her, no one was chasing her.

"Stop!" the cop barked as she ran up to him, crying madly those same words of hers.

"Shoot him!"

Marissa grabbed at the cop's holstered sidearm with her right hand, frenzied in her emotional state. As the officer pivoted to break the hold she had on his pistol, the damn thing popped out of the triple-retention holster and into her grip.

Panicked, the officer grabbed her forearm and with his free hand reached for the gun itself, yelling her ear in the process.

In two hair-seconds, Marissa managed to squeeze the trigger, the Sig Sauer P-226 automatic going off like thunder.

The cop was off her, so she turned back toward the woods, throwing the handgun up in a one-handed aim. She then squeezed the trigger again, firing wildly into the dark woods where Ray had pursued her.

Firing off 14 rounds of 9mm into the woods felt good in the release of hatred, but Ray didn't come out, nor did she see him anymore. Dropping the hot and empty gun to the asphalt, she instinctively turned back toward the cop car.

The officer whose gun she grabbed was sprawled out on his back. In the dismal haze of morning's light, she could see the dark ooze of blood exiting his throat, where she had accidentally shot him!

One Minute After Midnight

"Jeezus, no!" she screamed up to the heavens as vengeful rain fell without end. Only at this moment did she feel cold, standing naked over a cop she'd killed by accident, in her frenzy.

Panic threatened to consume her psyche at this moment as everything fell eerily silent and she couldn't hear anything but her own rapid heartbeat.

"No," Marissa groaned as she turned and ran back towards the woods again, forgetting about her bat-wielding husband for now, fleeing the homicide scene in panic, her only thoughts being to get to the house and her car!

She failed to see another person in the police car, for the officer had a civilian "ride-along" in his passenger seat and that civilian had hunkered-down when the shooting began.

"Marissa...I don't believe it," Giles Visor said to himself as he watched her bare form disappear back into the woods again.

He keyed the police radio, speaking into the mike clear and concise.

"Signal-thirteen, officer down...commuter parking lot near mall...." Giles said into the mike, then hopped out the cruiser to see the mortally-wounded officer he was riding with.

"Damn!" the plain clothes rider said as soon as he knelt beside Officer Davis, throat spewing blood like a water fountain.

Marissa Torelli had grabbed the officer's gun, shot him, then shot wildly at the woods. Had she gone insane? Giles wondered as he stood up again, looking at the woodline where she had vanished.

As the rain increased its deluge, Giles stood over the slain officer in nervous thought. He knew what he had to do, though.

Ray wondered what the gunshots were for as he sauntered out from the woods behind Marissa's house here in Aynor. He hadn't pursued her to that other end, stopping when he fell down, and decided to double-time it back here.

Rex: had he killed the young man after all with that blow to the head? He had no idea what transpired once Marissa cleared that other end of the woods. All eh could think about was Rex as

Ken Knight

he walked to the back door again, breathing heavy and soaking wet.

To hell with Marissa, he thought, she'll surely get in trouble for running naked in public; probably even get arrested, he hoped.

Re-entering the house, he headed up the stairs again, noticing how the upper floor was furnished and hospitable to someone staying there awhile. He placed his bat down against the corner wall as he stepped to the bedroom door again.

Rex wasn't there where he had fallen!

"Rex?" he called out in surprise, guessing the younger man had regained consciousness and wandered off in the house. How far could he get on foot, with braces on his legs?

He must have "recovered" under Marissa's care here at her grandmother's family home. She was a nurse, after all, and she had access to medical supplies like the rotating braces on his legs and pain killers.

Damn, all this just to blackmail me? He marveled in the thought.

He walked back to the stairs and called for Rex, but no answer came.

So damn tired, he told himself as he wandered back inside the bedroom where Rex had obviously stayed.

Pictures of his parents were on the dresser, both of them elderly ad, according to Marissa, dead. Maybe she lied about them, too? Maybe the elderly parents of Rex Matthewson were still alive? Maybe Marissa killed them, too, he thought.

"I gotta get outta here," Ray said out loud as he sat on the end of the bed, wet and cold from exposure to the storm outside. Figuring his truck had only about 10 more miles worth of gas left in it, he couldn't get far.

Taking Marissa's BMW was tangible, but he didn't need a grand-theft-auto rap either.

So, he just sat there, feeling the weight of hopelessness again, that heavy burden of realization that tells one he is in-over-his-head and sinking fast.

One Minute After Midnight

Now, he was back to square one, like before last June: Broke, evicted, and facing no prospects.

Remembering that he had $15 in his wallet, Ray thought that would, at least, buy him a meal at "Pedro's Diner" one last time.

He just sat there in oblivious reflection, regret beginning to fill his thoughts now. Despite what has transpired, he did like the comfort of Marissa's home and despite the woman, herself, her company at times. No, can't think like that!

Ray was feeling weary, sleep deprivation catching up to him suddenly, and he almost keeled over onto the bed but didn't.

Despite blurry vision now, he recoiled in horror as he spotted Marissa in the doorway now, leveling her gun at him. Her hair wet and slicked-back, she wore a man's flannel shirt 2-sizes too big now; in from the rain and aiming the Glock-17 she kept in her purse at the man she once loved.

"My god," he sighed in defeat, lowering his head in his hands. He expected her to open fire any moment.

"Hunh, who are you to call upon God, you impotent little man?" she chimed in a slightly hoarse voice.

"Here we are, Raymond…at a crossroads, where I've got you backed into a corner as always…and you still refuse me," she continued in contempt, eyes black from runny mascara.

"If you're gonna kill me, just do it; it's been your goal all-along," Ray sighed in surrender, throwing up his hands in gesture.

"You little prick…I loved you and wanted to give you a life with me…in spite of your rejection of my affection, dammit …you should've been grateful," Marissa sneered, holding the gun out in her extended grip, sights on his face.

"You can't make someone love you," he said angrily, not wanting to say it again.

"Obviously, I was wrong and now I've got nothing to lose by killing you…." Marissa spoke in a hiss, leveling the gun toward his groin now.

"Where's Rex?" she asked suddenly, noticing the body no longer where it dropped.

"I don't know, he must've gotten up and split," Ray answered as his eyes teared up in the stress, unable to move.

"No matter, 'cuz I was gonna kill him anyway before you barged in, the lousy retarded motherfucker...hmmh, good-bye, Raymond," Marissa snarled in virulent hatred, beginning to squeeze the trigger.

Ray closed his eyes, hoping it to be quick.

A sickening "thud" sounded once more, and Marissa pulled the Glock's trigger as she went down from the blow across her scalp; the gun popped off a round into the bed's mattress, just missing Ray.

Rex stood feebly in the doorway, wielding the bat in triumph as Marissa flattened out-cold on the carpet below.

"I'm not retarded...I'm Irish," rex said with a twisted smirk, looking down at the felled woman who had been his doctor as well as jailer.

"Jeezus Christ, Rex!" Ray snapped in delighted surprise, looking at the husky, hobbled young man with leg braces.

Rex grinned at Ray as he stumbled into the room, stepping next to the fallen Marissa, the gunshot still ringing in his ears.

"Man, I am glad to see you...and I'm goddamn sorry, too, really....I didn't mean to do what I did to you, Rex," Ray spoke wearily, fighting to stand up now.

Rex dropped the bat and laughed slightly, eyeing Ray intently as he rubbed the healing cut on his bald head.

"'S okay, Ray...no sweat, just hurt a little, and she wuz gonna kill us both," Rex spoke in jovial tone, smiling at the wet, worn-out man.

"Yeah, she was going to kill us," Ray said as he stepped over Marissa, then knelt down beside her as she lay on her back, out cold.

Touching a hand to her neck, he felt for a pulse and found a weak one. She was alive, but for how long after a blow to the head like that?

Rex definitely hit her harder than he had hit Rex with that bat.

One Minute After Midnight

Her face looked almost peaceful as she lay there unconscious, her pretty face dormant and relaxed. For that moment, Ray felt pity for his debauched bride, running a hand across her soft cheeks.

"Marissa," he sighed, shaking his head in pity. He then leaned in and kissed her.

"C'mon, Ray...she's asleep now. We should get the hell outta here...I know where some money is," Rex spoke in irritated angst, staggering to the door.

The word "money" got Ray's full attention.

He followed Rex slowly down the stairs to a closet next to the bathroom. It wasn't even locked, which surprised Ray considering his wife's penchant for security.

But the lock box was, by a key.

"How much money is in here?" Ray asked Rex, noticing the man still hadn't put a shirt on yet.

"Marissa said it was my reward for playing-ball, never said the amount of money," Rex answered hesitantly, not wanting to make Ray angry again.

"Well, go get a shirt on, man, while I bust this open," Ray snapped as he took the strongbox into the kitchen, looking for instruments to pry the lock.

Rex ran back upstairs hurriedly, stopping in his bedroom of the past 7 months. The shirt Marissa was wearing was his favorite flannel, so he proceeded to remove the garment from the naked woman.

"Sorry, Marissa...you shouldn't have said...those things," Rex spoke to the unconscious female, taking his shirt back.

When Rex came back down the stairs, Ray had the strongbox open, and was counting off $100 bills.

"There's just a thousand dollars here plus a check book I can't do anything with," Ray said in disappointment as Rex walked up to him at the front door. "And you had to brag that shirt...." Ray added, knowing the shirt Rex now wore was what Marissa had been wearing earlier.

Ken Knight

"Thousand dollars...I'm rich," Rex chimed in excitement, making Ray laugh.

"Unh-hunh, you're rich all right...." Ray chuckled mockingly, pocketing the big wad of bills into his jeans' pocket.

"Let's get out of here, Rex," he said next, stepping out the door with Marissa's care keys, deciding to take the BMW anyway, since his truck was low on gas.

Rex followed at a slower pace due to his healing legs and the metal braces he still wore. He got in on the passenger side, mentioning how long it's been since he rode in a car.

Ray sat behind the wheel, still weary, but his anxious ardor kept him awake, so he keyed the ignition of Marissa's BMW and shifted into reverse to back out.

A scheme was opening in his mind as he drove out of there, back onto Rt. 501. He could flee and the most he'd be wanted for would be assaulting his wife, and he doubted Marissa would involve the cops now that Rex was with him!

No, now he felt free as a bird, and free of her, finally. If she dies from that blow to the head, sure he would be a suspect, but how could it be proven he hit her over the head?

No, Ray thought, if the cops give him shit, he'll just give them Rex, who did hit Marissa over the head with the bat. Either way, now was time to leave Dillon, as well as South Carolina, forever.

Driving along the highway in the drenching rain, Ray glanced at Rex in the passenger seat for a second, curiosity peaking in regards to what happened immediately after 12:01 a.m. on June 4, 2000.

"Rex, buddy, please tell me what happened the night of your accident, how'd Marissa take care of you?" he asked the retarded man in the seat next to him.

Rex looked at Ray with his crossed-eyes and nodded in agreement, still breathing heavy, rubbing his bald head with his right hand. A sizable bump swelled where Ray had hit him with the ball bat, along with the gash that no longer bled.

One Minute After Midnight

"I was hit by a truck...that night back in June...ran over my legs and broke my knees...she came up to me and got me into someone's car...then, we drove to her house where Marissa fixed-up my legs," Rex explained in stuttering speech.

"Never took you to a hospital, notified your parents?" Ray asked softly.

"My mother died when she thought I was missing and ...my father is in a retirement home in...Florida," Rex answered, shaking his head as if not to know what a hospital was.

Marissa had nursed Rex back to health all by herself. Surely she had the know-how and access to medical supply, but to do so all in the name of winning herself a husband?

No, it was for her inheritance money, too, Ray told himself, as he drove. It couldn't have been just for him, he told himself again. Rex didn't seem to know who the driver was, who hit him on June 45th, and that was a relief. Marissa probably never told him who hit him, why bother?

The more Ray thought about it, Rex couldn't testify against him in court, anyway, because he was mentally incompetent.

Marissa could call the cops on him, but what would she tell them...how would she explain it all now that Rex was with him?

Ray sped up along Rt. 501 now, eager to get back to the house in Dillon as the rain increased its deluge. Marissa likely survived that blow to the head because he wasn't lucky enough otherwise. The worm was starting to turn, in his favor.

Marissa groaned in the pain, her senses a polyglot mush as she opened her eyes in attempt to regain her faculties. Moving her numb right hand up to her head, she felt wt, sticky blood at the scalp, and swelling.

She rolled over on her right side slowly, feeling cold as hell all of a sudden. Could it be shock? She wondered. A blow to the head, she thought, and it wasn't bad enough to incapacitate, thankfully.

Rex, she thought in realization. It had to be Rex who struck her, who else was in this house?

Ken Knight

"Unnh, damn you...Ray, Rex...I shoulda killed both of you," she whined in emotion, fighting to sit up now. The room was spinning, her mind numb with pain and queasy dizziness.

She began to cry as she sat up against the foot of the bed, realizing she was naked and alone in the old homeplace here, thunder booming outside.

"Why, Ray...why couldn't you love me, so none of this would've happened?" she cried out in agony of the moment. As her vision focused better, she glimpsed the pistol lying on the carpet two feet to her left.

Ray didn't take it with him, leaving post-haste like he did. She reached for it, crying violently now.

Never before had the feeling of helplessness become so profound, so horribly real to her. It had all fallen apart, all of her plan, her life, and she had accidentally killed a cop on top of it all; all because of Raymond Torelli.

She cursed him in profane ardor, holding the Glock-17 in her right hand weakly. Hatred burned white hot for the man she married, a man who betrayed her at every turn and rejected her no matter how she appeased him.

"Fuck you, Raymond Torelli...fuck you!!" she screamed at the top of her lungs, raging as she held her bun to her chest, shaking in painful anger.

The cops would be after he now, she thought, and she'd have to face at least a life sentence in prison for accidentally shooting that officer back in the commuter parking lot. All she wanted was his gun to shoot Ray who pursued her with a bat. It was a frenzy of fear and rage which caused that to happen and with the worst possible luck: a cop lays dead by her hand!

Breathing rapidly to the point of hyper-ventilation, Marissa thought about that horrific scene back there. No witnesses as far as she knew, so it might be awhile before the police would be on to her. She dropped the man's gun, though...fingerprints!

Sobbing diminished, she straightened up and fought to stand up now, despite dizziness and off-balance equilibrium, he head

One Minute After Midnight

throbbing with pain. Blood trickled down her right ear, and she didn't bother to wipe it off as she staggered up on bare feet.

Cursing out loud in pain and rage, Marissa failed to hear the door click-open downstairs, even as she stumbled out of the bedroom in aimless direction. Nausea worsened, as if she was going to pass out again.

Two men clad in black suits and boots with bavaclava-black masks over their heads, stood on the foyer inside the doorway now, looking and listening for their target.

One spotted her at the top of the stairs in the dark household, staggering naked with a gun in hand.

"This chick can't seem to keep her clothes on, careful...she has a Glock in her hand," the one man in black whispered to his partner. They were hired to do a job and it required this woman be alive.

The two men in black moved in stealth, seeing that one Marissa Torelli obviously didn't know they were present.

Marissa walked into the bathroom, turning on the light to try and see her head wound in the mirror of the vanity.

Despite the creaky wooden staircase, the two goons ascended to the top without noise, catching sight of their prey in the lit bathroom now, her back to them.

Marissa put the pistol down for a moment, looking at her haggard reflection in the mirror. My god, she thought at the sight of her smeared face, swollen left cheek and bleeding head of mangled hair, is this what I've become?

To hell with the dead; she thought only of her own situation now, her own future and it was too bleak to imagine.

Even if she ran, her home, money, car would be gone and she'd be a fugitive wanted in connection with a cop's death, and Ray would be the prosecution's star witness!

Tearing up again, she palmed her handgun once more, raising it to her face, barrel touching her right temple. Ending her life was better than going-on facing prison and loneliness, her plans all destroyed due to her husband. Crying in agony, she

Ken Knight

stood before the vanity mirror with the gun to her head, forefinger on its plastic trigger.

"Fuck it," Marissa sighed in defeat, finger slowly starting to depress the Glock's trigger.

A sharp shock of pain bolted into her torso, down her spine in split-second lightning, her arms going numb, gun falling from her grip. Marissa shrieked slightly, then stumbled backward, only to be hit by the electric stun-gun once more.

The masked man watched the naked broad shake violently, her face a contorted mask of surprise as she collapsed backward into the bathtub like a lifeless rag doll, ripping down the shower curtain as she landed on her back in the porcelain basin.

"Just in time," one of the goons in black said as they both stepped up tot the tub looking down at the sprawled-out Marissa Torelli, who was semi-conscious still.

"Yeah, if she had offed-herself, we wouldn't bet paid," the one holding the electric stun-device said matter-of-factly.

"Go get the bag,...so we can carry her ass outta here," the man with the stun gun told his partner, who promptly left the bathroom to get the item from their car outside.

Marissa could barely hear them, her eyes squinted-open with blurry vision now, pain wracking her body in stinging fury.

A man in black, again! She thought in agony, unable to move and hoping she will die.

When the second man in black returned with a large-sized sleeping bag, the other one was dragging the naked and wounded Marissa Torelli out of the bathroom by one ankle, pulling her bare body across the floor on her back. She was too weak to even yell out a protest.

The one man unzipped and opened the sleeping bag while the partner just stood over the helpless female on the floor, hands on his hips.

"She's got a nice body on her, too bad she's bought-n-paid for," the stun-gun man said to his partner in black.

One Minute After Midnight

"Yeah...waste of a good-piece-of-ass if you ask me. Oh, well...it's just a job," the one with the sleeping bag answered as he stretched out the bag next to her.

"Yeah, and an easy one at that, so let's get done an call the boss," the one standing over her said as he knelt down, grabbing an arm to roll Marissa into he sleeping bag.

Marissa suddenly realized these two intruders were the same two who assaulted her days ago at her home in Dillon.

Could they really be working for who they mentioned back then? No fucking way, she thought, but they were obviously going to kill her and she wanted to die, so it doesn't matter.

The two men zipped up the sleeping bag around the naked Marissa, covering her completely, even over the head.

With the one end open, she could breathe but was unseeable, which is what they wanted.

"You carry her to the car and keep her in the back seat with you," the one with the stun-gun said to the younger man.

"Of course," the man said in sarcasm as his older partner started down the stairs now. The younger man then hoisted the limp woman in the sleeping bag over his left shoulder, rising to his feet with a grunt. Carrying her down the creaky stairs, he kept thinking about the $10,000-a-piece he and his partner would be paid, all for "setting-up" this sexy bitch named Marissa. He hurried to the car outside as the sky began to clear, rain continuing.

In the back seat of the Lincoln Towncar concealed by tinted windows, the man holding Marissa relaxed, the bagged woman across his lap while the other man drove out of the driveway, back on the road. The driver removed his mask, revealing a Caucasian head of gray hair and a Roman face of stern expression. His name was Marty, a hired-gun employed for kidnapping this time.

The man in the back seat removed his mask to reveal a blond, blue-eyed head with a sweating expression of relief that the hard part was over. His name was Pat, partner-in-crime to the older man behind the wheel.

Ken Knight

Marty handed the younger thug a capped hypodermic needle over the seat to use on the woman in the bag because she would likely awake too soon. It was 30cc's of Demerol, a pain killer which will put her back into slumber.

Pat took the needle, then unzipped the sleeping bag half-way to see the nude brunette beneath. He smiled as he snaked a hand along her soft skin, across a thigh to her taut stomach, then down to her crotch. Cheap thrills.

He then felt her soft, full breasts and rolled her over in the bag, hands on her well-formed ass.

"That's the spot," he snickered as he uncapped the needle. Pat carefully stuck the thin needle into Marissa's left buttock and injected the serum.

"No pain," he whispered to his quarry, dropping the needle in the ashtray on the car door. Marissa was already out, so with some Demerol, she would stay that way, at the mercy of her captors.

"How fare we gotta go, Marty?" Pat asked the older operative in the front.

"About fifty miles or less...to Myrtle Beach, where we hand-off that bitch and get paid," Marty answered as he drove onto Rt. 501 eastbound, speeding up quickly.

"Cool, 'cuz I wanna go to one of those strip-clubs there," Pat chimed with a chuckle.

"Eager to spend your cut that fast?" Marty laughed in reply.

"Man, I'd rather get freaky with this hussy...she's so fine...but she's meat for the boss, and where else am I gonna see naked chicks with bit titties?" pat chortled jokingly, still molesting the unconscious Marissa in the sleeping bag.

"You've got a point youngster, bitches don't like to fuck-for-fun nowadays, it seems," Marty retorted in humor, relaxing now as he drove.

"Hmmh, yeah...but at least this job was easy enough," Pat sighed as he squeezed Marissa's boobs with both hands now, aroused by her physique under his control.

One Minute After Midnight

Too bad that rich money-bags in Myrtle Beach wants her, he thought. He noticed a gold wedding band on her left ring finger, surprised to find such a ring on this chick because he didn't think she'd be married! Pat then slipped the wedding band from her finger and pocketed it.

Ken Knight

Chapter 15

9:00 a.m.

The house didn't seem the same as he rummaged through it with Rex in tow, grabbing clothes and personal effects to stuff into one big suitcase. Maybe it was the fact that Ray was fixing to leave this place forever and the woman who made him live here for seven months of slavery. When he got the brown leather suitcase full and bulging, he stopped at the foot of the bed where he had slept with Marissa.

A moment of flashback rolled through his tired mind suddenly as he stared at her silk pillows, satin sheets and huge comforter on the bed Marissa made for them to share.

The times they laid in each other's arms here, made love. Nights of lewd abandon ending up on the floor, in the bathtub, on the sofa downstairs, fucking like rabbits. That is what he'll miss, Ray decided, even though he couldn't love the woman who snared him.

"'Bye, Marissa," he said softly to the bed, again feeling a little sorry for her, in spite of her.

"C'mon, Ray...we gotta go...c'mon, dis place iz creepy," Rex announced in slurred speech, standing in the doorway.

"Yeah, go get in the car," Ray retorted harshly, not looking at the younger man. Just as he started out the door, Ray glimpsed his multi-color floppy clown hat over on the dresser Marissa used.

He walked over and grabbed the clown hat, thinking of Rosemary and how she called the costume stuff like the "clownage". Damn, she was a beautiful, bubbly young woman who was pure sunshine in the flesh.

Making love to her was the best, and he knew he'd never have it that good again because "Jiggles" was gone, thanks to his wife.

He pocketed the floppy clown hat.

Ken Knight

"Damn you, Marissa...for all of this," Ray sneered out loud as he descended the stair with Rex.

"She wouldn't let me leave dat house for anything, and even had some man check on me to make shore I did nawt leeeve de house," Rex spoke in garbled quickness, following Ray to the front door.

"What man, what was his name?" Ray snapped in surprise, facing the mongoloid face of Rex Matthewson.

"Ah...don't know hiz naaame, but...he wuz an Africaaan...Americaaan," Rex answered, stuttering.

"A Black guy?" Ray quipped din surprise.

Rex nodded in the affirmative. About the only Black man Marissa could have used for such a thing was the one she cussed-out when he hit on her to try and see if she'd leave Ray, and that was the gullible Giles Visor!

It couldn't be, he thought as he stood in the doorway of the huge $250,000 home, thinking in agony.

She could have used him just like she used that dork, McCracken, against Ray! No way, he kept thinking in response to the mind-popping scenarios. Marissa hates Blacks, he remembered, because she used more racial epithets than he ever thought would come from the mouth of a wealthy Jewish chick like her.

What a conspiracy, he thought as he exited the house with the staggering Rex behind him, his leg braces slowing him considerably.

Rex looked at Ray with a painful expression as they got into the BMW to leave.

"What's wrong?" Ray snapped, keying the ignition.

"Knees hurt," Rex said hesitantly.

"Get used to it," Ray sighed as he shifted into drive and spun tires out of the driveway, eager to leave Dillon County and this house far behind.

He thought about the retarded man seated next to him, and considered the fact that the kid had no money, no luggage, and nowhere to go. Rex was about his size, only a little flabby, so he could fit into some of his clothes, but Rex can't stay with him, no.

I'll have to dump him off somewhere, Ray told himself in his mind, driving up Rt. 501 westbound as the sunlight began to break the overcast sky.

Ray hit the radio, tuning to the only rock channel in the area, driving the speed limit toward Hamer. He couldn't help but to think of Marissa as he drove, and how she conspired, toiled, even murdered to keep him. A woman like Rosemary would have had to simply ask him to marry her! He thought.

All this was Marissa's fault, he kept telling himself, all her doings, her sick plans!

Now, he had only to worry about his next path in life, where to go from here, minus Marissa and Rex.

Rex was chirping about how Marissa treated him like a little boy and threatened to kill him if he left that old house in Aynor, but Ray wasn't really listening. His thoughts were focused on where he could go now and how he can get hold of more money. A thousand dollars won't go very far, even for just one man.

I could sell this BMW, he thought, probably get at least $15,000 for it, black market.

"Can we stop and ...eat?" Rex asked hesitantly not feeling good about his new friend's mood now. He was hungry, too.

"Uhh, yeah, gotta fill up with gas, anyway; I'll stop at South Of The Border," Ray answered casually.

Rex smiled in approval, because that was his favorite "playground": South Of The Border!

Driving faster along 501, they passed a little country store, then a long stretch of country road, then a post office for Hamer, SC. The theme park was just ahead, and Rex laughed in delight.

Ray saw "Pedro's Diner" off to the right and now that it was 10:05 a.m., he knew they were just opening. He pulled off into the parking spaces and stopped, shifting into park.

"all right, let's go grab some chow," Ray said as he opened his car door, while Rex hurried out his end.

Ken Knight

"My favorite lunch," Ray said as he walked up to the doors, seeing Rex run through them first. This might be the last time here for a long time, so he wanted to see the place once more.

A chilling memory came to him as soon as Ray entered the air-conditioned joint. This is where Marissa "proposed" to him with a choice of either marrying her or going to jail for running over Rex.

Funny how things turn out, because here he was returning here over 7 months later with Rex Matthewson, alive!

Rex sauntered up to the counter and took a stool there, precisely where Ray usually sat to eat. Ray walked up behind him and patted Rex on the back to get his attention.

"Hey buddy, I'm going to the rest-room…you go ahead and order, and I recommend the grilled-chicken sandwich," Ray spoke politely to Rex.

"Okay," the younger man said cheerfully, watching Ray walk around the corner to the men's room. The smell of frying food made both of them hungry.

When the waitress behind the counter stopped in front of Rex, he grinned at her boyishly, and she returned the smile, asking what he would like to order. He told her, and then she brought him a glass of iced tea.

Inside the small men's room, Ray took a piss and washed his hands, then splashed water on his face. Leaning on the sink, he stared at himself in the cheap mirror.

Tired, with bags under his eyes and a pair of hollow cheeks staring back at him, Ray shook his head in dismay.

Here I am at Pedro's Diner again, homeless and nearly destitute with no prospects, he told himself in sarcasm.

Part of him almost expected Marissa to come walking into the place with a smile on her pretty face and a new "deal" for him. No, that option was dried up and gone and he was glad, too.

I got Rosemary killed, he thought as he continued to stare at his reflection. If he hadn't have made love with her, Marissa

One Minute After Midnight

wouldn't have caused the accident, and the lovely lady would be alive now.

He had heard she was cremated because she was so tore up in the crash.

What one person's momentary decision can do to others...how one wrong turn on a dark road at night can affect your life and those you care about ...how a moment's joy can become a curse for later....

I've died and gone to hell, he thought as he continued to stare at his wet face and unwashed hair. I'm a man who is handsome and employable, yet, who is broke and homeless all by my own choice.

Freedom has its price, and he was paying it, starting today.

Ray closed his eyes and remembered what a high school history teacher once told him and the rest of the junior class that year:

For a man, 90% of his life is spent for a woman—either trying to find one, impress one, provide for one, and keep one. A man works at jobs he usually loathes to pay for female attention and buys a house with a thieving mortgage-payment so a woman can "nest" and raise her litter of kids.

Women don't know how good they have it. With this way of life, most men lead in pursuit of them!

That was what Marissa had done to snare him, he thought next. She toiled, schemed, and even destroyed to keep him as her husband. She had assumed a "male" role in a way by getting financially wealthy and doing whatever it took to get the mate of her choice.

Normally, all a woman of her physically-endowed stature had to do was walk into a mall or a nightclub and men would flock to her, and she'd choose one or two lovers. Whereas a man like Ray could go cruising, nightclubs, bars, grocery stores, etc. and still go home alone because most of the good women are with other men, and the "available" ones are either unwed moms, dykes, or that new breed of female who is afraid of men because the media tells them to be.

Ken Knight

Why couldn't Marissa just walk into a nightclub and find her mate amongst the endless array of swinging dicks? No, she came charging into his fucked-up life and took it like a thief. Now, he had to flee like a fugitive and knew it was no other way.

If only I'd turned her down back then, and opted for the police to find out about the hit-n-run. I might be in jail right now but Rosemary would still be alive, he though in angst.

Funny how one decision, ever so slight, may make you or break-you-in-half and even result in the demise of someone close to you due to your decisive skill!

Life's a bitch, then you marry one.

He opened his eyes an nodded to his mirror image. It was part his fault, this mess. Rex wouldn't be walking on hobbled legs and Rosemary would still be performing as Jiggles the Clown if he hadn't been drinking the night of June 4th, 2000 and driving along Myrtle Drive in Dillon at 12:01 that stormy evening.

Marissa took advantage and put the icing on the cake. I could live with that. "Cut your losses and start over elsewhere," he whispered to himself as he walked out of the bathroom in his still-damp jeans and flannel shirt, not even looking over at Rex as he bolted out the door with car keys in hand.

He had a thousand dollars in his pocket and Marissa's BMW, enough to get a ball rolling, and he couldn't take Rex with him. Leaving the handicapped man behind here at "Pedro's" was the only reasonable option in his mind.

Running out to the car, he got in and started the engine hurriedly. He shifted into reverse and maneuvered onto the road slowly, seeing a traffic stoppage up ahead, just shy of the Rt. 95 Junction.

"Damn, fuckin' traffic," he sneered in disgusted impatience as he pulled up to the 18-wheeler truck waiting in line behind a dozen or so cars to get onto Rt. 95.

Ray looked in his rear-view mirror and saw someone coming out of the diner 100 yards behind him. It was obviously Rex, limping as he was.

"Fuck him, I'm free, white, and twenty-two...and my new life starts today," ray said out loud indignantly.

Rex stood in the diner's parking lot in angst, seeing the car Ray drove on the road now, leaving him behind! "Ray...Ray...don't leave," he sniffed in disappointment, wanting to cry.

He then looked down the other direction of Rt. 501, seeing a huge truck rolling fast toward the "South Of The Border" Theme Park and Rt. 95. Rex liked those "big rigs" as he called them, the huge Interstate 18-wheelers.

The lone driver of that truck hit his brakes as he drove parallel with the diner off to his right, then heard a loud hydraulic "snap", and his air brakes didn't engage.

"Jeezus!" the driver yelled in shock, his brakes failing at 45 mph. Ray glanced up in the rearview mirror to see the huge 18-wheeler barreling down on him too fast to stop.

He froze in his seat, the chill of realization mapping all reflexes as the grill of the truck filled the rearview mirror.

"No," Ray managed to utter as the truck struck the rear-end of the BMW; crunching metallic sounds.

Between the idle tractor-trailer and the incoming 18-wheeler, the BMW was crushed like an empty beer can in a second's timing of carnage. Ray was launched through the windshield, and his head exploded like a melon on the back door of the trailer ahead of him.

Rex cringed as the wreck occurred, its loud rupture hurting his ears, and he burst out crying, realizing what had just happened to Ray Torelli. No way someone could survive that! And Rex knew it. Ray was gone and he stood there outside the diner alone.

"Ray...no," he bellowed in despair, watching the twisted wreck up ahead as people from all over ran up to see if anyone was still alive in the BMW.

The driver of the truck with no brakes survived because of his seat-belt.

He turned toward the diner again as some of the other customers came running out. Nothing like a savage car accident to entertain everyone!

Rex stumbled back inside, crying childishly in sorrow over what he just witnessed. Ray was dead and he was all alone, even Marissa was out of reach now. Where will I go? Eh kept asking himself in mind-numbing dismay.

But, for a moment of clarity, he felt suddenly, strangely...free! He was on his own for the first time in his life, thanks to Marissa, Ray, and whoever the driver of that pickup truck was, who ran him over last summer.

Rex sat there on his stool with a glass of iced tea, crying still. This overwhelming situation was more than he was used to handling at one time. Freedom was both scary and exciting at the same time, but he knew his limitations; he knew he wasn't like other guys, guys like Ray.

Sirens could be heard outside the diner, as police and fire/rescue vehicles arrived to service the horrendous crash near the Rt. 95 Junction of Rt. 501 here at "South of The Border".

The crash was directly in front of a gas station, so an army of fire-fighters were dispatched, just in case.

Rex turned and saw a big bus pull up in front of the restaurant, seeing it clearly through the windows of the place.

He had seen a bus like that one before, his father once told him it was a private "tour bus". This one was candy-apple red and shiny. Then, Rex's attention was diverted as the waitress placed his lunch in front of him, a grilled chicken sandwich.

"This is on-the-house, honey," the obese waitress told him gingerly, seeing that he was upset. Rex thanked her twice.

Four, twenty-something females in country-western attire, two wearing cowboy hats, walked into the diner together, getting everyone's attention.

"Take a seat wherever you like," one waitress told them politely. Chirping like birds, the four ladies took the booth directly behind Rex at the counter.

One Minute After Midnight

Rex hadn't even seen the four flamboyant women because he was crying as he ate, but they noticed him.

The four country-girls were members of a County-Western band known as "The Dixie Dew", out of Selma, Alabama. They had just finished a one-week engagement at The Carolina Opry in Myrtle Beach and were on their way to Knoxville, Tennessee when they pulled over here to wait-out the traffic blockage up ahead.

The cute brunette with cowboy hat on her head noticed Rex was crying and that he was retarded by the way he looked. Her name was Trinity, and she prided herself in being able to cheer-up anyone, and since this poor guy was crying, she stepped up to him at the counter.

"Hey there, handsome," She spoke sweetly to Rex, getting his full attention. Rex wiped his eyes and spoke back with food in his mouth.

"What's wrong?" Trinity asked gingerly, touching a hand to his back. Rex always felt comfortable around women, so he told her in fluent sentences, everything in a nutshell. Trinity hadn't expected to hear this!

His parents were gone, his legs hobbled by a nurse who was going to kill him in the long run, his friend, Ray, getting killed in that accident blocking the road outside. His broke and hopeless position now, where he had no place to go. He told her his name finally.

All of it was told in Rex's simple way, but the country singer understood every detail, and it surprised her. Immediately, she liked this young man, though, and insisted Rex join her and her bandmates at the booth, telling him who they were.

He did so, sitting between Trinity and a buxom blond back-up singer named Amanda. All four of the ladies fawned over Rex girlishly, making him feel better.

They talked, ate, and Rex told his sordid tale for the four comely ladies of country. No pretty girls had paid him attention like these were, before! He started feeling better the longer he talked with them, almost forgetting about Ray Torelli, his

Ken Knight

smashed remains being pulled from the wreckage by EMS personnel now. Luckily for Rex, he didn't see the utterly destroyed corpse of Raymond Torelli, who died, seeing-it-coming.

Ray died quick but violently, his fate sealed by his last act of self-preservation, a selfish move to abandon responsibility once more.

The "Dixie Dew" girls were awestruck by Rex's story, all of them seeing him to be a rather harmless young man whose handicap limited him, thrown-to-the-wolves by selfish others. Their sense of charity welled-up strong at that moment.

"Hey...since you're on-ya-own here, Rex, why don't you come with us on-tour. We need another roadie...?" Trinity suggested impishly as she hugged him with one arm.

"Really?" Rex asked in wonder, looking out the windows at the big tour bus parked outside.

"Yeah, you can work for us, Rex, ride with us for the rest of your tour, which lasts another six weeks," Amanda spoke up in agreement with Trinity.

The leader of the band, a pretty brown-haired and chesty girl named Leigh, capped it off with the next statement. "Work for us; we'll pay you and you'll have fun, too...Where else you gonna find such an offer, honey?" she spoke sweetly, thinking of Rex in terms of how easily he could be used.

Trinity saw Rex as a non-sexual aide-de-camp who can be easily manipulated. He'd work hard for a reduced wage and not try to get in her panties, or any of the other girls, for that matter.

Amanda was a charitable girl, and simply wanted to help him out. The fourth "Dixie Dew" girl, a 21-year-old guitarist named Jen went along with her bandmates and asked Rex to join them.

Rex broke a smile and nodded in final agreement.

Minutes later, the five of them walked out of the diner to the big custom-tour bus, sunlight finally making its appearance.

"Here we are, Rex, our cozy bus," Trinity said as she pointed to the big custom bus as the other three girls boarded now. The

One Minute After Midnight

crash up ahead was being cleared-off now so the "Dixie Dew" girls got their orders-to-go and boarded their home-on-wheels.

Rex noticed the Honda scooter mounted on the back bumper rack of the bus, and asked Trinity about it before getting on.

"That's mine, but you can ride around on it later if you'd like," she told him sweetly as she ushered Rex into the big tour bus.

"Great, I like scooters...used ta haaave-wunn, ya know," Rex told her as he boarded the band's bus, marveling at its plush interior.

"Really," Trinity said, patronizing their new gopher. Rex was happy now, forgetting all about his braced legs, Ray, Marissa, and what had happened. Now, he would be part of a country band, "The Dixie Dew".

Rex sat next to Leigh on the bus, and someone handed him a cold can of beer. Opening the brew, he took a sip of the alcoholic beverage for the first time, actually liking it.

Leigh looked at the braces he wore on his legs and thought about it more.

"Those braces aren't permanent, are they?"

"Oh, no," Rex answered proudly.

"Cool," Leigh chimed, considering him useful despite his handicap. Rex smiled at Leigh as the bus roared back onto the road, heading for Interstate 95 north.

"You're a lucky guy, Rex. Don't disappoint us," Trinity told him from the next seat over, patting him on the shoulder.

He just kept grinning, happy to have a place now, an opportunity to survive on his own. And that scooter on the back; he couldn't' wait to ride again!

Ken Knight

Horry County Hospital
Myrtle Beach, SC
Jan. 25th:

Marissa slowly awoke from a dreamless sleep, her vision wearily-focusing on a ceiling and the fluorescent light overhead. In seconds more, she realized that she was lying on her back in a bed with an IV needle in her left arm.

This was a hospital room, and considering the events of the past two days, she wasn't surprised to end up here. The room was different in its interior though, so she guessed that she wasn't in Pennbrook Memorial Hospital now. Thinking hard in recollection, she tried tin vain to sit up. No good, still too weak.

She knew she had to be drugged to have been out like that. Her last memory of vivid detail was of those two goons in black attacking her in the bathroom of the old house.

Marissa felt her uncombed hair in disgust and found herself in a hospital gown beneath the sheet. How long she had been here had been any guess, but it can't be serious.

Her head was the only part of her that really hurt right now, in the form of a pounding headache.

Thoughts of what had transpired made it even worse, so she just laid there with her head on the pillow and felt helpless again. The police would be in to question her any time, she thought as she lay there, quiet and still.

She closed her eyes and thought of Ray, wondering where he was by now. It was dark outside the window and she couldn't help but to wonder. When she opened her eyes again, she saw someone slowly entering the room, letting the big door close behind.

Marissa gawked at the visitor in shock. The very appearance of this individual was something she never expected to see here, tonight.

"You...." She sighed in fearful awe, eyeballing someone from her past she had hoped to never see again.

One Minute After Midnight

Clad in a black, pinstripe two-piece suit with navy blue overcoat and a black silk tie with white dress shirt beneath, was a 5'9" statuesque and buxom Roberta Vazquez. Dr. Roberta Vazquez, assistant professor of biology and anatomy at South Carolina University.

"Good evening, Marissa," the Amazonian Hispanic woman spoke gingerly to the patient, smiling as she stepped to the end of the bed.

Marissa looked her up-and-down in surprise, the long, raven hair down to the shoulders and wavy, that pretty oval ace which looked too young to be 35, and those shiny teeth grinning back at her. Roberta Vazquez......

"Roberta, jeezuss...what are you doin' here?" Marissa spoke wearily in retort, trying to sit up again.

"Oh, I've come to see how you were doing and...to help you out," the statuesque Latina answered with a smile of avarice, touching her hands to the bed's collapsible railing as she spoke to her quarry.

"Help me...how's that, when I had hoped to never see you again, goddammit," Marissa sneered in contempt, angry, just looking at the woman again.

"That's certainly no way to speak to the one woman who holds your life in her hands, Marissa...." The visitor explained softly, eyeballing Marissa intently.

Marissa couldn't believe this: the woman had tried to seduce her into a lesbian love affair back when she was at the university. Marissa had gone out with her assistant professor once and they kissed but it didn't go any further.

Professor Vazquez pursued her student ardently and didn't halt her advances until Marissa filed a complaint against her with the dean's office. After that, Roberta Vazquez transferred to Eastern Carolina University, a more liberal school and Marissa graduated with honors at SCU.

Marissa had felt strangely guilty after that, and hoped to never see the gay female professor again.

She was the one who used the phrase, "I'm your only friend." She was the one who sent those goons to beat her up and kidnap her, no doubt about it, and now she had her here in a hospital.

"what are you doing with me, Roberta…why?" Marissa snapped in emotion.

"Oh, the things we do for love, my dear Marissa Borders," Roberta answered in her smooth American voice.

"Love?" Marissa sneered with a smirk.

"Yes, I still love you after all this time…though I tried to dismiss you after you nearly got me fired at SCU. I found my self wanting you more and more, and I was willing to wait for the right moment," Roberta answered softly.

"Right moment, what…so you could kidnap me like you did, you're sick?!" Marissa retorted in angst, tearing up again.

"Oh, I'm sick, when you took advantage of Ray Torelli's hit n' run of a retarded kid last year, blackmailing him into marrying you?" Roberta spoke matter-of-factly.

She knew. How the hell this woman knew about that was beyond comprehension. Marissa fell silent in realization, because if Roberta, the Dyke, knew about Ray, then what else does she know?

"Hmm…and let's see, your unlawful imprisonment of the retarded kid, the sabotage of one Rosemary Jones's vehicle which subsequently caused her death…the illegal computer hack job to destroy your husband's financial future, and to falsify death records," Roberta sounded-off in clarity, shocking Marissa further.

This was torture, she thought as she lay there…please let this be a dream!

"No, you can't prove any of that, there's no way," Marissa said in response, fighting off the urge to cry.

"You don't know what I can do, honey cheeks, or what I have to do-you-in, should I desire to," Roberta said softly, walking to the other side of the bed.

"How?" Marissa sighed in defeat.

One Minute After Midnight

"Baby, you've been my pet project since you graduated Nursing two years ago, and I've followed your every move, thanks to my cohorts," Roberta explained politely, smiling down at her prey in delight. Savor the victory, she thought.

"I know about Rex, Ray, Rosemary, and the hacker named McCracken...you leave quite a trail of broken lives, Marissa," Roberta said softly with a wink.

"Jeesus, what do you want then?" Marissa asked in a half.

"What do you think I want, baby" Roberta retorted in sarcasm.

"I have money...over a million dollars plus earnings, you can have half of it," she offered earnestly, hoping to buy-off this threat.

"Half-a-million, to forget everything?" Roberta quipped, not impressed at all.

Marissa nodded with a tear streaming.

"You're worth more to me than money, baby....Hmm, besides...I have made my own small-fortune writing two best selling 'self-help' books and a Gay Travelers' Guide, so I have a million in savings, too," Roberta said matter-of-factly, hands on her hips.

Marissa couldn't believe this. "Then, why are you hounding me, Roberta. Don't you know what I've already been through?!" she quipped indignantly, shaking a fist.

"It's okay, baby, play-ball with me and you'll never see a court room nor a jail cell," Roberta said softly.

"You can't prove all that, you can't," Marissa repeated sure of herself.

"I have to admit, a lot of it's circumstantial, but it'll still screw you over in court and ...there's one more thing I can prove which is the icing on the cake," Roberta said as she stepped over to the door, opening it for someone else to enter Marissa's room.

Marissa watched in dismay as a well-dressed Giles Visor slowly walked into sight.

"Hey there, Melissa," Giles spoke softly to her with his boyish smile. Insult to injury, as he knew she hated when people "accidentally" calls her Melissa. This is unreal…..

"What…is this?" she sighed in disbelief. "This can't be happening."

"Ah, yes, Marissa, Giles here has helped us come together like this, and has earned my favor by being at the right place at the right time," Roberta said, touching hand to Gile's back as they faced Marissa in the bed.

"How?!" Marissa snapped in anger.

"Sweetheart, I was a 'Ride-Along' with that police officer you shot and killed the other day…I was in the car and saw the whole thing, though no one else did …and I gave the police my statement with your vague description," Giles explained slow and smooth.

"Giles didn't tell your name but he could remember and re-tell the story later, claiming traumatic stress or whatever," Roberta spoke up, hugging Giles one-armed now.

"Migod, what do you two want?" Marissa asked with cotton mouth.

"Oh, Giles already ahs what he wants, thanks to me…he was hired by Dillon Sheriff's Department today," Roberta said softly.

"Yeah, a cop job like I always wanted, plus…got to fool around with you that night in the motel, so I'm happy," Giles said with a stupid grin.

"Really, so what's ya catch?" Marissa snarled at Roberta.

"Mmmh…something you can relate to, Marissa baby…a deal you forced on Ray Torelli seven months ago," Roberta sighed with a smile.

Marissa felt her heart sink in agony as the surreal situation began to sink in. This can't be happening! She wanted to cry out.

"You can go to prison-for-life as a cop killer, or…you can travel with me to Hawaii where we can marry as a couple, combine our finances and live very, very well, a sweet penance for everything you've done so far," Roberta explained softly.

Giles' smiled even wider, liking what Marissa had become ensnared in. he wanted to say to her: Who's the nigger now, bitch? But didn't.

"Marry you...are you insane, we can't...I'm still married to Ray, and gay marriages are...." Marissa stammered nervously.

"Legal in Hawaii, baby, and I dare say congratulations, you're now a widow," Roberta answered, handing her a local newspaper.

On the front page of the "DILLON DEMOCRAT" county newspaper was an article entitled: "Man killed in 18-wheeler crash, brakes on rig failed". Ray Torelli age 23, died instantly when his BMW was sandwiched between two tractor-trailers on Rt. 501 Junction with I95. The one truck's brakes failed, causing the accident.

"Ray is dead...jeezus, killed in a car accident with my car...migod, he's gone," Marissa said as she lowered the paper in shock.

Roberta smiled at the widow in kinky delight, noticing no real sorrow in her expression now. Ray had betrayed his wife in rapid succession and paid in fate's fury.

"See how accidents can be a girl's second-best friend?" Roberta said to Giles, patting him on the back-side.

Marissa felt strangely relieved over the news of her husband's demise. After all she did for him and all he did against her, she was relieved Ray Torelli was gone forever, making her a widow.

"Now you're free of that ingrate loser and free to make your next grand decision," Roberta continued.

"Fuck you, get out," Marissa groaned, her headache increasing.

"Then, you go to jail for killing that cop, accident-or-not, and Giles here is the prosecution's star-witness," Roberta sneered in contempt. Giles just stood there in his designer jeans, cowboy boots and western dress shirt, smiling at Marissa.

"I don't believe this shit," Marissa moaned with emotion, wanting to break down.

"Believe it, because I get what I want in life, baby, one way or another, and I want you with me, period," Roberta spoke firmly as she stepped to the bedside, dark eyes burning into her weakened prey's.

"I'm not gay, dammit, Roberta...I am not a fuckin' lesbian," Marissa snarled with tears streaming down her red hot cheeks.

"That doesn't matter, Marissa, you'll adapt in time, and you might just learn to enjoy sex with me," Roberta added.

Giles had to laugh at that remark, unable to hold back. Roberta flashed him a mean look, signaling for him to go.

"No, I'll give you all my money, please!" Marissa pleaded, crying now.

Giles waved at Marissa and turned to leave the room. He had what he wanted, not caring about the dead cop or the others affected by Marissa Borders. What they didn't' tell Marissa was that Roberta had also paid him a cool $50,000 as an incentive to keep silent about the cop's death. He had the job he wanted, and that was enough for Giles, not to mention the satisfaction of hoodwinking Marissa.

Roberta watched Giles leave and made sure he was down the hallway before saying anything else.

"Sorry, baby...you mean too much to me, and don't worry about that village-idiot, Giles Visor, because I've got him in-a-corner, too...besides, cops get killed all the time, so who knows what his future holds?" she chimed humorously.

"Bitch, I don't' want you in my life anymore...take my money instead," Marissa pleaded angrily.

"Careful, baby, remember who I am in this situation; your only friend," Roberta added with a smile.

She had a point, Marissa thought in angst; Ray was dead, Giles an opportunist stoolie, and who else would back her up considering the murder charges for that cop and maybe Rosemary? Never before had she felt so betrayed and alone.

Just like the blackmail perpetuated on Ray, Roberta offered "marriage" or jail. Life-without-parole or become the "wife" of a Lesbian author and PhD., and for a moment, Marissa considered telling her college teacher and suitor to go to hell.

She wasn't gay; she had accidentally shot the policeman, and Rosemary's crash was written off as a "loss-of-control" by the police. Roberta had wanted to bed her back in college and now she wanted to own her ass. Marissa had scoffed at Roberta's advancements back then, much like Ray had spurned her back in high school.

It felt like some deity's revenge for her sins, as if she had come full-circle only to face a vicious circle of consequences. Now, she was being blackmailed into marrying someone she didn't love, with the only other option being prison and utter ruin.

"Damn you," Marissa said under her breath at her lesbian suitor. She reminded herself of Ray, because he usually said 'Damn you,' instead of 'I love you'."

Roberta smiled in response, not fettered by the rejection of her love.

"I still love you, baby, no matter what and…I'm doing this for us, for our future, where no man stands in our way to happiness," Roberta added softly, touching a hand to Marissa's tear-wet face.

"But I'm not gay, Roberta," Marissa repeated.

"Doesn't matter, because you belong to me now…unless you want to be tried, convicted, and sentenced for shooting that policeman?" Roberta retorted frankly.

"It's an accidental shooting," she stammered.

"Tell that to a jury," Roberta chuckled.

Marissa wiped her face and stopped sobbing, composing herself.

"Giles worked for you the whole time, didn't he?" Marissa whined in realization.

"Yes, and I had him innocently meet Ray at a bar, falling right into Ray's foolish plan to subvert your fidelity to him, and then you conned him into doing your bidding by fucking his

Ken Knight

brains loose...what little brains he has...why it all worked out well for me," Roberta continued pacing the room.

"You were watching me all-along," Marissa sighed, closing her eyes and wanting to die.

"Pretty much, but you made it easy, and that idiot cowboy, Giles Visor, was the ace-in-the-hole, lucky enough to have been riding-along with that cop you accidentally killed, witness you in action," Roberta said softly.

"He can still talk...nothing's guaranteed, believe me, I know. Giles won't keep a secret like that," Marissa said in calmer demeanor now, folding her arms.

"He's affable and careless, I know, but don't worry, baby, for like you already know, accidents happen to anyone, even rookie cops who know too much," Roberta told her quarry in easy stride.

Was Roberta going to kill off Giles somehow? Marissa wondered. She hoped so, but the thought of Roberta being that "influential" in shady activities, scared her even further. Like Marissa was with Ray, Roberta was willing to kill for love.

"Men are expendable, often disposable at any turn...that's why I cannot love one of the apes...and, I'm willing to use them and lose them, which is the way you should be," Roberta explained further.

She was evil, Marissa told herself. Then, again, what does that make her with all she has done to the lives of others? Without doubt, Roberta was much like Marissa in her inner-soul.

Others were insignificant for the most part, only self and self-preservation mattered most! My god, she thought, this can't be true.

"I might be pregnant, ya know," Marissa spoke up suddenly.

"So, abortion is still legal the last I checked...no problem," Roberta chimed in cold demeanor.

Marissa just sat there, staring at the woman who had her by-the-throat quite literally, and there was nothing she could do about it.

One Minute After Midnight

"Marry me in Hawaii, then we'll take a luxury cruise to Mexico for our honeymoon and start our new lives together...." Roberta said out loud sharply, pulling a folded parchment out from her suit pocket, dropping it to Marissa's blanket.

It was a plane ticket and travel plans for Wednesday, 2 days from now. Marissa looked up at the clock on the wall and wondered how Roberta got into this hospital so late. The clock read 12:01 a.m., on minute after midnight, and Marissa surrendered to fate's hand.

"Okay," she sighed with tears falling again.

Roberta smiled in triumph, nodding to her conquest sweetly. Marissa's face was wet with tears of defeat and she silently asked God why this was happening to her, after all the other horror.

"Your doctor says you have a concussion but...you'll be released in the morning; I made sure of that," Roberta added, matter-of-factly.

"Meet me in Hawaii at the Springs Hotel Casino in Honolulu Wednesday night by eight, or...you will be a wanted woman, an arrest-warrant with your name on it," Roberta continued, pointing to the plane ticket and hotel reservation in Marissa's hands.

Marissa nodded, sniffing back tears. She looked at the beautiful Roberta Vazquez as the Amazonian author backed slowly toward the door now, eyeing her still.

"Roberta...why me?" Marissa asked meekly.

"I love you, baby...always have, and I get what I want in life...you know how it is girl; how we can be attracted to one person and no one else can match up," Roberta told her softly.

"Yes," Marissa groaned in agreement, looking down at the plane ticket.

"Now, get some sleep, baby, and don't worry about anything or anyone, Marissa, because we are gonna start everything," Roberta said next, opening the door to exit.

Ken Knight

"I'll see you in Hawaii, Marissa," the raven-haired woman said as she stepped out into the hallway of the Progressive Care Wing.

Marissa heard the door click-shut and began to cry now, alone in the room with her thoughts.

Ray was dead, and who-knows what happened to Rex., and now she was the object of a blackmail plot!

It felt strangely "good" to know that Ray was dead, the bastard. If he had just stayed with her, none of this would have happened like it was. She hated Ray Torelli and was glad he died like that in a car accident with her BMW. A fitting end.

Being "married" to a lesbian was something she had never imagined, never wanted, but now she had to face it or face jail for killing that cop.

She had been "curious" back in college and that was the only reason she dated her Asst. professor, Ms. Vazquez back then. She wasn't a lesbian, though, but now it was a choice of that "life" with Roberta or prison, just like she did to Ray 7 months ago!

Marissa sobbed uncontrollably now, crying in hopelessness of the situation, lying in the hospital bed, unable to save herself from a woman who was too much like herself.

She surrendered, crying in defeat. Part of her wanted to die, then again, Roberta offered her a "new Life" with her. A life with someone, like what she wanted with Ray and couldn't' achieve.

Marissa straightened up and stopped sobbing after a minute, thinking of other possibilities, other far-off options. Roberta had her by the short-hairs, and so she had to give-in, at least for now.

One Minute After Midnight

Springs Hotel
Honolulu, Hawaii:

"Now, I pronounce you wife and wife..kiss one another in equal devotion," the Episcopal Priest spoke in grinning eulogy, eyes on the two women before him in this hotel banquet room.

Roberta and Marissa leaned in and kissed each other lovingly as Roberta's dozen guests stood up and clapped lightly for the two celebrants.

As the couple turned to walk away from the priest greeted by the witnesses, Marissa glanced at the ring on her finger now, a new wedding band.

Equality of two. What a singular misnomer, Marissa thought as she walked with her well-dressed bride to the table with the tiny wedding cakes on it. She had little choice but to be here today.

Dressed in evening gowns, the two female "brides" stood for photos and to cut their cake. Marissa was glad Roberta wanted a simple ceremony with little pomp. No, Roberta had also insisted they not consummate their relationship until tonight, on the ship.

My parents are going to disown me, she thought as she toasted with her "bride". Marissa was smiling and cheery-faced in spite of the situation, her head still hurting in headaches today.

Damn this, she thought in retrospect, still hoping this was a nightmare and that she'll wake up. Maybe prison wouldn't be better than this, true, but it still didn't change the fact that Marissa was being forced into lesbianism by the influential Dyke Professor/Author.

She remembered what Roberta said about "accidents" happening to anyone. She hoped the worst kind of accident found Giles visor soon. Being "hoodwinked" like that hurt worse than Roberta's blackmail.

Ken Knight

Onboard "The Pacific Sea King"
170 nautical miles southeast
of Honolulu, Hawaii
11:50 p.m.:

This whole thing was still surreal. Marissa even considered jumping over the rail into the raging ocean below, but it just wasn't in her tonight. Tonight was the first night of her "honeymoon", as well as the first in her future with Roberta. This can't be happening.

The cabin they were assigned to was luxurious at least, even had a fridge and tiny liquor cabinet, not-to-mention a king-sized bed with genuine fur comforter, even a tiny porch to step out onto, and watch the ocean.

Standing by the little desk over in the corner of the suite, clad in a bathrobe now, Marissa enjoyed a cigarette during these few minutes of solitude while her "wife" was in the bathroom, getting ready for tonight's first lovemaking between them. That was the only "traditional" thing about Roberta, wanting to wait until their wedding night/honeymoon to get-it-on. Marissa had never been with a woman before, of course, and she was nervous as hell, as well as reluctant.

This entire cruise ship was booked-full on no one but lesbian vacationers for this trip, in the first place. Sure, there were a few male passengers on-board, but they were gay as well as some of the prettiest motherfuckers she'd ever seen in male form.

Marissa didn't know they had all-gay cruise trips chartered, and yet, here she was, almost 200 miles from land with a lesbian wife in legal matrimony; she couldn't believe it!

Taking a long drag on her menthol cigarette, Marissa thought about after this 2-week cruise and how she might get the upper-hand over Roberta.

It had to be possible, some way to rebuke Roberta and avoid the ax she held. Marissa stepped over to the head of the bed slowly, smoking as she tried to relax now.

One Minute After Midnight

She untied her bathrobe, opening the garment to remove it, letting it drop to the rug below. Completely naked, Marissa sat down on the fur comforter on the big bed, blowing smoke toward the ceiling. Running a hand through her short, neck-length brown hair, she thought of Ray again and silently hoped he was roasting on a spit in the pits of hell right now. She had found out that she had not gotten pregnant that last time with him.

Can't even do that right, can you, you hairy wap? She thought in contempt of her late husband. Maybe a pregnancy might have made Roberta change her mind, who knows?

She put her cigarette in the ashtray on the night stand and relaxed on the fur comforter, feeling slightly-aroused now, trying to "psyche" herself up for tonight's unconventional sex she was about to participate in.

The bathroom door clicked-open suddenly, and Marissa looked up to see Roberta Vazquez emerge in a blue silk bathrobe around her statuesque body.

This can't be happening, Marissa thought again. I'm not gay, she silently told herself as Roberta untied her silk robe slowly, opening the garment to reveal her buxom, statuesque physique.

Roberta possessed the body of a goddess, an Amazon with at least a 40DD bust and a 5'9" muscular-taut frame which naturally intimidated Marissa.

The Hispanic Amazon smiled slinky at her naked body on the bed, hands-on-hips in sensual pose.

Marissa forced a smile, staring up at the raven-haired beauty approaching the bed now. She looked at those huge breasts in awe of them, nervously quivering in anticipation.

"Forever starts tonight," Roberta said softly with her sexy smile. Marissa was speechless as her wife knelt onto the bed.

Marissa raised up enough to kiss Roberta as their hands met, and the two lovers entwined quickly on the fur.

"Forever...." Marissa sighed in fearful realization, enveloped in Roberta now.

This can't be happening, Marissa thought while Roberta squeezed and kissed her breasts in smooth, fluid foreplay.

It hadn't been a year since she first blackmailed Ray Torelli into marriage, and all the events transpired between then and now….

I'm trapped, she thought in defeat, and it's my fault. I did this, from day-one when Ray struck Rex with his truck in that thunderstorm….I took advantage of Ray's stupidity and bad luck, and he refused to even try to love me like I loved him….

I murdered Ray's mistress and accidentally killed a police officer, all to keep the man I married, against his will. And now her husband was dead, and the woman who was a terror during her college years…was between her legs.

Marissa gave-in to her new "lover" now, allowing Roberta to take her body like the ambitious former professor had always wanted to….

And for some strange reason, it felt good to be conquered.

-The End-

Also by Ken Knight:

CRYPTX

CRYPTX is modern fear and old horrors; where two lovers make their living robbing the graves and empty houses of the dead, finding that by disturbing the rest of the deceased, they become susceptible to the horrors of those lives long-gone…..While grave-robbing was their "victimless" crime, the couple take a priceless heirloom belonging to the most secretive and brutal Mafia Family on the east coast. They become the hunted, pursued by Mob Shooters and a beautiful, curvy female Assassin who specializes in exotic poisons. But the real danger lies inside of a century-old crypt in Dillon, SC. Where the grave-robbers seek an aristocratic medallion buried with a disgraced Prince…and in the deep, muddy tomb lies a powerfully-malignant spirit that will devour whoever enters.

Available at www1stBooks.com and Amazon.com or order it from your local bookstore!

Ken Knight